A Precarious Gamble

GENTLEMEN of LONDON

Laura Beers

Chapter One

England, 1813

Lord Hugh Calvert was a failure from the moment he was born. He was the second son, the spare. He could never live up to his elder brother, Nathaniel, the Earl of Hawthorne, or his parents' ridiculous demands for him. So, he had stopped trying long ago. He decided he would live for himself rather than for others. He would take his own destiny in his hands, ignoring all the naysayers along the way.

With a drink in his hand, he knew he had every reason to be happy, but he was miserable. He had made a fortune at the card tables, but he couldn't seem to stop gambling long enough to enjoy his spoils. He felt trapped in his life, and he saw no way out of the same blasted cycle.

Not that he would ever admit that, especially not to his brother. Nathaniel loved nothing more than to lecture Hugh about his wayward behavior, and he grew tired of hearing the same drivel over and over. Perhaps he should purchase an estate far away and go try to make it on his own. It might give him the reprieve that he so desperately craved.

Hugh brought the glass up to his lips and took a sip of his drink. He needed a clear head for the tables, but he also wanted to forget those painful memories that seemed to haunt him the moment he closed his eyes at night.

As he set his glass down, he saw his friend, Lord Grenton, walking towards him. He had an obnoxious grin on his face, and Hugh sighed. His friend seemed to radiate happiness right now, and the glare was maddening.

Grenton came to a stop in front of the table and pulled out a chair. "I suspected you would be here," he said as he sat down.

"I usually am," Hugh replied dryly.

Grenton caught the eye of a passing server and indicated that he would like something to drink. He brought his gaze around, and Hugh caught a glimpse of pity in the depths of them.

"I'm glad that I caught you alone," his friend said.

Knowing that he was about to hear some unsolicited advice, Hugh spoke up first. "How is your wife?"

That was the right thing to say. Grenton's obnoxious grin came back. "Georgie is well," he replied with pride in his voice. "She is at the orphanage as we speak."

"Do you not take issue with her working now that you two are married?"

"She is overseeing the orphanage until we can find a replacement for her," Grenton shared.

"That is going to be a difficult feat."

"I agree, but it is not impossible," Grenton replied.

"Since when have you become such an optimist?" Hugh asked.

Grenton chuckled. "I believe it was the moment I married Georgie. She changed me for the better."

"I'm glad that you are happy." Hugh meant his words, but he had no desire to ever fall prey to the parson's mousetrap. Marriage was not in the cards for him—and he should know, cards were his forte. He may be miserable, but at least he didn't have a wife to answer to.

"Thank you," Grenton said. "We are departing for my cottage in Scotland tomorrow morning."

"How long will you be gone?"

"If I have my way, a fortnight."

A server placed a glass in front of Grenton and turned his attention towards Hugh. "Would you care for another one, my lord?"

"Not at this time," Hugh replied.

The server tipped his head in acknowledgement before he walked away.

Hugh took a sip of his drink, then asked, "Who will run the orphanage while Georgie is away?"

"She's asked Miss Ashmore to tend to it."

"That's an interesting choice," Hugh murmured. "Does Miss Ashmore not care for her reputation?"

Grenton shook his head. "I have discovered that Miss Ashmore is an anomaly amongst women. She does things in her own way."

"I do hope the *ton* doesn't ostracize her for that," Hugh said. "Women are held to a different standard than men. They are expected to fall into line."

"That they are."

Hugh pushed his nearly full glass away from him. "I have enjoyed our chat, but I'm afraid the tables wait for no man."

"Before you go," Grenton started, "I was hoping to speak to you about an important matter."

"Which is?" Hugh asked with a weary look.

Grenton grew solemn. "Last we spoke, you seemed rather despondent, and I was wondering how you are faring."

"You do not need to concern yourself with me," Hugh said brusquely.

Grenton didn't react to his harsh tone and pressed on. "I know a thing or two about being miserable, and—"

"Who said I was miserable?"

"It's written all over your face," Grenton replied with a knowing look.

Hugh released a frustrated sigh. "I appreciate what you are trying to do, but I am well. I have no complaints about my life."

As Grenton opened his mouth to reply, Nathaniel and Lord Haddington approached the table, with Lord Graylocke trailing close behind.

"Look who we found loitering outside," Nathaniel announced as he gestured towards Graylocke.

"Welcome home," Hugh said as the trio seated themselves.

Graylocke smiled. "Thank you," he replied. "I came home to the surprise news that Grenton married while I was on my wedding tour."

"It's true," Grenton said. "Georgie and I were wed a little over a week ago."

"Why haven't you left on your wedding tour yet?" Graylocke asked.

Grenton threw his hands up. "I have been trying to convince my wife, but she's been preoccupied with the orphanage. However, I managed to convince her to depart tomorrow morning for our cottage in Scotland."

Graylocke gave him an odd look. "Why is your wife so interested in the orphanage?"

"Because Grenton married the headmistress," Nathaniel interjected.

"You married a woman who was in servitude?" Graylocke asked. "That's a bold choice, even for you."

"Georgie ran away from her brother, Lord Wakefield, because he was forcing her into an arranged marriage with Ransdale," Grenton explained.

"Lord Ransdale is a known rake and a despicable person overall," Graylocke remarked.

"Georgie shared your sentiments and refused to marry the

man," Grenton said. "From the moment she came to the orphanage, she disrupted my life, but in a good way."

Graylocke smirked. "You *are* in love."

"I am," Grenton admitted cheerily, "and I have never been happier."

Hugh groaned. "Can we please skip the declarations of love?" he asked. "I don't have the stomach for it."

A server placed drinks for all on the table before he walked off to serve another table.

Grenton reached for a glass. "Perhaps it is time for you and Haddington to secure brides."

"That sounds like a terrible idea," Hugh said. "I am doing just fine on my own."

Haddington raised a glass. "I agree with Hugh, and I rarely do," he remarked. "A wife will bring a whole host of new problems that I do not have time for."

Nathaniel took a sip of his drink before saying, "I think you are underestimating the power of a good woman in your life."

"I don't dispute that is what *you* needed, but I need a wife like I need a thorn in my side," Hugh said.

"I just feel—"

Hugh cut his brother off. "You do not get a say in my life. If I say I don't want a wife, then you must accept that."

"You need an heir," Nathaniel attempted.

"No, *I* don't. You do, though," Hugh said, "and I have no doubt that Dinah will provide you with a number of strapping boys, making this a moot point."

Nathaniel wasn't ready to concede. "What of the fortune you have amassed from gambling?"

"I will leave it to your daughters, and they will be heiresses in their own right," Hugh replied. "It will help them select a suitor in the marriage mart."

"Hugh…"

He shoved back his chair and rose. "If you will excuse me, I am tired of this interrogation."

"It's hardly an interrogation," Nathaniel said.

"It feels like one," Hugh stated. "Besides, my presence is required at the Gilded Crown. I hope to triumph tonight at the tables."

"What if you lose?" Haddington asked.

Hugh gave him an amused look. "That won't be an issue. I rarely lose."

"I assume that you will stagger home in the early morning hours," Nathaniel remarked, taking a sip of his drink.

"So what if I do?" Hugh asked. "There is no harm in that, and last I checked, you do not get to dictate my actions."

"You're right," Nathaniel remarked. "Do as you want, just as I know you intend to."

Hugh pushed his chair in. "Finally, you are beginning to see reason."

Grenton rose. "I will walk you out. It is time I retrieved Georgie from the orphanage anyway."

Neither of them spoke as they skirted the tables and headed towards the main door of the club. A liveried servant opened the door and they stepped onto the pavement. As they walked towards Grenton's coach, his friend asked, "Would you care for a ride to the Gilded Crown?"

"I would prefer to walk."

"It wouldn't be a bother," Grenton pressed, stopping by his coach. A footman promptly opened the door.

Hugh took a step back. "A walk will clear my head."

Grenton looked unsure. "It's really no trouble."

Hugh put his hand up. "Save your breath," he said. "I am fine."

"You don't seem fine."

"I am the same man you have always known."

"But I'm not," Grenton said. "Georgie opened my eyes to a life that I always thought was out of my reach."

"I am happy for you, but your life is not my life. I am content being on my own."

"You deserve a chance at happiness."

"I thank you for your concern, but it is unnecessary."

"I don't think it is."

Hugh eyed him silently, irked by the compassion expressed in his friend's eyes. "You should go be with your wife and not worry about me."

Grenton appeared as if he was going to press the matter, but thankfully, he relented. "As you wish," he said. "But I am always here if you need me."

"I appreciate your kind offer."

With a tip of his head, Grenton stepped into his coach, and Hugh watched as the footman closed the door behind him. He remained standing there until the driver merged the vehicle into traffic.

Hugh shoved his hands in his pockets and started walking down the street. He wished that his friends would just let him be. He didn't want to bother them with his burdens; they were his own. And no matter what he did, nothing would change that.

Hugh held his cards in his hand as he watched the other players at the table. He had always been good at reading people, which proved useful at times like this. They were playing Three Card Brag, a game of chance he had always excelled in.

He watched as Mr. Ahearn wiped sweat off his brow with an already saturated handkerchief. It was a tell-tale sign that he was about to go out.

Turning his attention to Mr. Gaudin, Hugh found that his beady eyes were staring intently at him. The man was trying to intimidate him into folding, but he had no intention of doing so.

Lastly, Hugh evaluated his third opponent, whom he wasn't familiar with, Mr. Cadell. He was a tall man, with his dark brown hair brushed forward, most likely to distract from his large, protruding ears. His narrow shoulders were squared, and he appeared confident with his hand.

But Hugh knew he held a winning hand, and he had no intention of losing the large pot on the table in front of him.

The dealer turned to Hugh. "Your turn, my lord."

Keeping his cards close to his chest, Hugh reached into his jacket pocket and pulled out a hundred-pound note. "I brag," he said, tossing the note into the center of the table.

Mr. Ahearn sucked in a breath before tossing his cards onto the table. "I fold," he said dejectedly.

The dealer shifted his gaze to Mr. Gaudin. "Sir?"

Mr. Gaudin's lips pursed as he looked down at his hand. Hugh was unconcerned. Mr. Gaudin was just putting on a show. He had no doubt that he would fold when he realized that he couldn't win this hand.

Just as he'd anticipated, Mr. Gaudin sighed as he dropped his cards to the table. "I am a smart enough man to walk out of here with some of my money."

All eyes turned to Mr. Cadell, who was clenching his cards tightly in his hand. Hugh expected him to fold, but, to his surprise, Mr. Cadell tossed his remaining coins towards the center. "I'm in."

The dealer glanced down at his offering, maintaining a stoic expression. "I'm sorry, but you must make a minimum bet that equals Lord Hugh's. If you are unable to do so, your only option is to fold."

Mr. Cadell's eyes remained fixated on the large pot, which was now valued at almost five hundred pounds.

"Sir," the dealer prodded. "Do you wish to fold?"

With a quick glance at his hand, Mr. Cadell turned his

attention towards Hugh. "I have something that you might want that is worth well over a hundred pounds."

"I doubt it," Hugh said.

Mr. Cadell leaned forward in his seat and lowered his voice. "I have a ward who is going to come into some money soon."

"How exactly would that benefit me?" Hugh asked.

"You would be responsible for all of her finances, and you can skim from the top," Mr. Cadell said as if he were offering him a great prize.

"I would never do something so dishonorable," Hugh responded. "Besides, I do not wish to be responsible for a ward."

Mr. Cadell's eyes darted to his cards before turning to Mr. Gaudin. "What say you?" he asked. "Would you care for a ward as part of the pot?"

"It doesn't really matter whether he would care for a ward or not," Hugh said. "He's already passed."

Mr. Gaudin eyed Mr. Cadell curiously. "Who is your ward?"

"The daughter of Sir James Wymond," Mr. Cadell replied.

Now Mr. Cadell had Hugh's attention. "Did you say Sir James Wymond?" he asked.

Mr. Cadell nodded. "I did," he replied. "Were you acquainted with him?"

"No, but I attended Eton with his son, Stephen," Hugh replied. "Last I heard, he'd joined the Royal Navy and was captain of his own ship."

"That is true, but his ship went down and he was lost with it," Mr. Cadell shared. "He has been gone for over six months, but the probate court won't release Miss Wymond's inheritance."

"Do you know why that is?" Hugh asked.

"They claim that Mr. Wymond hasn't been gone long

enough to declare him dead," Mr. Cadell said. "I have petitioned the court, repeatedly, but they are standing firm on their decision."

"Did they say when the funds will be released?" Hugh asked.

"When he's been gone for a year."

Hugh lowered his cards to the table. "May I ask why you are so anxious to get rid of your ward?"

Mr. Cadell shrugged one shoulder. "She is a drain on my finances."

Hugh lifted his brow. "You aren't trying very hard to convince me to take Miss Wymond off your hands."

With a smirk, Mr. Cadell said, "That is only if you win— which you won't."

"You seem pretty confident in your hand," Hugh said.

"I am," Mr. Cadell responded.

"And what if I don't accept the wager?"

Mr. Cadell glanced over his shoulder. "I am sure someone here will want her. She is a pretty enough thing, and they could have some fun with her."

Hugh followed Mr. Cadell's gaze, and he saw plenty of disreputable men that he had no doubt would pay for the pleasure of Miss Wymond's company, forcing her to submit to appalling things.

Mr. Cadell's eyes landed on Mr. Hudson, who was the vilest of men. This was a man who had no qualms bragging about his exploits with women.

"Hudson!" Mr. Cadell shouted, "I have a proposition for you!"

Hugh felt a surge of protection for the girl, despite having never met her. As a gentleman, he couldn't sit by and let Mr. Cadell sell her off to Mr. Hudson, or anyone else, for that matter. After all, he was well aware of the type of men who frequented gambling halls. No! He may not have gotten along with her brother, but he couldn't stand by and let Miss Wymond be treated as no more than a commodity.

He tightened his hold on his cards and said, "I will allow you to wager Miss Wymond."

Mr. Cadell brought his gaze back around and gave him a smug smile. "You are hoping to have a go with her, then?" he asked.

"My reasons are my own," Hugh remarked dismissively. He couldn't wait to wipe that smug look off Mr. Cadell's face.

The dealer spoke up. "The wager has been accepted," he said. "It is time to show your cards."

Mr. Cadell lowered his cards to the table and arrogantly announced, "Flush."

"That is a good hand," Hugh admitted as he glanced down at his cards.

With a chuckle, Mr. Cadell reached forward and started retrieving the pot. "This isn't the first time I've played with such high stakes and won."

"But you didn't," Hugh corrected.

Mr. Cadell froze. "Pardon?"

"You didn't win," Hugh replied as he placed his cards down on the table. "Running flush, which beats your flush."

"That's impossible," Mr. Cadell said, his face growing pale. "You must have cheated!"

"I assure you that I did not."

Mr. Cadell turned towards the dealer. "He cheated!"

The tall, thin dealer shook his head. "There is no evidence that he cheated, and I would encourage you to keep your voice down. This is a respectable gambling hall."

Mr. Cadell scoffed at the dealer. "You must be in on it," he accused. "No one can be as good at cards as Lord Hugh is."

Hugh shrugged off Mr. Cadell's comments as he started collecting his winnings. "I've had a lot of practice, I suppose."

Mr. Cadell shoved back his chair and pointed his finger at him. "You tricked me into wagering my ward!"

"Why would I do that?" Hugh asked, uninterested.

"This was your plan all along," Mr. Cadell declared. "You wanted her for yourself!"

Hugh let out a sigh as he saw more heads turning their way. "Now you are just embarrassing yourself. I didn't even know you were wagering your ward until after I bragged."

"I don't care!" Mr. Cadell roared. "I won't let you take her from me. She is mine!"

Hugh sat back in his chair and put his hands up. "Look around you," he encouraged. "Everyone here will testify that I won the game fairly. You shouldn't have wagered what you couldn't lose."

"Don't patronize me," Mr. Cadell spat. "The Court of Chancery made me her guardian."

"Then I shall petition the court to turn guardianship over to me," Hugh said.

"They will never grant that."

"You seem to forget that I am the son of Marquess Montfort, and my father wields tremendous support in Parliament." Hugh rose. "You will bring Miss Wymond to me, or else I will have you thrown in debtor's prison for not honoring your bet."

Mr. Cadell reared back. "You wouldn't dare."

"I would, without the slightest hesitation." Hugh gave him a knowing look. "Who do you think the magistrate will side with?"

Mr. Cadell remained rooted in his spot as his face grew splotchy. "I will deliver her to your townhouse tomorrow, but this fight is far from over."

"If I were you, I would just give up," Hugh said. "You do not have the funds to fight me, and I doubt that the Court of Chancery will look kindly on you wagering your ward in a game of cards."

Without saying another word, Mr. Cadell stormed off towards the main door as everyone in the room seemed to watch his retreat.

As Hugh deposited his winnings into his jacket pocket, his friend, Lord Simon Thompson, approached him, a drink in his hand.

"What was that noise all about?" Simon asked as he came to a stop next to the table.

"Nothing but a sore loser."

Simon took a sip of his drink as he leaned against the table. "How much did he lose?"

"It wasn't how much he lost, but whom he lost."

"Now I am confused."

Hugh turned to face his friend. "He wagered his ward, Miss Wymond, in the game."

"Miss Wymond," Simon repeated. "As in, the sister of Stephen Wymond?"

"Yes," Hugh said.

Simon frowned. "But didn't you hate Stephen?"

"I did, but that doesn't mean I could sit back and do nothing to help the poor girl. Mr. Cadell had designs to sell her to Mr. Hudson."

Simon set his drink on the table. "It is a good thing that you intervened, but what are you going to do with a ward?"

"I will give her to my mother."

"She isn't a pet, you know," Simon said. "You can't just pass her off until someone wants her."

"I am well aware, but my mother will know what to do with her."

Simon furrowed his brow. "What do you know about Miss Wymond, other than she is Stephen's sister?"

"Nothing, really."

"I have a feeling that this is going to fail spectacularly for you," Simon said with a shake of his head, "and I can't wait to watch it unfold."

"You aren't being very helpful."

Simon chuckled. "I'm sorry," he responded. "I've had too much drink to care."

Hugh brushed past his friend and started walking towards the main door. Simon caught up and met his stride. "How do you think your father will respond to you taking on a ward?"

"I have no doubt that he will be furious and disappointed in me."

"Isn't he always, though?"

"That he is," Hugh said as he stepped through the opened door. "I am just a grand disappointment, so what's one more thing to add to the list?"

"You are being much too hard on yourself."

Hugh stopped on the pavement and turned towards his friend. "Nathaniel was born lucky, but I was just lucky to be born."

"I doubt that."

"My mother almost died in childbirth, and my father can't seem to forgive me for that," Hugh said.

"Has he told you that?"

"In so many words." Hugh put his hand up to signal a hackney. "It is time I go home and get some sleep."

"But the night is still young," Simon said.

"Not for me."

Simon glanced at the worn-down hackney that came to a stop next to the pavement. "Where is your coach?"

"My father decided I wasn't allowed to use the coach to go gambling anymore," Hugh grumbled as he stepped closer to the shabby vehicle.

After he shouted up the address to the driver, Hugh opened the door and stepped inside, ignoring the pungent odor that attacked his nostrils as he did so. He moved to open the window but saw that it was broken.

Hugh ran a hand through his dark hair as he wondered how in the blazes he was going to explain to his family what he had just done.

Chapter Two

Hugh descended the stairs of his townhouse after a fitful sleep. He wished that he could blame his decision of taking over the responsibility of Miss Wymond on a night of drinking, but he had been completely sober when he made that wager. He rarely drank when he played cards. He only drank afterward to celebrate his wins, which was quite frequently.

As he walked through the entry hall, the butler stepped out of one of the rooms and greeted him cordially. "Good morning, my lord."

"Good morning," Hugh said. "Has anyone come down for breakfast yet?"

"Yes, Lord Hawthorne is in the dining room," Balfour informed him.

Hugh tipped his head in acknowledgement before he headed towards the dining room.

"I see that you wore your finest for breakfast," Hugh joked as he walked over to the buffet table.

His brother's worn blue jacket was tattered at the sleeves, and it made no sense to wear the old thing. But Nathaniel would never be accused of being a dandy, unlike Haddington. He could easily afford new clothes, but never seemed to bother getting any. Hugh wondered what Dinah thought of her husband's wardrobe.

Nathaniel glanced up from reading the newssheets. "You are up early."

"I had a lot on my mind."

"Anything you wish to discuss?" Nathaniel asked.

"Yes, actually." Hugh accepted a plate from a footman and piled it high with food, then sat across from his brother. "I did something intolerably stupid last night."

"Did you lose at cards?"

"No, I won."

Nathaniel gave him a baffled look. "Then what is the issue?"

Hugh arranged his napkin on his lap and picked up his fork. "Do you remember Stephen Wymond?"

Nathaniel let out a chuckle. "How can I forget Stephen?" he asked. "You two hated one another."

"We did," Hugh said, seeing no reason to deny it. "He always had a pompous attitude that I found very vexing."

"You two were at odds with each other from the moment you arrived at Eton. I can't recall how many fights I broke up between you two."

"If I recall, I beat him pretty soundly each time."

"You were pretty evenly matched, but I never understood why you couldn't just ignore one another."

"It's impossible to ignore someone like him," Hugh said. "Just the sound of his voice grated on my ears."

"I still question the headmaster's decision to force you to room with him."

"It was supposed to bring us together, but it made us hate each other even more," Hugh shared.

Nathaniel reached for his teacup and took a sip. "Why do you bring up Stephen?" he asked. "If I recall correctly, he left Eton and went to the Royal Naval Academy."

"That is what I remember as well, but I just learned that his ship went down six months ago, with him on it."

"That is most unfortunate."

"It is," Hugh agreed. "I found him bothersome, but I would never wish death upon him, or anyone."

Nathaniel removed his napkin from his lap and dropped it onto the table. "If you will excuse me, I have work I need to see to."

"I won Stephen's sister in a card game," Hugh blurted out as his brother rose.

Nathaniel stilled. "I beg your pardon?"

"Her guardian, Mr. Cadell, wagered her, and I won the pot," Hugh explained. "He should be delivering her today."

Nathaniel returned to his seat. "What in the blazes were you thinking?"

"I was thinking that I had to help Miss Wymond because Mr. Cadell wanted to sell her off to raise funds to play," Hugh said. "I couldn't just sit back and do nothing to help her."

"I find that honorable, but what are you going to do with her?"

"I was hoping Mother might tend to her."

Nathaniel lifted his brow. "You can't just pass her off to Mother and wash your hands of her. Miss Wymond is now your responsibility."

"What am I to do, then?" Hugh asked. "I know nothing about being a guardian."

"How old is she?"

Hugh winced. "I don't know."

"You didn't bother to ask?"

"I was a little preoccupied."

Nathaniel stared at him with disbelief on his features. "Do you not care that your actions reflect on the family, whether good or bad?"

"I do not need another lecture—"

"I think you do," Nathaniel said firmly. "You have a ward

now, whether you like it or not. You need to step up and be the guardian that she deserves."

"How am I supposed to do that?"

"Well, for starters, you will need to discover if she will reside in the nursery or in a bedchamber," Nathaniel said.

"I shall find out today when she arrives." Hugh put his fork down and reached for his teacup. "Mr. Cadell did mention that she has an inheritance, but it is still tied up in probate court."

"Did he say why?"

"Stephen has only been gone for six months, so they haven't legally declared him dead yet."

"How much is her inheritance?"

Hugh shrugged. "I'm not sure."

"You don't know much, do you?" Nathaniel mocked.

Hugh was about to respond when their father stepped into the room and greeted them. "Good morning. It is good to see both of my sons awake this morning."

No one spoke as their father stepped up to the buffet table and filled a plate. After he sat at the head of the table, he glanced between them and asked, "Whatever is the matter?"

"Nothing is wrong," Hugh attempted. "We are just having a pleasant breakfast."

Nathaniel gave him a pointed look. "You may as well tell him."

"Tell me what?" his father asked accusatorily.

Hugh knew he needed to proceed cautiously, or his father's temper would go from an ember to an inferno in seconds. "Last night, I won a small fortune at the card tables."

"How lovely," was the muttered response. "I'm glad that the education I paid for is going to good use."

"What did you win?" Nathaniel prodded.

Hugh hesitated but pressed on. "I won Miss Wymond."

Their father visibly tensed. "Would you care to repeat that, son?" he asked in a gruff voice.

"Her guardian wagered her and lost," Hugh replied, shifting uncomfortably in his seat. "If I didn't accept the wager, he would have sold her to Mr. Hudson to allow him to come up with the funds to continue the game."

Their father remained silent, but his hard and unyielding expression said enough. "How could you do something so dishonorable?" he finally demanded. "Have I taught you nothing about how to treat a woman?"

"Father—"

"You do not get to speak! I knew your gambling would one day hurt our family's reputation, but to do this..." His father's voice trailed off as he shook his head. "This is inexcusable. How can you be a guardian when you can barely take care of yourself?"

"I am not an invalid," Hugh stated. "I have secured a fortune at the card tables."

"Yes, and I am so proud," their father said dryly. "You were trained for years to be a barrister, but instead you spend your nights at gambling halls."

"I've made more money gambling than I ever would have as a barrister," Hugh defended.

"Being respected by your peers is more important than money."

Hugh huffed. "You have the luxury of saying that, but I don't. I am merely the second son. I inherit no estate, no source of income."

"I have made allowances for you," their father said. "You will be comfortable for the remainder of your days, assuming you live prudently."

"I don't want any of your money. You can keep it, or better yet, give it to Nathaniel. Heaven knows he needs more money."

Their father shook his head again. "What did we do wrong with you?" he asked. "You were such a promising young man."

Hugh shoved back his chair and rose. "I don't have to listen to this."

"Yes, you do," their father said. "You're the one who went and got yourself a ward. What do you intend to do with her?"

"I don't know," Hugh admitted begrudgingly, "but I will know more once I meet her."

The only sound in the room was their father's heavy breathing as he fought to control his emotions. Eventually, he spoke.

"Do you know if Miss Wymond is related to the late Sir James Wymond?"

"She's his daughter," Hugh confirmed.

"I was friends with Sir James Wymond," their father said as he leaned back in his chair. "He was a decorated war hero and fought for the rights of the men and women in the rookeries. I was saddened to hear about his passing last year."

Their father rose from his seat and continued. "To honor my friend's memory, I will do right by his daughter and ensure she is taken care of."

"You're going to help me?" Hugh asked in surprise.

"I am, but only if your mother agrees to it."

"Thank you—"

His father put his hand up, stilling his words. "Do not take my willingness to help as approval of your actions. Your behavior has tainted this family."

Without saying another word, his father departed from the dining room, leaving behind a plate full of food.

Hugh stared at the empty doorway. "That went better than I expected."

Nathaniel rose. "I daresay you are lucky that Father agreed to help," he said. "You are not in a position to take a ward."

"Why does everyone treat me as if I am an imbecile?" Hugh asked. "I have secured my own fortune, and I did that all on my own."

"By gambling."

"Who cares how I did it?" Hugh questioned.

Nathanial came around the table. "You could be so much more than what you currently are."

Hugh let out a groan. "Now you sound like Father."

"At least one of us does."

Hugh took a step back. "I thought we had an understanding. I don't ask about your questionable behavior, and you don't ask about mine."

Nathaniel put his hand up. "You are right. I shouldn't have said anything."

"No, you shouldn't have," Hugh agreed as he walked over to the door. "I need to speak to Balfour and inform him that my ward will be residing with us soon."

My ward.

What in the blazes had he been thinking? He didn't want a ward, but he had little choice in the matter now.

———————

Miss Marielle Wymond's back was rigid as she sat in the coach. Why was this happening to her? *Again?* Her life had been upended when her father died nearly a year ago and she was left alone in their country home with only the household staff to tend to her. Then, six months later, she received a letter that her brother's ship had gone down and he was presumed dead.

Months thereafter, Mr. Cadell arrived and announced that he was her guardian. He was a distant cousin, but he'd made it clear that no one else wanted her. The rest of her family had turned their backs on her because her inheritance was tied up in probate court. As Mr. Cadell pointed out, repeatedly, she was penniless and an utter burden to his household, despite her living as frugally as she could.

Marielle wasn't a fool. She knew that Mr. Cadell had eyed her inheritance with immense interest for the month that she lived with him. Once the probate court released the funds, Mr. Cadell would control her inheritance, and she was fearful that he would spend it without regard to her future or well-being.

As awful as her life was, she never imagined Mr. Cadell would gamble her away. How could he have done such a thing? She was being sent to live with Lord Hugh Calvert, an inveterate gambler of the *ton*. She had never met him, but she'd read about his antics in the Society pages. There were rumors of his immense wealth, but she'd learned long ago to dismiss rumors, as most were unsubstantiated.

Mr. Cadell spoke up, drawing her attention. "I am sorry that I put you in this position," he said, his words sounding at least somewhat remorseful.

Marielle kept her attention on the window and admired the large townhouses that lined the street without replying. She didn't feel the need to be solicitous, not after what he'd done to her.

"I understand that you are angry, but you will need to be respectful to Lord Hugh. He has the power to make your life very difficult."

"Only until I reach my majority in seven months," Marielle said, turning to face him. "Then I will be free to do as I please."

"I cannot say for certainty that your inheritance will be released by then, so you may as well accept that you will be relying on Lord Hugh's good graces, at least for a while."

Marielle glanced down at her clasped hands in her lap. "Was I so awful that you had to get rid of me?"

"Of course not," Mr. Cadell said. "I thought I had a winning hand and could finally recoup what I had lost."

Marielle knew she should bite her sharp tongue, but she was angry. "You wagered me to a complete stranger, without a thought or a care about my welfare!"

Mr. Cadell's expression hardened. "I am your guardian, and I will do with you whatever I see fit!"

"But you aren't my guardian anymore, are you?" she challenged. "You lost that right."

Mr. Cadell leaned forward. "You're lucky I'm in a forgiving mood this morning, or else I would make you regret such insolence."

Marielle knew that she had pressed Mr. Cadell too far and it would do her no good to continue fighting with him. She just needed to prepare herself for her meeting with Lord Hugh. One thing she had learned was that if she expected nothing, she would never be disappointed.

The coach stopped in front of a three-level whitewashed townhouse. Marielle wondered pessimistically what fate awaited her behind those walls.

A footman opened the door and Mr. Cadell exited first, then reached back to help her out of the coach. She accepted his assistance and hesitantly stepped onto the pavement, where she stopped to admire the opulent building.

Mr. Cadell tucked her hand into the crook of his arm and encouraged her forward. Marielle felt as if her feet were made of lead, but she managed to put one foot in front of the other.

The main door opened and a man with a warm disposition greeted them. "May I help you?"

Mr. Cadell removed a calling card from his pocket and extended it to the butler. "Lord Hugh is expecting me and Miss Wymond."

The butler glanced down at the card before opening the door wide. "Do come in, Mr. Cadell," he encouraged.

They were led to a room adjacent to the entry hall.

"If you would care to wait in the drawing room, I will inform Lord Hugh of your arrival."

"Thank you," Mr. Cadell said.

Marielle stepped into the room and withdrew her hand from Mr. Cadell. The room was elaborately furnished, and she briefly admired the ivory-colored walls with golden sconces. She walked towards a table in the rear of the room and picked up a small vase that had drawn her attention.

Mr. Cadell came to stand next to her. "Whatever are you doing?" he whispered. "It is impolite to show interest in someone's decorations."

"I am merely looking at it."

"Well, don't break it."

Marielle resisted the urge to shake her head at his ridiculous command. Her country home had been filled with the finest exports, and she had learned at a young age to be careful when handling them.

As she gently set the vase back down on the table, a rich baritone voice came from the doorway.

"Good morning, Mr. Cadell."

"Good morning, Lord Hugh," Mr. Cadell greeted.

Marielle closed her eyes as she attempted to garner the strength to meet her new guardian. She slowly turned and found herself rendered speechless. Lord Hugh was a tall man with broad shoulders, dark hair brushed to the side, a strong jaw, and a straight nose. She didn't know what she'd supposed Lord Hugh would be like, but she hadn't expected him to be so young. Or so handsome.

Lord Hugh glanced at her before he turned his attention back to Mr. Cadell, clearly waiting for an introduction.

Mr. Cadell cleared his throat. "Lord Hugh, allow me to introduce you to my—er, I mean, your—ward, Miss Marielle Wymond."

Lord Hugh bowed. "It is a pleasure to meet you, Miss Wymond."

Marielle dropped into a curtsy. "Likewise, my lord," she murmured.

Lord Hugh watched her for a long moment, and she resisted the urge to squirm under his scrutiny. "Marielle is a lovely name, but it isn't one I've encountered before."

"I was named after my grandmother," Marielle replied. "She was French."

"Ah," Lord Hugh said. "That would explain it, then."

Marielle's eyes grew downcast as the silence grew awkward. She was at a loss for words. What did one say at a moment like this?

Mr. Cadell looked at her with something like regret in his eyes. He shifted his gaze to Hugh and asked, "May I have a word?"

Lord Hugh gestured towards the door, indicating that Mr. Cadell should go first. They stepped into the hall and shut the door. Marielle walked closer to the door, being mindful to stay hidden. What did Mr. Cadell wish to discuss with Lord Hugh?

She could hear hushed voices but couldn't quite make out what was being said. She was about to give up when Mr. Cadell raised his voice.

"I won't let you get away with this!" he shouted. "Miss Wymond belongs with me, not you!"

"You shouldn't have gambled her away," came the surprisingly calm and collected reply.

"You just want to have your fun with her and toss her aside," Mr. Cadell accused. "I won't let you do that!"

Marielle gasped. Is that what Lord Hugh intended to do with her?

"I think it is time for you to leave. You are no longer welcome in my home," Lord Hugh said, his voice taking on a commanding edge.

"Can I at least say goodbye?" Mr. Cadell asked.

"You lost that right when she became my ward."

There was complete silence for a long moment, then Marielle heard footsteps stomping away, followed by the front door being slammed shut.

She had yet to move from her location when Lord Hugh reentered the room. He cast her a disapproving look.

"Were you eavesdropping?" he asked.

Blatantly lying to her new guardian didn't seem like the most promising idea.

"I was," she said, "but I barely heard anything."

Lord Hugh perused the length of her, his expression giving nothing away. "You are much older than I had expected."

Unsure of what to say to such a ridiculous comment, she murmured, "I'm sorry."

"There is no reason to apologize." He glanced towards the door. "What Mr. Cadell accused me of wasn't true. You are safe here. I promise that no one will hurt you."

Marielle nodded. What else could she do? He seemed sincere, but she still felt nervous. He wasn't being very welcoming. She surmised that he must not be pleased that she was here. She had felt an urge to run from him. She didn't think she feared him, but he unsettled her in a way that no one else ever had.

"Sorry for my delay," a woman's voice said from the doorway. "I just received word that you've arrived."

Marielle turned her attention to the older woman with fading blonde hair, grateful for the interruption.

The woman stopped before her and smiled.

"Welcome to our home," she greeted. "My name is Edith, and I am Hugh's mother."

Marielle dropped into a curtsy. "My lady."

"We do not stand on formalities in our house," Edith said with a wave of her hand. "You must call me Edith."

Marielle relaxed somewhat. "Then it would only be fair if you called me Marielle."

"What a lovely name," Edith remarked. "I am sure you are tired from your journey. Would you care for me to show you to your bedchamber?"

"That would be lovely."

"Follow me, then," Edith encouraged as she turned and departed from the room.

With a parting glance at Lord Hugh, Marielle hurried to catch up to Edith's quick stride. They proceeded towards the large staircase that dominated one side of the entry hall.

"This townhouse has been in our family for generations," Edith shared as she placed her hand on the iron railing.

"It's beautiful," Marielle remarked as she admired the ornately painted ceiling.

Edith glanced over at her. "I know it can be daunting to live in a new place, but we want you to feel at home here."

"That is most kind of you, my lad... Edith," she corrected.

"I must admit that I have only just recently learned of the circumstances that have led you to our home."

Marielle gave her a weak smile. "I only learned of it myself when Mr. Cadell instructed my lady's maid to start packing for me."

"Did you bring your lady's maid with you?"

Marielle nodded. "I did," she replied. "I do hope that isn't an issue. Grace has been with me for many years."

"Not at all." As they started walking down the hall, Edith continued, "I have selected a room for you near my bedchamber. It has recently been redecorated."

Edith stopped in front of a wooden door and reached for the handle. Marielle followed her into the room, and her eyes grew wide as she took in the size of the bedchamber. It was very large, with a four-poster bed along one wall, a fireplace opposite it, and two large bay windows. The walls were a pale green, and the floral curtains blew delicately in the breeze.

"I do hope you like this room," Edith said.

Marielle clasped her hands together. "I love it!" she gushed. "It is fit for a queen!"

Edith laughed. "I am glad that you approve. My daughter-in-law, Dinah, helped me decorate it."

"Is that my cue?" someone asked from the doorway.

Marielle turned to see a beautiful, blonde-haired young

woman, who wasn't much older than herself, walk into the room.

Edith gestured towards the young woman. "Marielle, allow me to introduce you to my daughter-in-law, Dinah, the Countess of Hawthorne."

Marielle dropped into a curtsy. "My lady."

Dinah gave her a welcoming smile. "I would prefer it if you called me Dinah."

"Only if you will call me Marielle."

"I have so many questions for you," Dinah said as she sat on the edge of the bed, "but I do not know where to begin."

"Perhaps it might be best if we let Marielle settle in before we bombard her with questions," Edith suggested.

Dinah nodded. "That would be the polite thing to do."

Edith turned to Marielle. "Would you care for a bath?" she asked.

Marielle perked up. "I would love a bath! The water was always so cold at Mr. Cadell's townhouse," she admitted, "and I had to bathe in the kitchen near the hearth just to keep warm."

"You will find a much different experience here," Edith said as she walked towards the door. "I shall see to the preparations."

"Thank you," Marielle acknowledged.

"Are you coming?" Edith asked Dinah.

Dinah seemed hesitant. "I suppose so," she said as she rose from the bed. "But that doesn't mean I don't have a list of questions to ask Marielle."

Marielle grinned. "I promise to answer every one of them later."

Her response seemed to appease Dinah, who followed Edith out of the room. Once she was alone, Marielle dropped down on the bed. This room reminded her so much of the one she had at her country home, and it made her slightly nostalgic.

Her bedchamber at Mr. Cadell's had been cramped and dark, the only window facing an alleyway. If she was lucky, she would never have to see Mr. Cadell again. That was one dark stain in Marielle's life she wished she could blot out.

Perhaps having Lord Hugh as her guardian wouldn't be as terrible as she'd previously thought.

Chapter Three

Hugh sat in the parlor with a long-forgotten drink in his hand. His ward was a beautiful young woman and not at all what he had expected. Frankly, he hadn't known what to expect. With her blonde hair, pale skin, and wide green eyes, Miss Wymond could be the diamond of the first water this Season.

But a man wasn't supposed to notice those things about his ward. She was now his responsibility. What a daunting thought! For so long, he had only worried about himself, but everything was different now.

His mother walked into the room with a purposeful stride.

"Here you are," she said. "I have been looking for you everywhere."

"I assure you that I wasn't hiding."

His mother took a seat across from him. "What in the blazes were you thinking, son?" she demanded.

Hugh lifted his brow. "Language, mother," he teased.

"I only use bad words when I am angry," she said, "and I am truly and utterly angry at the moment."

Hugh leaned forward and set his nearly full drink on a table. "I assume this is about Miss Wymond."

"What else would it be about?" his mother asked. "You

were foolish enough to gamble and won a ward in the process."

"I did, but my intentions were honorable," he explained. "Mr. Cadell is a scoundrel. He was going to sell her off to raise funds. What would you have had me do?"

Some of the anger left his mother's expression. "I suppose you did the right thing, but we have a bigger problem."

"Which is?"

"Miss Wymond is a beautiful young woman and needs to be introduced into Society," his mother said.

"Do you think that is truly necessary?"

"It is, and I think it would be best if I took charge of her care."

Hugh tried to keep his eagerness out of his voice and expressions. This was precisely the outcome he had been hoping for. "If you think that is truly necessary."

"I do, but I will expect you to do your part as her guardian."

"That won't be an issue."

"What do you know about Miss Wymond?" his mother asked, leaning back in her seat.

"I admit that I know very little about her," he replied. "I hadn't expected her to be so…" His words trailed off as he tried to find the right words. He couldn't very well admit to his mother that he found his ward to be quite beautiful. "…tall."

"I do not think Miss Wymond is overly tall."

"I had just expected someone shorter."

His mother gave him an odd look. "Well, I am glad she didn't disappoint you in regard to her height."

"Height is important for a young woman." Bother. Why couldn't he keep his mouth shut?

"If you say so," his mother said. "I think it is more important for a young woman to be clever and have a quick wit."

"I would agree with that sentiment."

His mother nodded approvingly. "We shall have to host a ball in Miss Wymond's honor."

"Why exactly is a ball necessary?"

"Miss Wymond is the daughter of Sir James Wymond and is now your ward. A ball will help her position in Society."

Before Hugh could reply, his father stormed into the room with newssheets in his hand. "Your antics have made the morning newspaper."

"How is that possible?" Hugh asked.

His father stopped next to his mother's seat. "Now everyone knows how you acquired Miss Wymond as your ward," he said. "Your activities have embarrassed this family again."

His mother reached for the newssheets and perused the article. "Well, what is done is done. We must proceed cautiously so as not to damage Miss Wymond's reputation any more than it already has been."

"Do you not care for my reputation?" Hugh asked.

His father scoffed. "Your reputation has been tainted for years, but you can recover simply by marrying a respectable young woman and taking your rightful place in Society."

"I don't care about Society," Hugh said.

"You will have to, because you are now Miss Wymond's guardian," his mother said. "You will be expected to escort her to social events and keep a watchful eye on her."

Hugh groaned. "That sounds miserable."

"This situation is entirely of your own making," his father said. "If you want me to feel sorry for you, you will be sorely disappointed."

"I did all of this to protect Miss Wymond," Hugh asserted. "You should be praising me instead of criticizing me."

"You are a blasted saint," his father mocked.

Hugh rose. "Nothing I do will be good enough for you, will it?" he demanded.

"You are wasting your life," his father said, shaking the

newssheets in front of him, "and making a mockery of our good name!"

"I'm sorry that you feel that way, but I refuse to live as you see fit," Hugh said. "I am not that man, nor will I ever be."

"What happened to you?" his father asked. "You were a successful barrister, and now you are throwing your life away."

His mother abruptly rose and placed a hand on her husband's shoulder. "Perhaps it would be best if we all took a moment to consider our words more carefully."

"That isn't necessary, Mother," Hugh said. "I have no desire to continue this conversation."

"The moment things get too serious, you run away," his father said. "You have to accept that there is more to life than gambling."

"Gambling gives me a reprieve."

"From what?"

Hugh tossed his hands up. "From this!" he shouted. "From you!"

His father took a step closer to him. "There is nothing wrong with your life, but I daresay that there is something wrong with *you*."

Hugh narrowed his eyes. "You pretend you know me, but you don't know anything about me," he countered. "You have never even made an attempt to understand me."

"What is there to understand?" his father asked. "You gamble nearly every night, and you gave up on a respectable career because you aren't disciplined enough for it!"

Hugh had heard enough. "I refuse to remain here and be insulted."

He didn't bother to wait for his father's reply before he headed for the door. His father didn't know what he was talking about, but it stung nevertheless. He didn't quit being a barrister because he was undisciplined. He'd quit because he had been too good at his job.

He ascended the stairs and started for his bedchamber.

The library door was ajar, and he peeked inside. Miss Wymond was sitting in front of the hearth, immersed in the book in her hand. She was dressed in a pale yellow gown, and her hair was piled on top of her head with small curls framing her face.

Hugh stepped into the room. It would probably be best if he let her be—arguing with his father never put him in a good state of mind—but he hadn't really had a chance to speak with his ward yet. This was as good an opportunity as any to learn more about her.

Miss Wymond glanced up and a tentative smile came to her lips. "Lord Hugh," she acknowledged.

"I see that you found the library."

Miss Wymond's eyes left his and roamed the bookshelves that lined the room. "I have never seen so many books before," she said. "I couldn't believe all of the first editions I found in your collection."

"My family has been collecting books for generations."

"You are lucky to have such a treasure in your home."

Hugh walked closer to her. "I never considered that before," he said. "Frankly, I do not have much time to read anymore."

"What a shame. Reading is a fantastic way to transport to another time, another place." Miss Wymond glanced down at the book in her hand. "Mr. Cadell didn't have much of a library, and he refused to purchase more books. He said it was a waste of time because no man wants a well-read wife."

"That was wrong of him to say so. You are more than welcome to read as much as you would like while you are here."

"Thank you, my lord."

Hugh gestured towards the chair next to her. "May I?"

"You may," she replied.

"I knew your brother," Hugh shared as he sat down.

"You did?" Miss Wymond asked, her eyes lighting up.

"I must admit that Stephen and I were at odds from the moment we arrived at Eton," Hugh shared. "We couldn't stand one another."

"Why?"

Hugh shrugged. "Does it truly matter now?"

"I suppose not."

He offered her a weak smile. "I was sad to hear of his passing," he said. "Despite our differences, I never wished for him to have such a tragic end."

Miss Wymond glanced down at her hands in her lap. "I know that his ship went down and that he is presumed dead. But is it pathetic of me that I still have hope that he will be found alive?"

"It is unlikely; you must know that."

Miss Wymond let out a breath. "I know, and I must sound incredibly foolish, but I can't help but hold onto hope."

"I don't think you sound foolish at all."

Miss Wymond brought her gaze up. "You don't?"

"You must have loved your brother very much to hold on to such hope."

"I do love him, very much," Miss Wymond said, her voice betraying her emotions. "He was the best brother I could have ever asked for."

"Then hold on to those good memories."

Miss Wymond reached up and fingered the gold locket hung around her neck. "I remember his smile," she said. "He had a serious demeanor, but when he did smile, it always reached his eyes."

"It is the little things that take up the most room in our hearts."

Miss Wymond bobbed her head. "I agree with that sentiment."

He could hear the love in her voice as well as see the pain lurking in her eyes. It was evident she missed her brother very much. A silence descended over them, and Hugh found that everything he wanted to say seemed inadequate at the moment.

He rose. "I should let you get back to reading."

Miss Wymond gave him a grateful smile. "Thank you for allowing me to speak about Stephen. The more I speak of him, the more I remember how blessed I was to have him in my life."

"You are always welcome to speak to me about Stephen."

"Thank you, my lord."

"I would prefer if you called me Hugh."

Her eyes grew wide. "I wouldn't dare."

Her reaction was oddly charming. "I am your guardian, and I do not want you 'my lording' me every time we speak."

"You must call me Marielle, then."

He smiled. "I would like that very much."

Marielle returned his smile, and the room seemed a little brighter.

"I shall see you at dinner," Hugh said, taking a step back.

"I am looking forward to it… Hugh."

He chuckled. "You might want to practice saying my name."

"I shall do so."

With a tip of his head, he departed from the library and headed down the hall towards his bedchamber. It was only then that he noticed he was still smiling.

Marielle lounged on the settee with her book before a crackling fire. The sun had just set, and she was waiting for her lady's maid to come help her dress for dinner. A knock signaled her arrival.

"Enter."

The door opened and her lady's maid stepped in the

room, a gown draped over her arm. Grace was short, thin, and redheaded, and she always seemed to find something amusing.

"I've come to dress you for dinner," Grace said, placing the gown on the bed. "I thought you would like to wear your blue gown with net overlay. I assume you want to make a good impression this evening."

Marielle put the book down and rose. "I do," she said as she walked over to the dressing table and sat down.

Grace removed the pins from her hair and started brushing her blonde tresses. "I must admit that I am glad that we're here."

"Why is that?"

"This townhouse is so much nicer than Mr. Cadell's, and the staff is much more hospitable," Grace replied. "It's like a breath of fresh air."

"I am of the same mind."

Grace put her brush down. "By all accounts, it appears that the servants enjoy working here and Lady Montfort doesn't make any ridiculous demands."

"Unlike Mr. Cadell."

Grace shuddered. "I did not like that man," she admitted. "He treated you terribly, along with the household staff."

"Those days are behind us," Marielle said. "With any luck, we will never have to see Mr. Cadell again."

"I hope so." Grace started pinning Marielle's hair up. "I did hear the most interesting thing downstairs."

"Which was?"

Grace took a step back. "One of the footmen overheard Lord Hugh saying that he saved you from Mr. Cadell because he was going to sell you off to the highest bidder to raise funds."

"How distasteful! But I am not at all surprised by Mr. Cadell's despicable behavior," Marielle murmured. "I shall have to thank Lord Hugh for his interference."

A short time later, Marielle was dressed, and the dinner bell could be heard echoing from downstairs. A knock came at the door and Grace crossed the room to answer it. She dropped into a curtsy at the sight of Lord Hugh.

Hugh was dressed dapperly in a dark blue jacket with a crisp white waistcoat and matching cravat. His hair was brushed forward and his long sideburns were neatly trimmed.

"I have come to escort you to the drawing room," he said, remaining in the hall.

"I appreciate your thoughtfulness." Marielle walked over to the door and Lord Hugh stepped back. "Frankly, I am not sure if I could have found the drawing room on my own."

Hugh offered his arm. "I was worried that might have been the case."

A shiver went up Marielle's spine as she placed her hand on his arm. Good heavens, what was that about? Had she been so alone that her heart was playing tricks on her? It would not do well for her to develop feelings for her guardian. Marielle put the disturbing thought behind her and chalked it up to nerves.

"Did you have an enjoyable afternoon?" Hugh asked as he led her down the hall.

"I did," she replied. "I spent the afternoon reading in my bedchamber, and I even had a nap, which I am quite fond of."

"You are fond of naps?"

"I am. I don't sleep very well at night."

Hugh glanced at her. "I am sorry to hear that."

Marielle shrugged. "I haven't slept well since my father passed. I can't seem to quiet my thoughts long enough to fall asleep."

"I can relate to that," Hugh responded. "No matter how hard I try to suppress certain thoughts, they resurface in my dreams, haunting me. Sleep isn't often restful."

"You do understand."

"I have found a perfect solution, though," Hugh said as they began descending the stairs.

"Which is?"

"I stay out all night, and I'm usually too exhausted in the morning to do anything but sleep deeply."

"That sounds like a terrible idea."

Hugh gave her an amused look. "You do not mince words, do you?"

"I do not," she replied. "I was raised to voice my opinion."

"That's good."

They stepped into the drawing room, where they found Dinah standing close to a blond man. They were gazing longingly at one another; it wasn't hard to deduce that this was her husband.

Hugh cleared his throat.

Dinah turned her head and smiled. "Good evening, Hugh."

"I am used to your antics, but I'm afraid Marielle is not," Hugh said lightly.

"You are welcome to purchase your own townhouse," Lord Hawthorne said.

Dinah elbowed his ribs. "Be nice to your brother."

"Yes, my love," Lord Hawthorne said, reaching for his wife's hand. "I will behave, assuming he does."

Dinah turned toward Marielle. "Have you been introduced to my husband, Lord Hawthorne?"

"I have not," Marielle replied.

Lord Hawthorne tipped his head. "I would prefer it if you would call me Nathaniel, considering you are my," his voice tripped, "brother's ward."

"You must call me Marielle, then."

Dinah gestured towards the settees. "Shall we sit and become more acquainted as we wait for Edith and William?"

Hugh led Marielle to the settees and dropped his arm, claiming the spot next to her once she was seated.

Dinah gave Marielle an expectant look. "I'm afraid that I know nothing about you, other than what Hugh has told me, which is really nothing."

"What would you like to know?" Marielle asked.

"Where do you hail from?"

Marielle smoothed her gown. "I grew up in Brightlingsea at our country estate. It's a coastal town in Essex."

"How delightful," Dinah said.

"My father owned a shipyard and built brigs for the Royal Navy," Marielle shared.

Hugh interjected, "What happened to the business?"

"It is still quite profitable, or so I have been told by Mr. Cadell," Marielle replied. "The probate court approved my father's man of business overseeing all of our family's assets until they rule my brother legally dead." Her voice grew quiet at the end.

"My condolences for your losses," Dinah murmured.

Marielle waved her hand in front of her. "It has been six months since my brother's ship went down. I keep telling myself that if he was alive, he would have been found by now, but I still hope for a miracle."

"There is nothing wrong with that," Dinah said. "Without hope, we have nothing."

Marielle gave her a grateful smile. "In seven months, I'll have reached my majority and the court should rule in my favor, and I will inherit my father's holdings."

"You will be an heiress," Hugh said.

"I will, but I do not wish to be married and lose my father's company to my husband," Marielle said. "My hope is that I can run it."

"A woman running a company?" Hugh asked. "That is quite unorthodox."

Marielle lifted her chin. "Just because something is unusual doesn't mean that it is wrong."

"I think that is wonderful," Dinah said with an encouraging smile. "Why can't a woman run a business?"

"For many reasons, my love," Nathaniel replied. "Just think of the scandal it would cause."

"I am not afraid of hard work," Marielle said.

Hugh shifted to face her. "You may not be afraid of hard work, but women of your station aren't meant to sully their hands with work."

"I understand your concerns, but this is my father's company; it was his legacy. I intend to honor my father by continuing his work," Marielle responded.

Dinah bobbed her head. "I find that admirable," she said. "Do not listen to the naysayers."

"I have no intention to." Marielle decided to change the direction of the conversation. "May I ask how long you two have been married?"

Dinah exchanged a smitten look with Nathaniel. "A little over two months now," she said.

"Did you take a wedding tour?" Marielle asked.

"We did not," Dinah replied. "Nathaniel had work that he had to see to, but we intend to once the Season is over."

Edith stepped into the room. "I have just spoken to Balfour, and dinner is ready to be served," she announced.

"Will Father not be joining us?" Nathaniel asked, rising.

"He sent word that his meeting at the House of Lords was running late and for us to start without him," Edith replied.

Hugh rose and held his hand out to assist Marielle. Once she was standing, she withdrew her hand and walked over to Edith.

Edith eyed her with approval. "You look lovely," she said.

"Thank you," Marielle replied. "I haven't worn this gown in so long that I am glad it still fits."

"Whyever not?" Edith asked.

"Mr. Cadell was rarely home for dinner, so I frequently ate in the kitchen with the household staff," Marielle replied.

Edith's eyes went wide. "You ate in the kitchen?"

"I did," Marielle replied, wishing she could take back her words. What they must think of her now!

Edith seemed to recover quickly. "Well, we do things differently in our household," she said. "We eat dinner together as a family."

"That sounds wonderful," Marielle said. "I haven't eaten dinner as a family for so long."

"What about when your father was alive?"

Marielle sobered. "He was quite sick towards the end, and he spent most of his time in his bedchamber."

Edith placed a comforting hand on her sleeve. "You have my sympathies, my dear," she said. "You must be an exceptionally strong young woman to have overcome all that you have and still have the ability to smile so genuinely."

"I appreciate you for saying so," Marielle responded.

Edith lowered her hand. "Sometimes the people with the greatest hardships are being prepared for something extraordinary."

Hugh came to stand next to her. "You must excuse my mother. She missed her calling as a philosopher," he teased.

Edith laughed. "Maybe I will write a book one day."

"That would be quite scandalous of you," Hugh said.

"I would read it," Marielle responded. "I hope one day it will be acceptable for a woman to write a book and use her own name."

Dinah spoke up from behind her. "Until then, we can enjoy the books written anonymously by 'A Lady'. Reading her books is a guilty pleasure of mine."

"Mine too," Marielle said. "I do hope we will one day discover her true identity."

"I wonder if she's someone I know," Dinah said. "Wouldn't that be grand?"

Edith gestured towards the entry hall. "It might be best if we continued this conversation over dinner."

Hugh offered his arm to his mother. "Allow me to escort you to the dining room."

"Thank you, son," Edith said, placing her hand on his arm.

As Marielle trailed behind, she found herself grateful for the situation she found herself in. It wasn't ideal, but she would be happy here until she received her inheritance.

Chapter Four

Hugh assisted his mother into her chair before he claimed his seat next to Marielle.

As he placed his napkin on his lap, his mother smiled broadly at Marielle and announced, "I have decided that we will be throwing you a ball."

Marielle shook her head. "That isn't necessary."

"But it is," his mother asserted. "You haven't had a Season yet, and it is time for you to take your place in Society."

"I have no desire to take a place in Society," Marielle said. "I want to live a quiet life in Brightlingsea where I will run my father's company."

Not deterred by her refusal, his mother pressed on. "It will keep the gossip at bay if we introduce you to Society."

"What gossip?" Marielle asked.

Hugh shifted in his seat to face her. "The morning newspapers discovered that you were wagered in a card game and that I won," he explained.

"I see," Marielle said, lowering her gaze to the table. "That is most unfortunate."

"It is, but the gossips will move on to something more

interesting once they realize there is nothing to report on," Hugh remarked.

Marielle brought her gaze up and met his. "Do you think I should have a ball?"

"I do," he replied. "I think it would be a very good thing."

Hugh watched in fascination as a myriad of emotions crossed her face before she nodded. "If you think it is a good idea, then I will trust you."

He sucked in a breath. They hardly knew one another, but somehow, she trusted him. How was that possible?

His mother clasped her hands together. "What wonderful news!" she exclaimed. "I hoped for this outcome, so I have already begun the preparations. The ball will be held next week."

"Isn't that a little ambitious?" Hugh asked.

"Not for me," his mother said. "We'll make Marielle's ball the event of the Season. I have no doubt that it will be a crush."

Dinah spoke up from the other side of the table. "I can help with the preparations, as well."

"I shall take you up on that," his mother responded. "We have a lot of work that we need to see to, but the most important is that we must commission Marielle a new ballgown at once."

"Will a week be enough time to create one?" Dinah asked.

"We will have to pay for extra seamstresses, but it is entirely possible," his mother said. "I have no doubt that Madam Blanchet will make an exception for Marielle."

Marielle's eyes grew wide. "Madam Blanchet is the most coveted dressmaker in all of London."

"That she is, but she is a friend of mine. I was purchasing her gowns long before she became a name to Society," his mother said. "I stumbled across her small shop and decided to go inside. Once I saw her designs, I knew she was exceptionally talented, and I have only worn her gowns since. It didn't take long before Society took note."

His father stepped into the room and took his place at the head of the table. "I apologize for my delay," he said.

His mother smiled from across the table at her husband. "We were just discussing the preparations that we need to see to for Marielle's ball."

"Very good," his father murmured, nodding to Marielle. "There is an abundance of interest in her at the moment, and I believe a ball would quell most of it."

"That is the hope," his mother said.

As the footmen placed bowls of soup in front of them, Dinah asked Marielle, "Were you educated by a governess?"

"Only for a few years," Marielle said. "My father thought it would benefit me to attend boarding school after my mother died."

"Which one did you attend?" Dinah asked.

"Mrs. Allard's Finishing School," Marielle replied.

His mother nodded in approval. "That is an impressive school, and I have no doubt that they saw to your complete education."

"That they did," Marielle agreed. "It was lonely being away from home, but I was fortunate enough to forge many strong friendships with the other students."

"I am sorry that your mother passed away when you were so young," Hugh said.

"Thank you," Marielle murmured. "It was unexpected, and I still dearly miss her. She was my whole world when I was younger."

"I take it that you two were close," Dinah said.

"My mother was everything I aspired to," Marielle said, looking reflective. "She was kind, loving, and could make me laugh at the drop of a hat."

"How old were you when she died?" Hugh asked.

"Thirteen," Marielle replied. "She fell off her horse and hit her head. Sadly, she never woke up after that."

"How terrible," his mother murmured.

Marielle quieted, her eyes moistening with unshed tears. "It was," she murmured.

Hugh gave his mother a pointed look. "Perhaps we could speak of something else," he suggested, earning a grateful look from Marielle.

His mother took his cue and turned her attention towards Dinah. "Would you care to go to the dressmakers tomorrow with us?"

Dinah smiled. "I would enjoy that very much," she said. "I might just commission a ballgown myself."

"Another one?" Nathaniel asked teasingly.

"One cannot have too many gowns," Dinah replied with a slight shrug of her shoulders.

"I am a smart enough man not to argue with that," Nathaniel said.

His father put his spoon down and met Nathaniel's gaze. "Did you have a chance to review the ledgers I left on your desk?"

"I did," Nathaniel responded.

"What are your thoughts?" his father pressed.

His mother interrupted Nathaniel's response. "It might be best if we didn't discuss business over dinner, for the sake of our guest."

His father looked displeased. "Marielle isn't truly a guest. She is Hugh's ward."

"That she is, but you could speak about business after dinner over a glass of port," their mother said.

"As you wish," his father stated.

His mother smiled at Marielle and asked, "Have you been able to settle in?"

"I have," Marielle replied. "I did venture from my bedchamber and found the library."

"You will find our library is quite extensive," his mother said.

"That it is. It puts the library at my country estate to shame," Marielle said. "I have never seen so many first editions before."

Hugh leaned to the side as a footman came to collect his bowl. "I encouraged Marielle to read any book that she desires in the library."

His father let out a slight huff. "There are some books in the library that are not appropriate for a gentlewoman, especially the books on politics and religion."

"I have no doubt that Marielle will use discretion when she chooses her books," Hugh said, turning towards her. "Won't you?"

"I will," Marielle replied.

Hugh turned back towards his father. "Does that put that issue to rest?"

"It does, but you have yet to begin to take your guardianship of Marielle seriously," his father replied. "Have you met with her solicitor?"

"I have not secured a meeting yet, but—"

His father cut him off. "What do you know about the terms of her inheritance?" he asked.

"Very little, but—"

"You are now responsible for Marielle, and I won't let you fail her," his father said. "At least, not how you have failed this family."

Hugh felt his jaw clenching. "I have not failed this family."

"Haven't you?" his father asked. "You spend your evenings gambling and your days sleeping off everything you drank."

"You know nothing about my life, Father," Hugh said, his voice rising.

"I know enough."

His mother interjected, "Can you two speak of this after dinner? We don't want to make Marielle uncomfortable."

"I just want Marielle to understand what kind of guardian she has," his father said.

"What do you mean by that?" Hugh asked.

A footman placed a plate in front of his father as he replied, "You have opened this family, and now your ward, to gossip."

"I did no such thing. I have only ever minded my business," Hugh argued.

"Do you think your presence can go unnoticed at a gambling hall?" his father asked. "You are the son of a marquess."

"I am aware of my lineage," Hugh growled.

"Are you?" his father asked. "You might want to start acting like it."

An uncomfortable silence descended over the table, and Hugh found himself fuming. No matter what he did, he would never be good enough for his father. He knew that, and so did everyone else. It was a wonder that he even kept company with his father anymore. They could hardly be in the same room without fighting.

To his surprise, Marielle spoke up, her voice starting weak but growing stronger. "I know precisely the kind of man that Hugh is," she said. "He saved me from Mr. Cadell, and I will forever be in his debt. As far as I am concerned, Hugh is my hero."

Hugh shifted his gaze to meet hers. "I am no one's hero," he admitted softly.

"You are mine. I heard that Mr. Cadell planned to sell me off to raise the funds to gamble when you stepped in," Marielle said. "Frankly, I couldn't have stayed a moment longer at Mr. Cadell's townhouse. He always eyed me with entirely too much interest."

"You are safe here," Hugh assured her.

"I know, and that is a wonderful feeling." Marielle turned

her attention towards his father. "I care not about Hugh's reputation, or the gossips, because he saved me."

A smile slowly spread on his father's face. "I like this one," he said. "You are incredibly naïve, foolish, perhaps, but you can hold your own, and I respect that."

His mother picked up her fork. "We best start eating this meat before it grows cold."

As everyone started eating, Hugh snuck a glance at Marielle. Had she meant what she said? He hoped she hadn't put him on a pedestal. He wasn't worthy of that kind of praise. If she ever learned the truth about him, she would know that he was selfish, dishonorable… not a hero. He didn't want to be idolized, but he wasn't sure he wanted Marielle to know his true nature, either.

With the sun streaming through the windows, Marielle sat at the long dining table as she enjoyed a cup of chocolate. It was an indulgence she'd missed when she lived at Mr. Cadell's townhouse. When she requested chocolate, he dismissed her by saying it was too expensive to waste on someone like her.

She set the cup down and returned to her breakfast. She wasn't sure if anyone would join her for breakfast, but she was secretly hoping that Hugh would. They hadn't spoken after she had stood up for him at dinner, and she hoped he wasn't upset with her for doing so. Most men did not like women fighting their battles for them, but she couldn't stand by and do nothing while his father berated him unjustly.

It was evident that there were hard feelings between Lord Montfort and his son, but she'd meant what she said. Hugh was her hero. He had saved her from Mr. Cadell, and no gossips could be worse than being in her former guardian's presence.

Marielle glanced at the empty doorway as she slowly ate her last bite. She had no more food in front of her, and she couldn't wait forever for Hugh to make an appearance.

As she wiped the sides of her mouth with a linen napkin, Dinah glided into the room with her husband trailing closely behind. Marielle noticed that Nathaniel's jacket was tattered around the sleeves and his boots were scuffed. It was an odd look for an earl, but it wasn't her place to say so. Maybe his wife's wardrobe took financial precedence over his own.

"Good morning, Marielle," Dinah greeted with a smile. "You're up early."

"Am I?" Marielle asked. "I suppose I got used to that when I lived with Mr. Cadell and ate in the kitchen."

Dinah sat across from her at the table. "I can't believe Mr. Cadell allowed such a thing."

"He didn't know," Marielle replied. "He tended to sleep in late and rarely spent the evenings in."

Nathanial put a plate in front of his wife before he sat down at the head of the table. "It is still odd that you spent so much time with the servants."

Marielle gave a half shrug. "It was far better than sitting in my room alone."

"How lonely you must have been," Dinah said, reaching for her teacup.

"It was not the best of times, but it was familiar," Marielle remarked. "After my father died, I lived alone in our country estate with only the servants to tend to me. It wasn't until after my brother died that Mr. Cadell came to retrieve me."

"That sounds awful," Dinah said with sympathy in her eyes.

"I had no choice but to carry on," Marielle responded, "but, yes, it was quite lonely."

Dinah took a sip, then asked, "Did you mean what you said to Lord Montfort last night over dinner?"

"About Hugh being my hero?"

Dinah nodded.

Marielle leaned to the side as a footman collected her plate. "I did, every word," she said. "I didn't like how Lord Montfort was speaking to Hugh."

Nathanial spoke up. "That will not be changing any time soon."

"May I ask why that is?" Marielle asked.

"Father and Hugh have been at odds for as long as I can remember," Nathanial replied. "It only got worse after Hugh stopped working as a barrister."

"He was a barrister?" Marielle asked.

Nathaniel bobbed his head. "He was one of the best, but he gave it up for a life of gambling."

"Did he ever say why?" Marielle inquired.

"If you ask Hugh, he'll tell you that gambling is much more lucrative than being a barrister," Nathaniel said, "but I am not inclined to believe him."

"Why not?"

Nathaniel grew solemn. "My brother worked hard to become a barrister. He wouldn't have just thrown that away without a good reason."

"Money is a good motivation," Marielle attempted.

"To many, yes, but not to Hugh," Nathaniel said. "He went into law knowing that he would never be overwhelmingly wealthy."

"People can change."

"Not that much," Nathaniel insisted. "Sometimes I hardly recognize the man that my brother has become."

Marielle reached for her cup of chocolate. "That is most unfortunate," she murmured.

"I commend you for speaking up for Hugh, but I daresay it did no good," Nathanial remarked. "My father's stance has not changed."

"I had to say something."

"I have discovered that it is best to let Lord Montfort and

Hugh exchange a few jabs and then try to redirect the conversation," Dinah interjected.

"I'm afraid I am not one to bite my tongue," Marielle admitted.

Nathaniel chuckled. "Neither is Dinah, but we have learned that some things will never change," he said. "My father will still fume at Hugh, who will escape to the gambling halls."

"That is awful," Marielle mused.

"I wish I had a magic cure that could fix our family's struggles, but I have long given up hope that my father and Hugh will ever get along," Nathaniel said.

The sound of the main door closing reached them.

"I see that Hugh is home," Nathaniel muttered.

Marielle lifted her brow. "He was truly out all night?" she asked.

"Yes," Nathaniel answered, "just as he is almost every night."

Before she could reply, Hugh stepped into the room with a silly grin on his face. Marielle eyed his disheveled hair and wrinkled clothing.

"Good morning," Hugh said cheerfully.

Nathaniel put his fork down. "You seem to be in a fine mood this morning."

"I won big at faro last night," Hugh announced as he walked over to the table and picked up a plate. "It was a good night; for me, at least. I can't say anything for the people I competed against."

Edith walked into the room with a disgruntled expression. "I do wish you wouldn't rob people of their hard-earned money," she complained.

"I didn't rob anyone," Hugh said smugly. "I played a game of chance, which I happen to be very good at."

"There must be a better use of your time," Edith said as

she sat down. A footman promptly came over to fill her teacup.

"Now you sound like Father," Hugh muttered as he sat down.

Edith sighed before turning her attention towards Marielle. "I do hope you don't mind spending the day shopping."

"I do not," Marielle responded.

"Wonderful," Edith said. "We shall begin at the dressmaker's and acquire you a whole new wardrobe."

"Oh, that really isn't necessary..."

"I noticed that your gowns, albeit lovely, are not in the height of fashion," Edith said. "They may have been suitable for the countryside, but they would never do here in London."

Edith had a point. It had been years since she'd commissioned a new gown. Fashion was the least of her concerns when her father's health was declining.

Hugh lifted his glass. "I think Marielle looks lovely just the way she is."

Edith gave him a shrewd look. "I can't help but wonder if you are just saying that because you don't want to pay for the new gowns or if you are being genuine."

"A little of both, I suppose," Hugh admitted as he lowered his glass.

"Just think of the family's reputation—" Edith started.

Hugh huffed. "Why does our reputation hinge on the gowns that Marielle is wearing?"

"Her clothing is a reflection of us, whether you like it or not," Edith remarked.

Hugh shook his head. "Nathaniel dresses like a pauper, but no one seems to give him much heed."

"I have already made my opinions known on Nathaniel's clothing," Edith said.

Nathaniel rose. "And with that, I shall bid you a good

day." He leaned down to kiss Dinah on her cheek. "I shall see you this evening."

After Nathaniel departed, Edith said, "We should depart soon if we want to be there when the dressmaker opens her shop."

Marielle put her napkin on the table. "I will just need to retrieve my bonnet," she said, rising. "I shall be down in a moment."

She departed from the dining room and had just started walking across the entry hall when someone called her name from behind. She turned and saw Hugh approaching, his expression unreadable.

He stopped a proper distance from her. "I just wanted to ensure you are all right with going shopping with my mother today."

"I am," she said. "Why do you ask?"

"My mother can be overbearing at times, but she always means well."

"I think she is charming."

Hugh chuckled. "Just wait until you get to know her better," he teased.

"I am grateful for everything she has done for me since I have been here," Marielle said. "She reminds me of how my mother used to fuss over me."

"She is good at that."

"You are most fortunate to have a mother like yours."

"That I am," Hugh agreed.

Marielle glanced up at his hair. "Were you mauled by a bear?" she ribbed.

Hugh's hand flew up to his hair and he attempted to smooth it down, but it still sprang back up. "Does it look that bad?"

"You've looked better," Marielle replied.

He smirked. "I'm glad you've noticed."

Marielle felt a blush creeping onto her cheeks. "That's not what I was insinuating."

"I know," Hugh said. "I just felt the need to tease you in return."

"You shouldn't do so in such a way. We hardly know each other yet," she chided lightly.

Hugh's face became more subdued as he asked, "Did you mean what you said about me to my father?"

"I did."

"I do not deserve your praise," he said with a frown.

"But—"

"I am not a man who goes about performing great deeds, and I will never be that man," Hugh said, taking a step closer. "It would be best to remember that."

Marielle cocked her head. "What kind of man do you think you are?"

"It doesn't matter," he muttered.

"To me, it does," Marielle replied quietly.

Edith's voice came from the doorway to the dining room. "Did you retrieve your bonnet, my dear?" Her question was innocent enough, but there was a firmness behind it.

Marielle took a step back, and only then did she realize how close they had been to one another. "I, uh, got distracted," she replied. "I will be right back."

Turning on her heel, she hurried up the stairs and down the hall. She opened her door and stepped inside, taking a moment to steady her breathing before snatching up her bonnet.

Why did Hugh have such an adverse effect on her? She wasn't normally so blunt, but words seemed to pop heedlessly out of her mouth when it came to him. He was her guardian, nothing more. She needn't be drawn in so carelessly.

Chapter Five

Hugh watched as Marielle hurried up the stairs. He would have to be careful with his ward. The other women of the *ton* didn't give him a second glance; his reputation prevented it. Marielle didn't look at him with disgust, however, but as her hero. She claimed that she meant her words, but she would no doubt come to regret them. He was not a man who was worthy of her notice. The less he associated with her, the better.

His mother's voice broke through his musings. "No, son," she said sternly.

"Pardon?" Hugh asked, turning to face her.

She approached him and kept her voice low. "It would be best if you kept some distance from Marielle for the time being."

"Why is that?" He'd been thinking the same thing but wanted to know his mother's opinion on the matter.

"Because I see the way you look at her."

Hugh furrowed his brows. "How exactly do I look at her?"

"She has beguiled you."

"I think not," he scoffed.

His mother didn't appear convinced. "You can deny it all you want, but you need to be careful. She is your ward."

"I am well aware of our situation." Hugh's words came out much harsher than he intended.

"Do not let your emotions get ahead of your duty," his mother counseled.

"I have no intention to," Hugh responded.

A knock came at the door, and Balfour appeared from one of the side rooms to open it, revealing Hugh's solicitor.

Mr. Donovan met his gaze and tipped his head. "May I speak to you for a moment, my lord?"

"We can speak in the drawing room," Hugh replied, gesturing towards the doorway.

After they stepped into the drawing room, Mr. Donovan turned to face him, wearing a solemn look. "Mr. Cadell has filed a petition to the Court of Chancery to sue you for the return of Miss Wymond's guardianship."

"That is not completely unexpected," Hugh said. "Did you give a response?"

"I did, but there is a chance that the case might go to trial."

"Let's hope it doesn't come to that."

"If it does," Mr. Donovan asked, "will you be representing yourself, or should I hire a barrister?"

"I will represent myself."

Mr. Donovan nodded in approval. "I think that is wise," he said.

"Until that time, I want you to utilize the Court's notoriously slow and convoluted proceedings to our advantage," Hugh instructed. "Miss Wymond reaches her majority in seven months, and then this will be a moot point."

"Consider it done," Mr. Donovan said.

"Mr. Cadell is only trying to sue for Miss Wymond's return so he can have access to her inheritance when it is released," Hugh said. "I refuse to let that happen."

"If I may say so, what you are doing for Miss Wymond is admirable."

Hugh brushed off his praise. "I am simply performing my duty."

"To you, perhaps that is all it is, but I imagine Miss Wymond thinks differently, considering you are protecting her from Mr. Cadell."

"We should use his lack of funds to our advantage," Hugh said. "It could be rather costly to take this to trial."

"With any luck, he will back down when he realizes that you intend to fight him over guardianship."

"That is the hope."

Mr. Donovan opened the satchel that was draped over his right shoulder and removed a piece of paper. "I looked into the estates that you requested information on."

"Did you find anything interesting?"

"They are all profitable but will require some extensive work to bring them up to snuff," Mr. Donovan said, extending him the paper.

Hugh accepted and perused it. "These profits are minimal."

"They will grow when you invest in new machinery," Mr. Donovan said. "Sometimes you must spend money to make money."

"I understand that concept more than you understand."

"Of course, my lord," Mr. Donovan remarked. "Would you like me to start negotiating on the prices for these estates?"

"Proceed with the estates in Essex and Dover," Hugh said, giving the paper back to Mr. Donovan. "Those have the highest profit margins and seem like the best investment at this time."

"Very good. Although, I should warn you that they are not as grand as your family's country estate."

"I have no illusions about that."

Mr. Donovan put the paper back into his satchel. "I highly recommend you tour the estates before you purchase them."

"I shall heed your advice and do so once you come to a tentative agreement."

"Will there be anything else?" Mr. Donovan asked, his hand on the strap of his satchel.

"Not at this time."

"Then I shall get to work, my lord," Mr. Donovan said.

Hugh sat down after his solicitor departed. He needed to go up to his bedchamber and go to sleep. He had been up all night gambling and was exhausted. He wasn't sure how much longer he could go on like this. He wasn't getting any younger, and his body was starting to protest the late nights.

He enjoyed winning at the tables, but his priorities were beginning to shift. He planned to buy up estates and enjoy the spoils of being a landowner.

Hugh's eyes were drooping as Balfour stepped into the room and announced, "Lord Simon would like a moment of your time, my lord."

"Send him in."

As he straightened in his seat, Simon stepped into the room with an unusually grave look on his face.

"Whatever is the matter?" Hugh asked.

Simon sat on the chair across from him. "Mr. Emerson was being rather vocal about losing to you after you left the Gilded Crown this morning."

"That isn't surprising. He lost nearly five thousand pounds."

"He claims you cheated."

"In faro?" Hugh asked. "Pray tell, did he say how I did such a thing?"

"No, but he is adamant that you will pay for what you did."

Hugh waved a hand dismissively in front of him. "I'm not terribly worried," he said. "Mr. Emerson isn't the first man to threaten me after losing a substantial sum, and I'm sure he won't be the last."

"This time seemed different," Simon said.

"In what way?"

Simon glanced at the empty doorway before saying, "Mr. Emerson is known for his unscrupulous business dealings, and I worry that he will make good on this threat."

"I'm not," Hugh replied. "He's just flapping his mouth."

Simon eyed him warily. "I daresay you are being entirely too blasé. Mr. Emerson isn't a man I'd want to trifle with."

"He shouldn't have gambled what he couldn't lose," Hugh said. "I did nothing wrong, and Mr. Emerson will realize that soon enough."

"Just be careful."

"I have every intention to."

Simon sighed. "I heard that Mr. Cadell filed suit to have his guardianship over Miss Wymond restored."

"I see that news travels fast."

Simon chuckled. "You should know that any tasty piece of gossip will cause a ripple through the *ton*."

"It's a waste of his time," Hugh said. "I have no doubt I will retain guardianship over Miss Wymond."

"Is her fortune as vast as everyone is saying?"

"I don't rightly know, but that is the least of my concerns."

Simon leaned back in his chair. "She is an heiress and will be the target of every fortune hunter and rake."

"Don't remind me."

"What do you intend to do with her?"

Hugh rose and walked over to the drink cart. "My mother intends to throw her a ball and introduce her into Society."

"Is that what you want?" Simon asked curiously.

"It doesn't matter what I want," Hugh replied, picking up the decanter. "It's what's best for Marielle."

"Marielle? How close are you to your new ward?" Simon asked, his question sounding more like an accusation.

"You are reading too much into it," Hugh said as he poured two drinks. "I am her guardian, and it is perfectly respectable for me to call her by her given name."

"I suppose so."

Hugh picked up the two glasses and walked over to Simon, extending him a glass. "How did you do at cards last night?"

"Awful," Simon admitted. "I think it's time I stop going to gambling halls, since I don't have your good fortune."

"Gambling is not for the faint of heart."

"No, it's not," Simon admitted. "May I ask what your secret is?"

Hugh took a sip of his drink, then replied, "You need to learn to read people and understand what they aren't saying."

"How do I do that?"

Hugh gave him a knowing look. "Every time you're bluffing, you lightly tap your foot."

"I do not!"

"You do, and it's because you're anxious about the hand," Hugh explained. "When you're relaxed and joking, I know you have a good hand."

"I hadn't realized I did that."

Hugh set his glass down. "People are creatures of habit. They tend to fall into the same routines without even realizing they are doing so. It is comfortable, safe."

"I'll need to change my tactics," Simon said. "Perhaps then I will start winning back the money I've lost."

"I wish you luck with that."

Simon tossed back his drink and put his empty glass on the table. "Now, I must hurry home," he said. "I have a meeting with our solicitor this afternoon. Father has immersed himself in politics and expects me to handle our business dealings."

"That is a great responsibility for a second son."

Simon frowned. "It should fall to my brother, but he's too busy chasing women all over town."

"Henry's a rake."

"I won't disagree with you there," Simon said, rising. "I would just be cautious around Mr. Emerson—at least for the time being."

"He doesn't scare me."

"He should," Simon responded before he walked out the door.

Hugh just leaned his head back and closed his eyes. He needed to make his way up to his bedchamber, but he'd rest for just a moment before he headed there.

Bonnet in hand, Marielle descended the stairs and headed towards the drawing room to wait for Edith and Dinah. She was rather excited to go shopping and commission new gowns.

She stepped into the drawing room, coming to an abrupt stop when she saw Hugh sitting in a chair, his eyes closed. She took the opportunity to admire his handsome face and noticed the faint stubble of a beard had begun to shadow his jaw. But of all his features, she liked his mouth the best.

Marielle shook her head at that wayward thought. She hardly knew the man; it wouldn't do to be enamored by him. It must have come because he saved her from Mr. Cadell.

Hugh's eyes opened, and a lazy smile formed on his lips. "Marielle," he greeted.

"I'm sorry for disturbing you," she said, embarrassed that she'd been caught staring.

"You did no such thing," Hugh replied as he rose. "You are a welcome sight to wake up to."

Marielle brushed off his compliment, knowing it couldn't be in earnest. "I'm about to go shopping," she blurted out. Why did she say that?

"I am aware," Hugh said. "I do hope you enjoy spending time with Mother and Dinah."

"I have no doubt that I will."

Hugh stepped towards her. "I am glad that you are here."

"You are?"

"Yes. I was just informed by my solicitor that Mr. Cadell intends to go to court to have you returned as his ward."

Marielle gasped. "Please say that won't happen."

"You need not worry," Hugh said. "I have no doubt that the Court of Chancery will rule in my favor."

"How can you be so sure?"

"I will fight for you, Marielle," Hugh said, fixing her with a level gaze. "As I told you before, you are safe now."

"I do not mean to be a burden."

"You are no such thing."

"Why are you helping me?" Marielle asked.

"Because you are my ward, and it is my duty." He leaned forward. "Besides, I daresay that my mother has grown rather fond of you in the short time she has known you."

"I have grown fond of her, as well."

Hugh gave her an encouraging look. "This is your home until you reach your majority," he said. "Do not concern yourself with Mr. Cadell. He is in your past."

"Thank you," Marielle said.

"You don't have to thank me for doing my duty."

"I feel as if I must."

"You are a delight, Marielle," Hugh said with a grin. "Now, if you will excuse me, I am going to retire to my bedchamber."

Marielle knew it wasn't her place, but she couldn't withhold the urge to ask, "Why do you stay out all night gambling?"

"Simple," he replied. "The gambling halls aren't open during the day."

"Do you enjoy gambling?"

Hugh's smile didn't falter, though it seemed to dim. "It is something I am quite good at," he said.

That didn't answer her question. "But do you enjoy it?" she pressed.

"I wouldn't say I enjoy it, but it has enabled me to amass a large fortune," Hugh replied.

"If you don't enjoy it, why do you keep doing it?"

Hugh was quiet for a moment. "I'm afraid you wouldn't understand my reasonings," he said.

"You will find that I can be rather astute."

"I don't doubt that, but the answer to your question is not so black and white."

"Oh?"

A pained look came to Hugh's eyes. "Gambling gives me a reprieve from my life," Hugh said, his eyes holding a pained expression, "even if it is just for a moment."

"Why would you wish for a reprieve?"

Hugh huffed lightly. "Now you're starting to sound like my father."

"I'm just trying to understand," she rushed out. "I meant no offense."

Turning, Hugh walked over to a drink that sat on the table and picked it up. He tossed it back before saying, "I do not think you can understand the immense pressure that I am under to succeed as a second son. My father can be relentless when it comes to reminding me of my duty."

"Is that why he was so critical of you at dinner?"

"It was," Hugh replied. "I am a failure in his eyes."

"That can't be entirely true."

Hugh nodded. "I'm afraid it is."

Marielle could hear the heartache in Hugh's voice, and her heart swelled with compassion. Not knowing what to say, she remained quiet, hoping he would continue to confide in her. Fortunately, she didn't have to wait long.

Hugh glanced at the door before saying, "He's always compared me to Nathaniel, and I always came up lacking."

"You are two different people, with two different destinies."

"Try telling him that," Hugh muttered.

Marielle took a step towards him. "Have you tried speaking to your father about this?"

"It'd be pointless to do so," Hugh replied. "He's just as stubborn as I am, much to my mother's chagrin."

"One of you needs to yield if you want the feud to end."

Hugh gave her a weak smile. "I know you are trying to help, but this has been going on for far too long to end so easily."

"That doesn't make it right to continue it."

"No, but it makes it predictable," Hugh said. "I know precisely what to expect from my father, so I am not disappointed by it."

"That's a sad way to live."

"Let me guess," Hugh said, "your father showered his love upon you unceasingly when he was alive?"

"He did, but—"

"Then your life is very different from mine. I'm afraid there is no comparing."

His words annoyed her, and she felt her back grow rigid. "My life has not been perfect, you know. I've lost my entire family and was forced to reside with Mr. Cadell."

"I did not mean to imply that your life has been easy, especially these past few months, but you were raised in a loving environment."

"That doesn't mean I can't empathize with what you are going through."

Hugh walked over to the drink cart and poured himself another. "I don't want your sympathy."

"Good, because you aren't going to get it."

Hugh looked at her in surprise. "Pardon?"

"Both of your parents are alive, and you have time to alter your course," Marielle said. "You don't have to continue going on as you have been."

"What if I don't want things to change?"

Marielle shrugged one shoulder. "Then you will continue to wallow in self-pity."

"I am not wallowing in self-pity," he said, tightening his hold on his glass. "You know not what you are speaking of."

"You have made something of yourself," Marielle said. "If your father can't see that, then that's his loss."

"I made something of myself by gambling."

"I am aware."

"Doesn't that bother you?" Hugh asked, eyeing her closely as he took a sip of his drink.

"Why should it?"

"Gambling is not a respectable way to earn a living. Surely you know that."

"Who decides if something is respectable or not?"

"I'm afraid we live in a Society that defines the rules quite ruthlessly," Hugh said.

"Then make your own rules; live life on your own terms."

"I stopped caring what the *ton* thought about me years ago, but that doesn't mean I can escape the consequences of my actions." Hugh came around the drink cart and said, "You will need to be careful not to overstep the boundaries, because your reputation is much more brittle than mine is."

"I understand that."

Hugh took another swallow of his drink before he went and set it down on the table. "You are a kind person, Marielle, and I hope Society won't taint you when you enter it."

"It won't," she replied with a tilt of her chin. "I know who I am."

"I used to know who I was," Hugh muttered with a small wince, "but I lost that long ago."

"It's not too late to rediscover it."

Hugh stared at her for a long moment. "Your eternal optimism is starting to grate on my ears, and it is time I depart before I say something I might regret." He walked towards the door but stopped next to her. "I did listen to what you said, but it is too late for me."

Marielle watched as Hugh departed from the drawing room. She hadn't meant to push him away, but she'd thought she could get through to him.

It was only a moment before Edith appeared at the doorway with a solemn look on her face. "I was shamelessly eavesdropping, and I heard everything." She stepped further into the room. "Hugh doesn't usually open up to anyone, so I was surprised by how frankly he spoke to you."

"It didn't do much good," Marielle said.

"I think it did," Edith replied. "I do believe what you said resonated with him, even if he brushed it aside for now."

Marielle smoothed down her gown. "Has Lord Montfort always been as hard on Hugh as he claims?"

"I'm afraid so," Edith said. "William always had high hopes for Hugh because he was the second son, as well. His older brother died from consumption when William was at Eton, and he became the heir. His life changed dramatically from that point on."

"But Nathaniel is healthy."

"He is, but William wants Hugh to always be prepared for the unexpected," Edith explained, "and he views gambling as a terrible vice."

"Even though Hugh has amassed a fortune on his own?" Marielle questioned.

Edith bobbed her head. "Doing one's duty isn't about making money," she said. "It's about doing what is right."

"I would agree, but I do believe Hugh is an honorable man."

"He is," Edith agreed. "But he is lost right now and has been for quite some time."

"How can we help him?"

Edith pressed her lips together as if at odds with herself, then said, "I'm afraid he stopped listening to me long ago, but it appears to be different with you."

"I'm not sure that is true."

Edith gave her a grateful smile. "I am glad that you are here, Marielle. I do believe you are a godsend to this family."

Dinah stepped into the room with a bonnet in her hand. "I do apologize for the delay..." Her words trailed off as she glanced between them. "I'm sorry. Did I interrupt something?"

Turning to face Dinah, Edith said, "Not at all."

"Balfour informed me that the coach is out front," Dinah said. "Shall we depart?"

"That is a brilliant idea," Edith replied.

Chapter Six

Hours later, Hugh sat at a table in the corner of White's and nursed his drink. He hadn't slept well, and had given up on it and gone to the club earlier than usual. He couldn't believe that he had conversed so freely with Marielle. What was it about her that caused him to speak openly? There was a familiarity about her that he could not explain, and her words were so calming, as if it was a balm for his soul. Or maybe he'd imagined that because of how tired he'd been after being up all night.

He stifled the groan on his lips. He was her guardian, and he would be mindful to remember that. He was supposed to be giving her advice, not the other way around. It would be best if he kept her at arm's length and avoided her for the time being. Frankly, he couldn't seem to trust himself around her. She was the first person in a long time who didn't seem disappointed in him, and when he looked deep into her eyes, he found that he wanted to confide in her, to please her. But that was a double-edged sword. If he told her the truth about him, then that light in her eyes when she looked at him would dim, and she would be disappointed, as well.

Marielle was a kindhearted young woman. It was obvious

that she cared deeply about others, wanting nothing in return. He feared for her when she entered Society. The *ton* was full of vultures that pounced on anyone who was different, and Marielle would definitely stand out.

Hugh took a sip of his drink. It would have been much easier if Marielle had been a plain, unassuming young woman, or better yet, a child. But nothing ever seemed to come easy for him. He'd had to work for everything he had been given, despite being raised with immense privileges.

He glanced up and saw Graylocke approaching the table with Nathaniel and Haddington following close behind. Graylocke was the only normal-looking one of the three. Haddington was dressed in his usual flamboyant clothing, with a bright green jacket and yellow waistcoat. Nathaniel surprised Hugh by wearing a jacket only somewhat ragged, though it was clearly out of date.

"You look terrible," Graylocke commented as he pulled out a chair.

"Thank you for that," Hugh muttered.

Nathaniel took a seat next to him. "It might have something to do with his ward."

Graylocke lifted his brow. "Yes, about that. Pray tell, when were you going to tell me that you won a ward at the tables?"

"I suppose the next time I saw you," Hugh remarked.

"I read about it in the newssheets," Haddington said, "and I had to re-read it to make sure I had read it correctly."

"Does reading not come naturally to you?" Nathaniel joked.

Haddington chuckled. "I just couldn't believe that our dear friend saddled himself with a ward," he said. "What is Miss Wymond like?"

"She is…" Hugh's voice trailed off as he tried to think of the right words. "She is pleasant enough."

"Pleasant enough?" Graylocke asked. "That's all that you can say about her?"

Hugh had a lot that he could say about Marielle, but nothing that he could say to his friends. If he did, he had no doubt that they would suspect he had feelings for his ward—which he didn't.

"Marielle defended Hugh to my father last night over dinner," Nathaniel revealed as he leaned back in his chair.

"She did?" Haddington asked.

"She even called Hugh 'her hero' for saving her from Mr. Cadell," Nathaniel replied with a nod.

"How did your father react?" Graylocke inquired.

Nathaniel grinned. "He took it rather well and announced that he 'liked this one'."

"That doesn't sound like your father," Graylocke said. "He isn't known for his overly pleasant demeanor."

"I was surprised, as well," Nathaniel responded.

"How did you respond when Miss Wymond called you 'her hero'?" Haddington asked Hugh.

Hugh shrugged half-heartedly. "I didn't give it much heed," he lied. He didn't want his friends to know how deeply it had resonated with him.

A server walked over to the table and placed drinks for all in the middle of it. "Will there be anything else?"

"Not at this time," Nathaniel replied as he reached for a glass.

As the server walked away, Hugh sipped his drink and hoped that the interruption would halt his friends' line of questioning. But he was not so lucky.

"I'm surprised that you let Miss Wymond fight your battles with your father," Graylocke said.

"I didn't ask her to speak up," Hugh grumbled. "She did that on her own."

"It sounds like Miss Wymond is a formidable woman, in addition to being pleasant," Graylocke commented, amusement in his voice.

"She is," Hugh agreed.

Haddington took a sip of his drink. "I've heard that she is beautiful, as well."

"I suppose she is pleasing to look at." Hugh pushed his empty glass away from him. "I don't wish to speak about Marielle anymore."

Haddington put his hands up in surrender. "Fair enough."

A silence descended over the table before Graylocke announced, "My wife received the invitation to your mother's ball."

"Did she now?" Hugh asked.

"It says that it's being held in honor of Miss Wymond," Graylocke said.

Hugh let out a frustrated sigh. "I thought we were going to stop speaking about Marielle," he stated.

"I was just trying to make conversation. I just wanted to know how you felt about the ball, since I know how much you hate social events," Graylocke remarked.

"They're pointless," Hugh muttered.

Haddington shook his head. "They are an important part of living in a civilized society."

"I disagree," Hugh said. "I tire of scheming parents trying to trap us into marriage with their maddening daughters."

"It does get tiresome, but it is important to attend," Haddington pressed as he tugged down on his yellow waistcoat.

"I care little about being seen," Hugh said. "I would rather be making money at the card tables."

"That's your problem, Hugh," Haddington remarked, "you've forgotten how to have fun."

"Winning is fun."

Haddington chuckled. "You are past hope."

Hugh looked up and saw Mr. Emerson approaching the table with a formidable look on his face. Botheration. What now?

Mr. Emerson stopped next to the table. "Good afternoon, gentlemen," he greeted cordially.

"What is it that you want, Emerson?" Hugh demanded.

Mr. Emerson smiled. "I see that we are past pleasantries, which is fine by me," he said. "It will make my message much easier."

"What message is that?" Hugh asked indifferently.

The smile faded from Mr. Emerson's lips. "I know you cheated, and I am giving you the opportunity to return my money."

"One can hardly cheat at faro," Hugh said sarcastically.

"It is entirely possible and happens often, and we both know that," Mr. Emerson said. "One of the other players saw you moving bets."

"They would be wrong."

"I don't believe that is the case."

Hugh pursed his lips together. "I don't cheat, and I am insulted by the insinuation."

"I am insulted by your mere presence," Mr. Emerson spat out. "You have until tomorrow to return my money, or you will regret it."

"It sounds like you are threatening me," Hugh said.

"I am."

Hugh slowly rose from his chair. "I beat you fair and square. You are just sore."

"You cheated!" Mr. Emerson spat, his face reddening.

"No, you're just bad at faro," Hugh countered.

Mr. Emerson removed a white handkerchief from his pocket and wiped his brow. "You have until tomorrow."

"I have no intention of returning your money."

Mr. Emerson returned the handkerchief to his pocket. "Then you will rue the day that you cheated me."

"Again, I did not cheat."

Mr. Emerson leaned closer. "How is your new ward doing?"

Hugh stiffened. "She is none of your concern."

"Isn't she?" Mr. Emerson asked. "I would hate for anything to happen to Miss Wymond, especially since she is about to enter Society."

Hugh vaguely acknowledged his friends standing up from the table. "You have no right to even utter her name."

Mr. Emerson's eyes left his and roamed over his friends. "I hope you do the right thing and return my money to me, for her sake."

"I cannot make this any clearer," Hugh said slowly. "I won that money fairly, and I intend to keep it."

Mr. Emerson took a step back and put his hands out wide. "Then what happens next is your fault."

"And what will that be?"

"You shall have to wait and see," Mr. Emerson sneered before spinning on his heel and walking away.

Hugh watched Mr. Emerson's retreating figure and tried to cool his boiling blood. How dare that insufferable man threaten Marielle!

"Do you believe Mr. Emerson will make good on his threat?" Nathaniel asked, returning Hugh to his immediate surroundings.

"I don't know," Hugh said. "I hardly know the man."

"How much did Emerson lose?" Graylocke asked.

"Five thousand pounds," Hugh revealed.

Graylocke let out a low whistle. "That is a substantial sum. No wonder Emerson is so angry."

"I didn't cheat," Hugh defended.

"I never implied that you did," Graylocke said. "Besides, I know you well enough to know that his claim has no merit."

Hugh returned to his seat and his friends followed suit. "I am sure he's just blowing off some steam. Once he calms down, he'll see the error of his ways."

"And if he doesn't?" Haddington asked.

"Then we will notify the constable of Emerson's threats," Hugh replied.

Haddington exchanged a look with Nathaniel before saying, "It might be best if you kept a watchful eye on Miss Wymond, at least for the time being."

"I don't think extra attention there is necessary," Hugh attempted.

"Hope for the best and prepare for the worst," Haddington said.

Hugh had to admit that Haddington had a point. "You're right," he responded. "I will see to it."

"I will make some inquiries about Emerson," Nathaniel said as he rose. He placed a hand on Hugh's shoulder. "Don't worry. We'll keep Marielle safe."

After his brother walked away from the table, Haddington rose. "I think I will do the same."

"Who are you making inquiries to?" Hugh asked curiously.

Haddington reached down and picked up his glass. "Just some acquaintances." He tossed back his drink, put the glass down, and headed towards the entrance.

Hugh turned to Graylocke. "Why does it feel like Haddington and Nathaniel are always trying to appease us?"

"Because they are," Graylocke said, bringing his glass up to his lips.

After being poked and prodded for what felt like ages, Marielle departed the dressmaker's shop with a sigh of relief. She was finally free from that fastidious dressmaker. Madam Blanchet had chided her for even the slightest movements. She'd been so excited to commission gowns this morning; now she was just glad it was over.

Edith stood beside her on the pavement. "I am so pleased that Madam Blanchet agreed to sew your gowns for this Season."

Marielle glanced back at the shop. "Is she always so... intense?"

"She is, but she means well."

"I doubt that. I think she took great pleasure in poking me."

Edith smiled. "I've never had an issue, but I do believe you will be pleased with the elaborate pieces she'll create for you."

"I do hope so, because I might be entirely covered in pinpricks. I'd hate for that sacrifice to go to waste."

Dinah laughed from behind her. "If only you had stood still long enough, it wouldn't have been an issue."

"I doubt it," Marielle said. "Besides, my legs were getting tired."

Edith batted her sleeve with the fan in her hand. "Achieving perfection is never easy."

"I didn't ask for perfection," Marielle responded.

"No, but I did," Edith said. "When you walk into your ball, I want everyone's eyes on you, and I want them to be insanely jealous of you."

"I do not wish for anyone to be jealous of me."

"Nonsense," Edith said. "I don't want anyone to outshine you at your own ball."

"I have never been comfortable being the center of attention," Marielle admitted.

"You will need to overcome that somewhat, because you are in the most envious position," Edith said.

"Am I?"

Edith turned to face her. "You are an heiress and a beautiful young woman. Any man would be lucky to have you as his wife."

"But what if I don't wish to marry?"

Edith waved her hand dismissively in front of her. "What you are experiencing is nerves, and that is expected."

"I don't think I am," Marielle said. "If I marry, then everything that my father worked so hard to achieve will belong to my husband."

"But you need a husband," Edith insisted.

Marielle pressed her lips together, then asked, "Do I?"

"You would willingly become a… a spinster?" Edith questioned.

"I would, if it kept my father's legacy safe."

Edith glanced over her shoulder. "This conversation is much too heavy to be discussing on the pavement. We shall continue it at home."

Dinah spoke up. "Shall we adjourn to the milliner's shop?" she asked. "I wonder what hats they have out today."

"That is a wonderful idea," Edith agreed as she started towards the shop.

Dinah came to walk beside Marielle as she followed Edith. "I used to think like you did," she said.

"What changed your mind?" Marielle asked.

"I fell in love," Dinah stated simply.

"What if love isn't enough?"

"Then you haven't found the right person."

"Surely it can't be that simple."

Dinah met her gaze and replied, "When you fall hope-lessly in love, you feel complete, as if you are right where you belong."

"I don't think I will ever be able to find that," Marielle admitted.

"Give it time," Dinah encouraged. "Love often finds us in the most unexpected places."

Marielle stopped outside the milliner's shop. "But what if I'm not looking for love?"

Dinah's eyes twinkled with merriment. "Then when you

do find it, it will make it that much more special," she said before she entered the shop.

Marielle followed Dinah inside and took stock of all the hats on display. She saw hats of all kinds, adorned with everything from flowers and fruit to ribbons and lace.

Dinah walked over to a table and picked up a covered straw hat with a simple red flower as adornment. "I think this would suit nicely for me."

Edith shook her head from across the room. "You need a hat that will garner more attention." She picked up a hat with bunches of grapes and vines artfully arranged around the band. "Like this one."

Marielle giggled. "Too bad the fruit is inedible, being made of wax. I can imagine a hat trimmed with real food would come in handy if I was hungry."

A round shopkeeper with a pleasant demeanor about her approached Edith and smiled. "How may I help you, Lady Montfort?"

"Miss Wymond requires new hats," Edith replied. "What would you recommend?"

The shopkeeper turned towards Marielle and perused the length of her. "We don't want anything too flamboyant, as it would distract from her beauty." She walked over to the table and picked up a hat with a cluster of strawberries and leaves on it. "Is this to your liking?"

Marielle scrunched her nose. "It's not unappealing, but I would prefer hats that didn't have fruit on them."

The shopkeeper replaced the hat and walked over to another table. Her hand roamed over the hats until they stopped on a straw hat that was adorned with a lone sunflower and matching ribbon. "This is an understated hat," she said as she picked it up.

Marielle walked over to the shopkeeper and accepted the straw hat. "I like how bright it is."

The shopkeeper hummed in agreement.

Edith apparently approved of it, as well. "Box it up for her while she continues shopping," she said.

Marielle handed the hat back to the shopkeeper with a murmured, "Thank you."

The bell over the door jingled as it opened and a tall, slender, brown-haired young woman stepped inside. Her eyes fastened on Dinah almost instantly.

"Dinah!" the young woman said enthusiastically. "I see that I correctly assumed you would be in here when I saw your coach parked down the street."

Dinah turned and a bright smile lit her face. "Evie!" she greeted. "What a pleasant surprise!"

Evie tipped her head at Lady Montfort. "My lady," she murmured respectfully, then turned towards Marielle. "And you must be Miss Wymond."

"I am," Marielle said.

Evie smiled, immediately setting her at ease. "I have read all about you in the newssheets."

Dinah gave Evie a disapproving look. "You shouldn't say such things."

"I am sure Miss Wymond knows she is being gossiped about," Evie said, "although it is through no fault of her own."

"You will have to forgive my sister," Dinah told Marielle. "She sometimes forgets her manners at the door."

"I find it refreshing," Marielle admitted.

The shopkeeper walked up to Evie with a box. "Your hat is ready, Miss Ashmore," she informed her.

Evie accepted the box and set it on the table. She opened the top and pulled out a plain brown bonnet with frayed ivory string. "It is exactly how I envisioned it," she said, holding it up.

"That is an interesting choice for a hat," Edith said.

Evie quickly returned the bonnet to the box. "It's perfect."

"You don't truly intend to wear that in public, do you?" Edith asked, concern on her features.

"My aunt would never allow me to wear this hat amongst polite society," Evie replied.

"Then why did you commission it?" Edith pressed.

Evie picked up the box. "I thought it might come in handy on occasion."

Dinah abruptly interjected, "Perhaps it's a gift for one of the servants. Speaking of, where is your maid?"

"I left her outside," Evie replied. "She is relentless and follows me everywhere."

"I have no doubt that is our aunt's doing," Dinah said with a laugh.

"It most assuredly is."

The shopkeeper approached Marielle with a stack of boxes in her hands. "Here are your hats, miss," she said.

"My... hats?" Marielle asked.

Edith nodded as she glided across the room. "I took the liberty of selecting a few for you," she revealed. "There is no need to thank me."

Marielle accepted the boxes from the shopkeeper, wondering how Edith had accomplished this so quickly and undetected. "Pray tell, did you select any with fruit on them?"

"You will have to see when we arrive home," Edith replied. "Come along, now."

As they exited the milliner's shop, Marielle extended the boxes to the footman that had approached her.

Dinah turned to Marielle and asked, "Have you been to Gunter's before?"

"I have, but it has been many years since I last frequented it," Marielle admitted.

"Then we must go, especially since it is just around the corner," Dinah insisted. "Besides, I am quite fond of their ices."

"You are fond of everything served at Gunter's," Evie teased.

"It's true," Dinah said with a slight shrug of her shoulder, "and I am not alone in that."

Edith bobbed her head. "Gunter's is a wonderful idea on this warm day," she said before she started walking down the street without looking back.

Marielle had just turned to follow Edith when a gentleman bumped into her. She stumbled back, but strong hands reached out to steady her.

"I do apologize," the man said as he withdrew his hands.

Marielle smoothed out her dress as she said, "You should watch where you are going..." Her voice trailed off as she brought her gaze up and got a good look at the handsome man, who had blond hair and thick eyebrows, which contrasted nicely with his blue eyes.

"I agree wholeheartedly," he said. "Please forgive me."

"You are forgiven," Marielle said, pleased that she had found her voice.

He smiled. "You forgive easily, for which I am grateful." He shifted his gaze towards Dinah and bowed. "Good afternoon, Lady Hawthorne."

Dinah's expression was unreadable. "I'm afraid I am at a disadvantage, since I am not acquainted with you."

"My name is Mr. Emerson," he said. "I am a friend of Lord Hugh's."

Dinah gestured towards Evie and asked, "Have you been introduced to my sister, Miss Ashmore?"

"I have not had the pleasure," Mr. Emerson said with a slight bow at the waist.

"And that person you ran into is Miss Wymond, Lord Hugh's ward," Dinah remarked.

Mr. Emerson met her gaze and his lips twitched. "Ah, so you are the lovely Miss Wymond. I was wondering when we would meet."

"If you will excuse us, Mr. Emerson," Dinah said firmly, "we were just on our way to Gunter's."

Mr. Emerson put his hand out and said, "Please allow me to escort you there."

Marielle saw hesitation on Dinah's face, but she nodded her permission. "If you wish."

As they started walking towards Gunter's, Mr. Emerson clasped his hands behind his back and matched Marielle's stride. "I must assume that Lord Hugh has not spoken of me before."

"I'm afraid not," Marielle replied, "but, in all fairness, I do not believe he has mentioned any of his acquaintances."

Mr. Emerson chuckled. "Lord Hugh has always been reticent."

Evie spoke up as she walked behind them with Dinah. "How exactly do you know Lord Hugh?"

"We frequent the same gambling hall," Mr. Emerson said dismissively over his shoulder.

"Frequenting the same gambling hall hardly equates to being friends," Evie pressed.

Mr. Emerson looked amused by Evie's comment. "I have heard you are rather inquisitive, Miss Ashmore."

"I am, and there is no shame in that," Evie responded.

"No, there is not," Mr. Emerson agreed, turning his attention back towards Marielle. "Are you enjoying the sights of London?"

"I'm afraid I haven't seen most of them."

"That is a shame," Mr. Emerson said. "Perhaps, if you are agreeable, I could show you around Town."

"You would have to ask Lord Hugh for his permission," Dinah interrupted.

"That won't be a problem," Mr. Emerson said as they stopped in front of Gunter's. "Will you please tell Lord Hugh that I say hello?"

"I will," Marielle said.

Mr. Emerson reached for her gloved hand and kissed the air above it before gently releasing it. "I hope to be seeing more of you, Miss Wymond." Mr. Emerson didn't wait for her to reply before he walked off.

Evie watched his retreating figure as if she were trying to sort out a puzzle. "What do you make of Mr. Emerson?" she asked Dinah in a hushed voice.

Dinah frowned. "I'm not quite sure."

"Neither am I," Evie said.

Marielle glanced between them curiously. "I thought him to be a kind man."

"Let's not dwell on Mr. Emerson a moment longer," Dinah said. "We have more important matters to discuss, such as what delectable treats we will choose."

Chapter Seven

Hugh had just returned from a ride when he saw the ladies exit the family's coach. He dismounted his horse and extended the reins to the awaiting footman.

His mother's eyes lit up when she saw him approaching. "Hugh," she said. "How was your ride?"

"It went well," he replied.

He watched as the footman removed the stacks of boxes that were secured to the back of the coach. "Did you buy out all of Cheapside?" he joked.

Dinah laughed. "Your mother took it upon herself to buy a few hats for Marielle, among other things."

"That does not surprise me," Hugh said, eyeing Marielle curiously. "Did you not select the hats yourself?"

"I did select one, but your mother acquired the rest before I knew what had happened," Marielle replied.

Hugh offered his arm to his mother. "I hope you didn't pick anything too ghastly for her."

"Of course not," his mother said. "Everything I picked was tasteful and entirely in fashion this Season."

"I'm afraid that doesn't grant me much confidence," he teased with a smile.

He dropped his arm when they stepped into the entry hall. "Were you shopping this entire time?"

"Mostly," his mother replied. "We did manage a stop at Gunter's for a scrumptious treat."

"I am glad to see that you have your priorities straight," he teased.

"If you will excuse me, I need to rest before I dress for dinner," his mother said before she walked off.

Dinah spoke up. "I believe I will follow your mother's lead and go rest as well."

She headed up the stairs, and Hugh turned to Marielle. "Do you not care to rest before dinner?"

Marielle shook her head. "I'm not tired."

"That's surprising. It would appear from the number of packages that you frequented every shop in London."

Marielle grinned. "Your mother was relentless today, but I did acquire the most beautiful things."

"That's good."

"We ran into a friend of yours," Marielle said as she untied her bonnet strings.

"Is that so?"

Marielle took the hat off and replied, "A Mr. Emerson, and he sends his greetings."

Hugh tensed. "Did you say Mr. Emerson?"

"I did," Marielle answered, looking unsure. "Is there an issue?"

"Mr. Emerson is no friend of mine."

"Then why would he say you were?" Marielle asked.

"Most likely to prove a point."

"What kind of point?"

"It matters not," Hugh said, waving his hand dismissively, "but I do not want you to associate with Mr. Emerson."

"May I ask why?"

"My reasons are my own," Hugh said curtly, "and as my ward, I expect you to follow my dictates."

"You wish for me to follow you blindly?"

"If I so desire, yes. Perhaps it is time that you learn your place."

Marielle pursed her lips together. "My place?" she repeated. "You cannot possibly be in earnest."

"I am," Hugh replied.

The main door opened, and Nathaniel walked into the entry hall. He glanced between them. "Am I interrupting something?"

Marielle turned to Nathaniel and smiled saccharinely. "Will you kindly inform your barbaric brother that I am not some puppet that he can manipulate with the pull of a string?" she asked before she hurriedly left the hall.

Nathaniel lifted his brow in question as he met Hugh's gaze. "What was that about?"

"It was nothing."

"Clearly, it was something," Nathaniel said. "Marielle appeared rather upset with you."

Hugh gestured towards the drawing room. "It might be best if we have this conversation in private, away from prying ears."

Once they walked into the drawing room, Nathaniel closed the door as Hugh walked over to the drink cart. "Would you care for a drink?" Hugh asked.

Nathaniel put his hand up. "No, thank you," he replied. "I need a clear head this evening."

"Suit yourself." Hugh poured himself a drink and picked up the glass. After he took a sip, he said, "Marielle informed me that she met one of my friends while shopping today."

"I'm afraid I don't understand the issue."

"It was Mr. Emerson," Hugh said, tightening his hold on his glass. "He told Marielle that we were friends."

"That's concerning," Nathaniel said, "but it still doesn't explain why Marielle is upset with you."

"I informed her that Mr. Emerson and I were not friends and told her to stay away from him."

Nathaniel gave him a knowing look. "It sounds as if you commanded her."

"Told her, commanded her, it's the same thing," Hugh said. "I am her guardian, and as such, she will follow my decrees."

Nathaniel's face went slack. "Dear heavens," he muttered. "Please tell me that you didn't say that to her."

"I did."

His brother walked over to the settee and sat down. "Women do not like being told what to do," he said. "You must make them believe your reasoning is their own if you want them to go along with it."

"I don't have time for games."

"It isn't a game, it's your new way of life."

Hugh sat across from Nathaniel. "But Marielle is my ward. She has no choice but to listen to me."

Nathaniel sighed. "Do you wish to be happy?"

"What does that have to do with anything?"

"There is an easy way to live and a hard way to live," Nathaniel said. "If you force Marielle to do your will, she will only come to resent you and will end up fighting you at every opportunity."

Hugh took a sip of his drink. "Then what do you propose?"

"You could start with telling her the truth."

"That is rather humorous, coming from you," Hugh scoffed.

"I may not be forthcoming with all the details of my life, but I have since learned that Dinah deserves to know the truth."

"Even if it may upset her?" Hugh asked.

"Even then," Nathaniel replied.

Hugh put his glass on the table. "How do you propose I tell Marielle that Mr. Emerson threatened her?"

"Do not attempt to pacify her. Tell her the truth and let her decide how to feel," Nathaniel advised. "You owe that much to her. It is concerning her wellbeing, after all."

"You make it sound so simple."

Nathaniel smirked. "I was once where you were, and I tried to control Dinah by ordering her about."

"How did she take that?"

"About as well as Marielle."

Hugh let out a groan. "I am going to have to apologize to her, aren't I?"

"If you are a smart man."

"I just wish she understood that I am trying to help her," Hugh said.

Their mother walked into the room with a purposeful stride and met his gaze. "Do you want to explain to me why Marielle is feigning a headache and requesting a tray be sent to her room for dinner?" she asked in an accusatory tone.

"Do I have a choice?" Hugh asked.

She put a hand on her hip. "What did you say that upset her?"

"I only asked her to stay away from Mr. Emerson."

"Why?"

"Do I need a reason?" Hugh questioned, reaching for his drink.

Their mother dropped her hand to her side. "This is worse than I thought," she said. "Marielle is not some simpering miss that you can lord yourself over."

"I am not lording myself over her," Hugh defended. "I'm her guardian. I'm trying to protect her."

"By controlling who she associates with?"

"Yes," he replied. "Mr. Emerson is not who he seems and associating with him could tarnish her reputation."

"And you told her this?"

Hugh shifted uncomfortably in his seat. "At the time I didn't think it was necessary."

Their mother stared at him for a moment. "You can't treat Marielle so distastefully. You are her guardian and need to treat her with respect. If you don't show her that courtesy, then how can you expect others to do the same?"

"I respect Marielle," Hugh insisted.

"It doesn't appear that way," their mother said. "I know you did not want to be her guardian, but we are all that she has. We're her family now."

Hugh tossed back his drink and set the glass down. "You're right," he said, rising. "I will go speak to her."

"I should warn you that she is rather upset," their mother said.

"That won't be an issue."

Nathaniel's eyes held amusement as he asked, "Have you ever tried to reason with a woman when she is upset?"

"I haven't," Hugh replied.

"Then I wish you luck," Nathaniel said.

"Surely it can't be that bad?"

Nathaniel rose. "Just imagine the worst possible scenario and double it."

"You are of little help," Hugh muttered before he walked over to the door. "I am sure that Marielle will be reasonable about this."

Hugh hurried up the stairs to the second level. He felt confident that Marielle would hear him out and they would find contentment in their relationship once again. This was just a simple misunderstanding, after all.

As he stopped in front of her door, it suddenly opened, and Marielle stood there with a valise in her hand, as shocked to see him as he was to see her.

"What are you doing?" he asked, brows furrowed.

"I am leaving," Marielle declared, holding up her valise. "I cannot stay here for a moment longer."

Hugh stifled a groan. So much for being reasonable.

———————— ∼ ————————

Marielle stared at Hugh with a stubborn tilt to her chin. She knew that she was being entirely perverse, but she did not care a whit. She'd submitted to every heartache and difficulty to this point admirably, but now she was beyond her limit. She refused to remain under the same roof as Hugh and let him treat her so unjustly. She knew now she should have made a stand with Mr. Cadell, and she wasn't going to make the same mistake with Hugh.

She expected him to grow angry now, combative even, but she hadn't expected him to smile. He leaned his shoulder against the door frame and asked, "Pray tell, where do you intend to go?"

"I will travel to my country estate."

"Brilliant," he said. "But how do you intend to get there?"

Marielle tightened her hold on the handle of the valise. "I shall take the mail coach."

"Have you ridden on a mail coach before?"

"I have not."

"It will be cramped, not at all what you are used to."

"So be it."

Hugh nodded. "Will you ride on the top or inside?"

"Inside, of course."

"That is wise, as you'll avoid the fickle nature of the elements. Though you might wish for that fresh air after being stuffed with other passengers and cargo for hours." He paused. "How will you pay for your passage?"

"I'll sell my mother's gold necklace."

"Smart. But where will you sell it?"

Marielle pressed her lips together. "I'll go to a jewelry shop and ask if they wish to purchase it."

"Will you not miss the gold necklace?" he asked. "I assume it has some sentimental value to you, as it was your mother's."

"It does, but I need the funds."

Hugh crossed his arms over his chest. "What will happen once you've arrived at your country estate?"

"I will be free to do as I please."

"Freedom truly is a blessing. Do you know how to cook?"

She paused. "Pardon?"

"Do you maintain a household staff there?" he asked.

"I assumed there was one."

"Perhaps they found new employment since their services weren't needed without anyone in residence."

Marielle frowned. "I should have enough funds left over from the sale of my mother's necklace to purchase food."

"That is a relief," Hugh said. "I wouldn't wish for you to starve."

Marielle stepped out into the hall and closed the bedroom door behind her. "I am more than capable of taking care of myself."

"I have no doubt, but your plan is riddled with holes."

"How so?"

Hugh straightened from the wall. "Your funds will no doubt run out, and you will be alone at your country estate."

"It is preferable to staying here."

"I doubt that," Hugh chuckled.

"At least no one would be telling me what to do."

"There are worse things," he cocked his head and raised his brows knowingly, "like starvation."

"I won't starve," Marielle argued.

Hugh uncrossed his arms. "Well, I can see that you are determined to go, so I won't stop you."

"You won't?" What game was he playing?

"I will even offer you the use of our coach."

Marielle stared at him in disbelief. "You will?"

"Yes," Hugh replied. "And you must not worry about your

lady's maid. We will ensure she is taken care of until you have the funds to pay for her."

"Thank you." She was confused, and wished her words were more confident, like the way they were before he agreed with her.

"I do not envy you," Hugh said. "With no household staff, you will be responsible for the care of a large country estate. You will be working from the moment you wake up until you go to bed."

"I hadn't considered that, but it won't be an issue."

Hugh bobbed his head. "Good." He gestured toward the stairs. "I shall walk you to the door."

"That is not necessary," she said as she started down the hall.

"It isn't safe for the coach to travel to your country estate until tomorrow," Hugh said, matching her stride, "so where do you intend to stay tonight?"

Her steps faltered but she quickly recovered. "A boarding house, I suppose."

"Which one?"

"I'll find one."

"Before or after you sell your mother's gold necklace?"

"After."

Hugh glanced over at her. "It will be dark soon. Are you not worried about walking the streets at night? What if the jeweler closes up shop soon?"

"I shall strive to hurry."

"As your guardian, I feel as if I must counsel against this," Hugh said as they descended the stairs. "My conscience dictates that I at least make the effort."

"I thank you for your concern, but you do not need to worry about me anymore."

His mother's voice came from the entry hall as they descended the stairs. "Why does Marielle have a valise?"

"She is staying at a boarding house tonight and traveling to her country estate tomorrow," Hugh explained.

Edith's mouth dropped open. "Surely you cannot be in earnest?"

"Marielle is determined to make it on her own, and I do not wish to restrict her." Hugh smiled over at his ward. "Isn't that right?"

His mother blinked. "You are mad."

Hugh shook his head. "Marielle is a formidable woman, and I am sure she considered all the problems that might arise from living entirely alone in a country estate." He met her gaze. "Haven't you?"

"I... uh..." Marielle started.

"I do hope that no highwaymen stop you along your journey. I doubt they will believe you have no funds," Hugh said. "That might be a little dangerous, but I will tell my footmen to inform the highwayman that you are insistent on making it on your own and need to keep your possessions."

Marielle stopped in front of Edith, trying to keep her face expressionless. She didn't dare admit that she was beginning to think this was a terrible idea after all. "Thank you for everything that you have done for me."

Edith looked panicked. "You can't leave," she contended. "Just think of what will become of you if you leave. Your reputation, your future, would be put into peril." She put a hand on Marielle's sleeve. "Will you not at least sleep on this monumental decision?"

Finally, someone was talking some sense. "That might be for the best——" Marielle started.

"Nonsense," Hugh interjected. "We don't wish to keep her. Marielle has made up her mind to leave us, and I support her decision."

"You do?" Marielle asked, feeling like a rock had settled in the pit of her stomach.

"I will not force you to live here," Hugh said. "I am not a tyrant."

"But, Hugh, it is evident that Marielle isn't thinking clearly at the moment," Edith pressed.

Dinah stepped into the entry hall and glanced at Marielle's valise. "Are you going somewhere?"

Marielle opened her mouth to respond, but Hugh spoke first. "She is going to a boarding house for the evening."

Dinah's eyes grew wide. "You cannot be in earnest?"

"I am," Hugh replied. "Marielle has determined to make it on her own, without my assistance, and I applaud her for it. Not everyone would give up food and a nice, warm bed to live in uncertainty."

Dinah frowned. "I'm going to get Nathaniel." She spun on her heel and hurried away.

Hugh held out his arm and asked, "Shall I escort you outside?"

Marielle's eyes darted to the proffered appendage and wondered how she was going to get herself out of this situation. She should admit that she was wrong, but she didn't want to give Hugh that satisfaction. But she truly didn't want to sleep in a boarding house, not when she had a warm, comfortable bed here with servants tending to her every need.

"Marielle," Hugh prodded, keeping his arm outstretched, "is everything all right?"

"I, uh, am not sure if I have enough time to find a boarding house before it gets dark." There. That was true.

Hugh glanced out the window. "I would be happy to escort you to one."

Drat. Why was Hugh being so accommodating?

"Perhaps I should do as Edith recommended and sleep on it," Marielle said, taking a step back.

"If that is what you would like to do," Hugh said.

"It is," Marielle rushed to reply.

"There is no shame in admitting that you were wrong," Hugh remarked as he withdrew his arm.

"Who said that I was in the wrong?"

"I think we both know that you had no intention of leaving the townhouse," he said with a smug smile.

"You're wrong," Marielle said.

Hugh gave her a look that implied he didn't believe her. "It's foolish to believe that a lady like you could ever handle living on her own."

"A lady like me?" Marielle repeated. "What is that supposed to mean?"

"You are used to everything being handed to you. You wouldn't know the first thing about taking care of yourself," Hugh replied.

Marielle squared her shoulders. "I have no doubt that I would get by."

"You would fail spectacularly," Hugh said.

"You do not know what I am capable of," Marielle responded with narrowed eyes.

Hugh held out his hand. "Hand me your valise, and I will see it returned to your bedchamber."

"No."

Hugh lifted his brow. "No?"

"I think I would like to take you up on your offer to help me find a boarding house," Marielle said with a stubborn tilt of her chin. "I find that I cannot stand to stay in your residence a moment longer."

"I know Hugh can be difficult," Edith interrupted, "but don't do anything that you might regret."

Hugh turned to his mother. "I'm not the one being difficult! Marielle is the one threatening to run off and live on her own. It's preposterous!"

"Why is it preposterous?" Marielle demanded.

"You don't know the first thing about cooking or cleaning, and it's highly likely the staff at your estate isn't there to take care of you," Hugh said, taking a step closer to her. "Just admit that you were wrong, and we can forget this whole tantrum ever happened."

"You would like that, wouldn't you?"

"I would, because this is the most idiotic situation I have ever been in," Hugh said.

Marielle brushed past Hugh. "I don't need, or want, your help."

As she reached for the latch, Hugh put his hand on the door and ordered, "You aren't going anywhere!"

"Yes, I am," Marielle said, turning around to face him, "and you can't stop me!"

Hugh leaned his face closer to hers. "I will lock you in your bedchamber."

"I will sneak out my window."

"Then I will nail it shut."

"And deprive me of fresh air?" Marielle tsked. "That is not a very gentlemanly thing to do."

Hugh clenched his jaw. "I will do whatever it takes to keep you safe."

"Am I supposed to thank you?"

"That would be a good start."

"Why would I thank someone who is trying to control me?"

"I am not trying to control you. I am trying to *help* you," Hugh asserted. "Surely you can tell the difference between the two?"

Marielle opened her mouth to make a retort when Nathaniel's voice boomed from behind Hugh. "You two are acting like unruly children!"

Hugh took a step back and turned to his brother. "Perhaps you can talk some sense into her," he said, clearly exasperated. "She wants to travel to her country estate and live on her own!"

Nathaniel's stern gaze shifted towards hers. "Is that true?"

Marielle squirmed under Nathaniel's scrutiny. "Yes, it is," she murmured, "but I am beginning to think I was acting too hastily."

Hugh huffed. "You think?" he muttered under his breath.

Edith came forward and slipped her arm around Marielle's shoulders. "Why do you wish to leave?"

"Because Hugh is being entirely unreasonable," Marielle replied with a glance at the offending man, "and is trying to dictate my every action."

"He is your guardian," Edith pointed out.

"I am aware, but I never asked for that," Marielle said. "I reach my majority soon, and once I do, I don't need a guardian."

"I never asked to be your guardian either, but here we are," Hugh gibed.

Nathaniel crossed his arms over his chest. "It is evident that you two need to talk and come to an understanding."

"That's unlikely," Hugh said. "We've been talking, but agreement seems impossible."

"I want you both to go into the drawing room, and I don't want you to come out until you two have talked through this," Nathaniel ordered.

"Surely you can't be serious?" Marielle asked.

Nathaniel uncrossed his arms and pointed towards the drawing room. "I would hurry if you want to be out before the dinner bell is rung."

Edith removed her arm from Marielle's shoulders and held her hand out. "I will see to your valise."

Reluctantly, Marielle handed the valise to Edith and started towards the drawing room, not caring a whit if Hugh followed or not.

Chapter Eight

Hugh watched as Marielle traipsed towards the drawing room with her chin held high. What a stubborn minx! She would have left just to prove a point if he'd let her. And what would have become of her if she'd wandered the streets alone? He shuddered at that thought.

He may not know everything about being a guardian, but he knew enough to know it wouldn't be good for Marielle to live on her own. It was best for her to stay here under his roof, where he could keep her safe. She may not want his protection, but he would give it to her, nonetheless. She was his responsibility until she reached her majority, and he was beginning to realize how important it was that he took his duty seriously.

Perhaps he should take his family's advice and apologize for upsetting her earlier. It was evident that she was still angry with him for ordering her to stay away from Mr. Emerson. But it was for her own good!

Why were women so complicated? If only they acted more like men and learned to keep their emotions in check. Marielle was being completely unreasonable. She was letting her emotions dictate her actions without fully thinking through the repercussions.

Nathaniel joined him by the door. "I wouldn't keep her waiting for too long if I were you," he advised.

His mother gave Hugh a disapproving look. "I agree with your brother," she said. "Don't dally and make the situation worse."

"Could it get any worse?" Hugh asked.

His mother patted the side of the valise. "I will see that this is returned to Marielle's bedchamber."

"Do you think that Marielle is acting irrationally?" Hugh asked Nathaniel as their mother walked off.

Nathaniel glanced at his wife, who shook her head. "I don't have a say on the matter," he answered.

Hugh sighed. "Where do I even begin with her?"

"Be the man she wants and needs you to be."

"I already am that man. I do believe I prevented her from being sold off to scoundrels like a bauble."

"Then prove it to her," Nathaniel urged.

"How do I do that?"

Nathaniel put a hand on his shoulder. "I would start with an apology."

"An apology?"

"Women tend to respond better to those than accusations," Nathaniel said as he withdrew his hand.

Dinah came closer and remarked, "It's true. If you go in there angry, then she will no doubt respond in a similar fashion."

"Am I supposed to ignore the fact that she threatened to run away?" Hugh asked.

"No, but you should ask yourself why she wished to do such a thing," Dinah replied.

Hugh ran a hand through his brown hair. "I already know the answer to that."

Dinah gave him an encouraging smile. "Then you can rationally—and calmly—discuss that with her."

"Why do women want to talk about their feelings?" Hugh asked. "Why not bottle them up and cast them aside? Or drown them in the contents of that bottle in privacy?"

"Emotions will only resurface later at the most inopportune times," Dinah said. "It is best to confront them head on."

"This sounds exhausting," Hugh muttered.

Dinah laughed. "It gets easier with time, but you must establish trust between you and Marielle if you want to work amicably together."

"I would prefer to give her a command and have her follow it," Hugh said.

"That would be easier for you," Dinah agreed, "but that is not what Marielle needs. She is not a docile young woman you can order around."

Hugh frowned. "I suppose it's best that I get this over with."

Nathaniel chuckled. "That's the spirit. We'll wait out here."

"Shamelessly eavesdropping," Dinah added.

Hugh started slowly towards the drawing room, not knowing what to expect. He knew he owed Marielle an apology for ordering her about earlier, but would that be enough to quell the situation?

He stepped into the drawing room and saw Marielle sitting on the settee. Her back was rigid, and she was staring daggers at him. This did not bode well.

Bracing his hands on the back of an upholstered armchair, Hugh attempted, "I can't help but wonder if I played a role in your tantrum."

Apparently, that was the wrong thing to say, because her eyes grew wide and she inhaled sharply.

"And I would like to apologize for anything that I may

have said that upset you," Hugh rushed out. There. He'd apologized. That should appease her.

Marielle crossed her arms over her chest and leaned back in her seat. "Pray tell, do you recall what you said that upset me?"

He shrugged. "I assume it has something to do with Mr. Emerson."

"Yes, and that was shortly before you told me that I needed to learn my place," Marielle informed him.

"Which you do," Hugh said. The moment his words left his mouth, he wished that he could take them back.

Marielle uncrossed her arms and slowly rose. "And what place is that?" Her words held a warning he'd be a fool to miss.

"I am your guardian, and you are my ward," he attempted. "I make decisions on your behalf, and you accept that it is for the best."

"What if it isn't for the best?" Marielle questioned. "Should I not have a say in the matter?"

"I suppose I could take what you say into consideration."

"How very generous of you," Marielle mocked.

Marielle's cheeks were flushed, no doubt from being angry at him. She looked like a vengeful goddess, ready to strike his inferior humanity out of existence.

They were just going in circles, and Hugh knew nothing would be resolved at this rate. He pushed off from the chair and stepped carefully away from the security it provided. "I think we got off on the wrong foot." He smiled, hoping the friendly expression would do something to cool her ire. "I have never been a guardian before, and I daresay that I have a lot to learn."

"That you do," Marielle said.

"Perhaps we could sit down and discuss how we can improve working together as we move forward." He gestured towards her seat. "Don't you think that would be for the best?"

Marielle looked hesitant but eventually lowered herself onto the settee. "I do," she finally said.

Hugh took a seat across from her. "It has come to my attention that I did not properly explain why I want you to avoid Mr. Emerson."

"You did not."

"Mr. Emerson lost a great deal of money to me, and he wants me to return it to him," Hugh explained.

"I assume he lost it through gambling."

"That he did," Hugh said. "He is terrible at faro and had the nerve to accuse me of cheating when he lost."

"It was wrong of him to do so."

"Mr. Emerson made some threats directed at me—and you."

Marielle furrowed her brows. "Why would he be angry at me?"

"Because you are my ward."

"But I had nothing to do with him losing that money."

Hugh nodded. "True, but that doesn't matter to someone like Mr. Emerson."

Marielle leaned back in her seat. "He seemed so pleasant when I met him," she said. "Do you think he would make good on his threat?"

"I don't rightly know," Hugh replied, "but I thought it would be best if you didn't associate with him, for safety's sake."

Marielle pressed her lips together, then asked, "Why didn't you tell me this earlier when we spoke?"

"I didn't want to worry you unnecessarily."

"If you had, then we could have avoided this whole misunderstanding," Marielle said.

Hugh grinned. "You may not have noticed, but I am unsure about how to properly be a guardian."

"You were doing just fine until you *ordered* me to stay away from Mr. Emerson."

"I admit it was not my finest moment, but I was furious that Mr. Emerson dared to approach you in the first place," Hugh said. "I don't want him anywhere near you."

"You could have explained that to me."

"I could have, but then I would have missed your impressive performance," Hugh said. "Would you have truly left?"

"I don't rightly know. I was angry and hurt, and I'm afraid I acted rather impulsively."

Hugh leaned forward in his seat. "While I am trying to figure out this whole guardian thing, you must strive to be patient with me."

"I will try."

"Just so you know, I would never have let you leave," Hugh said. "I care too much about you to let anything bad happen to you."

Marielle lowered her gaze to her lap. "Thank you," she murmured.

Hugh rose and moved to sit on the settee next to her. "I know I am terrible at showing my emotions, but I promise to be better from here on out." He waited until she brought her gaze up. "I think it would be best if you met me halfway."

"I can do that," Marielle responded.

"Good, because for the life of me, I can't predict what you will do next," he said with a wry smile.

Marielle let out a soft sigh before sharing, "Mr. Cadell controlled every aspect of my life, and I did not like it. He made me feel as if I didn't matter."

Hugh reached for her gloved hand. "You do matter, and don't you dare let anyone tell you differently."

"You are too kind," she murmured automatically.

"There is nothing kind about it," Hugh said. "You are a clever young woman, and Mr. Cadell was wrong to treat you so distastefully."

"I was raised to take charge of my own affairs, and I was worried that you would take that away from me, just as Mr. Cadell did."

"I can be a boor sometimes, but that doesn't mean I don't value your opinion," Hugh said.

Marielle smiled sweetly. "Thank you," she said.

Hugh's eyes roamed over her lovely features until they landed on her lips. Perfectly formed lips. He cleared his throat and brought his gaze back up.

"Shall we inform my mother that we have reconciled?" Hugh asked.

A crashing sound assaulted their ears, and glass shards flew into the room. Hugh turned towards the broken window and saw a large rock laying on the carpet. It appeared that a note was tied to it.

He had barely risen when Nathaniel stormed into the room with a pistol drawn. His alert eyes scanned the room, eventually settling on them.

"Are you all right?" Nathaniel asked.

"I am." Hugh turned towards Marielle. "Are you hurt?"

She shook her head and swallowed. "No."

Nathaniel walked over to the rock, the broken glass crunching under the weight of his Hessian boots. He leaned down, untied the string, and removed the paper. He read it and frowned before he extended it towards Hugh.

Hugh accepted the paper.

Return what is rightfully owed to me or you will lose more than a window next time.

Marielle gasped from where she'd been reading over his shoulder. "Do you think Mr. Emerson did this?"

"Who else would have done it?" Hugh groused as he crumbled the paper in his hand.

Nathaniel tucked the pistol into the waistband of his trousers. "This cannot go unanswered," he said. "Do you want me to take care of it?"

"No, this is my fight," Hugh said. He didn't need his older brother to fix things for him.

"Then I shall respect that, assuming Mr. Emerson doesn't make a habit of breaking my things," Nathaniel stated.

Hugh didn't comment on the fact that the townhouse wasn't actually his yet, and instead turned around to face Marielle. "It would be best if we depart from here until the glass has been cleaned up."

"I agree," Marielle replied, allowing him to lead her out of the drawing room.

The following morning, Marielle stepped into the dining room and came to an abrupt halt. Lord Montfort was sitting at the head of the table, reading the morning newspaper, his usual gruff look on his face.

He lowered the newssheets and glanced over at her. "Do you intend to just loiter in the doorway?"

Drat. He'd seen her, despite not making her presence known. "I haven't quite decided."

Lord Montfort gestured towards the chair next to him. "Come and sit," he encouraged.

Marielle walked over to the chair and sat down. She tried to think of something clever to say, but she was at a loss for words. It wasn't as though she was afraid of Lord Montfort, but rather that she didn't know him very well.

An uncomfortable silence descended over the table as a footman placed a cup of chocolate in front of her. She reached for the cup and took a long sip. Perhaps if she drank this chocolate slowly enough, Lord Montfort wouldn't expect her to engage him in conversation.

But she was not so lucky.

Lord Montfort held up the newssheets. "Would you care to read the Society page?"

"I would," she said, placing her cup back onto the saucer.

As he extended the paper to her, he said, "I would imagine you would find that preferable to attempting a conversation with me."

She gave him an apologetic smile. "Is it so obvious?"

"I have been around long enough to know that someone can't be that interested in chocolate." He winked at her. "But it might help if I was the one to start the conversation."

"It would," she said, already feeling herself relax.

"Did you know that I was friends with your father?" Lord Montfort asked.

"I did not."

Lord Montfort smiled. "He was a few years younger than me, but we met when we were at Cambridge."

"I hadn't realized."

"Your father always had a way with words, and I would pay him to help me write my papers," Lord Montfort shared. "I always knew he would make something of himself, and he did."

Marielle nodded. "He built his shipping company from the ground up," she said proudly. "He had to take out a loan to start the company, and he paid it back within six months. From then on, he just reinvested his profits until it started thriving."

"That is impressive."

"My father would recount the same story of how he started his business every year on the anniversary of the day he opened his doors," Marielle said with a smile.

"What he accomplished was no small feat."

"No, it wasn't, especially since he started it with only ten pounds to his name," Marielle agreed.

Lord Montfort wiped the sides of his mouth with his

napkin. "Were you aware that I recommended him to be knighted?"

"No, I wasn't."

"Your father could have been knighted for any of a host of reasons, but it was his work with the poor that inspired others," Lord Montfort said. "He hired laborers from within the rookeries, helping them out of poverty and giving them a fresh start. It was hard work, but it was honest work, which was something that many of his workers never had a chance at before."

Marielle reached for her cup and took a sip. "I hadn't realized that my father did that."

"He was not one to brag about his accomplishments," Lord Montfort said. "He kept his head down and got to work. That was one of the many things I admired about him."

"I appreciate you for saying so," Marielle said. "At times, I feel like his memory is slipping away from me."

"Have you written down your memories of your father?"

"Not yet."

"Do not wait too long," Lord Montfort advised. "The longer you wait, the harder it will be."

"It sounds as if you've experienced this firsthand."

A sad smile tugged at Lord Montfort's lips. "I have," he said. "My mother was a stubborn woman, and one year she insisted on residing at our country estate during the Season. I tried to convince her to come to Town, but she didn't want to leave the countryside. By the time the Season was over, she had passed on. The doctor said her heart gave out."

"I am so sorry," Marielle murmured.

"My grief was unrelenting, and I mourned her deeply. Years passed before I could even think of her without growing despondent. By then, my recollection had started to fade, and I was left wishing I had written down every memory, every conversation, that I could think of." Lord Montfort sighed.

"But it was too late for me. Don't make the same mistake that I did."

"I will strive not to."

Lord Montfort's eyes crinkled around the edges. "I daresay that this conversation is not going as I intended," he said. "It has grown far too serious for my tastes."

"I think it is just the right amount of seriousness," she joked.

With a glance at the empty doorway, Lord Montfort asked, "Has my son made a nuisance of himself yet?"

"He has not."

"Hm. I find that hard to believe, especially after everything that my wife has told me," Lord Montfort said, giving Marielle a pointed look.

A footman placed a plate in front of her and stepped back. Marielle welcomed the extra moment to gather her thoughts.

"Hugh and I have come to an understanding," she said as she reached for her fork.

"I'm pleased to hear that." Lord Montfort leaned closer to her, his eyes twinkling with mirth. "I heard that you threatened to sleep at a boarding house."

"I did."

"Bravo, child," Lord Montfort said. "I bet that really irked my son."

"I didn't do it to make him angry."

Lord Montfort chuckled. "Whatever your plan was, it worked splendidly."

Pushing the eggs around her plate with her fork, she admitted, "I didn't have a plan."

"You were playing a dangerous game, then," Lord Montfort said, leaning back. "A warrior cannot go into battle without a strategy to win."

"I wasn't in a battle."

"Weren't you?"

As if summoned by their conversation, Hugh stepped into

the room. Lord Montfort glanced up at him. "You don't look terrible, which leads me to believe you didn't stay out all night gambling."

"I decided to stay in last night," Hugh replied as he pulled out the chair next to Marielle. "I thought it would be for the best."

Marielle glanced over at Hugh and smiled. "Good morning."

Hugh returned her smile. "Good morning," he greeted back. "Dare I hope you slept well?"

"I did," she replied. "Did you? Sleep well?"

He shook his head. "I did not. I kept worrying about the note Mr. Emerson sent."

"I do not understand why no one contacted the constable and reported that," Lord Montfort interjected.

"There is no point. Mr. Emerson would just deny throwing the rock through our window," Hugh explained.

Lord Montfort frowned. "This is all your fault. If you hadn't taken Mr. Emerson's money—"

"I did not take his money," Hugh stated, cutting him off. "I won it fairly."

"Bah. You seem to think gambling is an honorable profession, but it is not," Lord Montfort said.

"I never said it was."

Lord Montfort pointed a finger at Hugh. "You are embarrassing this family the way you are carrying on at the gambling halls."

"I doubt that," Hugh responded.

"For the life of me, I do not know why you gave up being a barrister," Lord Montfort said. "From what I heard and saw, you were quite good at it."

"I was, but my life has taken a different path," Hugh responded.

Lord Montfort lowered his hand. "You have a ward that

you need to think of now," he asserted. "Why do you refuse to be respectable?"

"Father..." Hugh sighed. "Can we not do this now?"

"Why? Is this not a good time for you?" Lord Montfort asked dryly.

A footman placed a plate in front of Hugh, and he reached for his fork. "I would prefer to eat my breakfast in peace."

"And I would prefer to have a son who lived up to his duty." Lord Montfort shoved back his chair and rose. "If you will excuse me, I am needed at the House of Lords."

The silence was palpable after Lord Montfort departed, and Marielle opened her mouth to say something, but Hugh spoke first.

"Don't bother, Marielle," he urged.

"You don't even know what I was going to say."

Hugh shifted in his seat to face her. "I have no doubt that you were going to offer some words of encouragement."

"I was, but—"

"Nothing you say will change the fact that my father views me as a disappointment."

"He is wrong."

"Is he?" Hugh asked. "I spend my nights at disreputable gambling halls and my days sleeping off the effects."

"It sounds as if you agree with him."

Hugh's eyes grew guarded. "At times, I feel like the failure he believes me to be."

"I find it hard to believe that you are a failure."

"Nothing I do will ever please my father, so I stopped trying long ago," Hugh said. "I do what I want, when I want, and it is much easier that way."

Marielle cocked her head. "Are you happy?"

Hugh looked surprised by her question. "I'm not sure how to answer that."

"It's a simple enough question."

"Is it?" Hugh asked. "After all, is anyone truly happy?"

"Yes," Marielle said. "Being happy is a state of mind. You have to choose to be happy, every day."

"It isn't that simple."

"I believe it is," Marielle responded.

Hugh reached for his cup and took a sip of tea. As he placed the cup back on the saucer, he said, "Life is not about chasing rainbows and having tea parties. It's hard, unrelenting, and most days are dreary."

"That doesn't mean you can't be happy."

"I am past the point of being naïve enough to believe everyone deserves to be happy. I have made my bed, and now I have to lie in it."

It was evident that Hugh believed his words, but it made her heart ache. How could someone live without having some type of hope of a happy future?

Marielle decided to change the topic. "Were you truly a barrister?"

"I was," Hugh said, clenching his jaw, "but I do not care to discuss that phase of my life."

Marielle didn't wish to upset Hugh, but she couldn't help but prod a little more. Her curiosity was getting the best of her. "May I ask why that is?"

Hugh didn't speak for a long moment, and she thought he might refuse to answer. But finally, he spoke. "I learned there is a fine line between right and wrong, and it is almost indiscernible in a court of law."

As she opened her mouth to ask another question that would no doubt upset Hugh, Dinah stepped into the room with a bright smile on her face. "Good morning," she greeted.

"Good morning," Marielle said as she reached for her cup of chocolate.

Hugh rose when Dinah stepped into the room and waited by his chair until she sat down across from them. "How are you faring this morning?" he asked.

"I am well, but I'm afraid I must rush breakfast if I wish to arrive at the orphanage on time."

"What orphanage?" Marielle asked.

"It is the most charming orphanage in the rookeries," Dinah started, "and my sister is acting as the headmistress while Lady Grenton is in Scotland." She paused. "You should join me."

"In the rookeries?" Marielle asked skeptically.

Dinah bobbed her head. "You can help me read to the girls," she said. "Just think of how much fun it will be!"

It did sound better than sitting around the townhouse. Besides, she had never been to an orphanage or the rookeries before. It would be an adventure. Turning towards Hugh, Marielle asked, "May I go with Dinah?"

Hugh hesitated. "I don't know if that is the best idea," he said.

"Nathaniel always ensures that I am protected by sending more than enough footmen," Dinah interjected, "and it will only be for a few hours."

"Please, Hugh," Marielle said.

"All right, but I must insist that you be cautious," Hugh said, raising his hands in surrender. "There are dangerous men afoot in the rookeries."

Marielle pushed back her chair and rose. "What hat should I wear?" she asked, remembering that she now had an abundance of them. "Or do they wear hats in the rookeries?"

Dinah laughed. "I daresay that you are overthinking this," she replied. "I would recommend a simple bonnet."

"A bonnet," Marielle said. "I have those."

"Well, I should say so," Dinah said. "Hurry along. We must be quick if we want to arrive before the girls start their chores."

Chapter Nine

The coach jostled them about as it rolled down the uneven street. A terrible smell wafted through the window, and Marielle reached over to close it.

"It won't help," Dinah said. "You will just have to get used to the smell."

Marielle looked at Dinah like she was mad. "How can someone get used to such a foul odor?"

Dinah gave her an amused look. "It does take some getting used to, but now I associate the smell with fond memories of the rookeries."

Marielle arched an eyebrow. "You have fond memories of the rookeries?" she repeated. "I find that hard to believe."

"It's true," Dinah responded. "The rookeries are filled with hard-working people who are just trying to survive another day."

"Do you come to the rookeries often?"

"Not anymore, but I couldn't turn down Evie's offer to read to the girls, especially since I am a patron for the orphanage."

"What reason did you have to visit the rookeries before you were a patron?"

Dinah waved her hand dismissively in front of her. "I had some matters to take care of."

"Such as?"

"It was something of a personal nature, and I would prefer not to discuss it."

Marielle found it interesting that Dinah was being so secretive, but she had no right to pry further. It wasn't her place. But when had that stopped her before?

"Earlier you mentioned that Lady Grenton runs the orphanage," Marielle said, deciding it was best to switch to another topic. "How is it possible that a lady is running an orphanage?"

"That is a long story, and it is not mine to share." Dinah glanced out the window. "You will have to ask Lady Grenton when she returns from her wedding tour."

"Will you at least explain how your sister is running the orphanage while Lady Grenton is away?"

"That's easy; she volunteered."

"Why would she do such a thing?"

Dinah smiled. "My sister is rather unconventional, and she tends to do things in her own way."

"That is a fine trait to have, but is she not afraid of ruining her reputation if the *ton* finds out that she is spending her time at an orphanage in the rookeries?"

"Evie truly cares little about her reputation, but she understands what is expected of her nonetheless," Dinah said. "She is discreet when the situation requires it."

"Now you are sounding more like Lord Montfort."

"In what way?"

Marielle clasped her hands in her lap. "He seems to value duty above all else."

"He is a marquess."

"True, but he is so hard on Hugh."

"I agree, but it is for a good reason," Dinah said. "Hugh

can't keep going on the way that he has. Eventually, his luck will run out."

"Hugh just seems so…" Marielle's voice trailed off as she tried to think of the right words. "…lost. Despondent."

"I agree, but it is of his own making."

Marielle pressed her lips together before asking the one question that had been on her mind since breakfast. "Do you know why he stopped working as a barrister?"

Dinah adjusted the sleeves of her yellow gown. "I don't rightly know," she replied. "Nathaniel told me that he had just won a big case in court, and a few days later, he quit."

"What was the case about?"

"I'm not sure," Dinah said. "Nathaniel was rather vague."

"I just wish there was a way to help Hugh."

"You are helping him just by being you," Dinah responded. "I have noticed a real change in Hugh since you arrived."

"I wish that were true."

Dinah reached out to steady herself as the coach hit yet another rut in the road. "It is true. Hugh is starting to smile more."

"Truly?"

"I don't know why you sound so surprised. Sometimes all it takes is for someone to just be themselves to enact change."

Marielle scrunched her nose as the smell of excrement permeated the coach. "I daresay that the smell is getting worse."

"That means we are getting closer."

The coach came to a stop in front of a red brick building, and it dipped to the side as a footman stepped off the back perch. The door opened and the footman reached his hand in to assist them onto the pavement.

Marielle noticed the pavement in front of the orphanage was swept and free of debris. As they approached the door, it was opened, and a tall, older man greeted them with a kind smile.

"Good morning," he said, opening the door wide.

Marielle followed Dinah inside and they stopped in the modest entry hall. The faint sound of children's voices could be heard coming from upstairs.

The man closed the door and latched it before he turned back to face them. "Miss Ashmore has been anxiously awaiting your arrival, Lady Hawthorne."

"I am not surprised. Evie has never been one for patience," Dinah joked. "How are you faring, Wilson?"

"I am alive, so I can't complain too much," Wilson replied.

Dinah gestured towards Marielle. "This is Miss Wymond. She was gracious enough to accompany me today."

Wilson tipped his head. "It is a pleasure to meet you, Miss Wymond," he said. "I was given strict orders to take you to the office the moment you arrive." He turned on his heel and started to walk down a narrow hall.

It wasn't long before Wilson stopped beside a door and indicated that they should enter.

Marielle stepped into the office and saw Evie sitting at a worn desk, her head hunched over a ledger. A few pieces of her brown hair had escaped her simple chignon and curled around her face.

Evie glanced up and a bright smile lit her face. "Miss Wymond," she said. "What a pleasant surprise."

"Please, you must call me Marielle."

"Then you must call me Evie." She rose and came around her desk. "I was wondering if Dinah would ever arrive."

Dinah gave her sister an amused look. "I am right on time."

"Our aunt would be so disappointed that you just said that," Evie said. "She always says it is better to be early than late."

"Again, I'm not late," Dinah pointed out.

"No, you aren't, because I had you arrive thirty minutes early," Evie responded. "I couldn't risk traffic delaying you."

Dinah sat down on the chair in the corner. "Well, I am here now, and I'm ready to read to the girls."

"Thank you for doing so," Evie said. "They have been yammering on about little else since they heard you were coming."

"Is that so?" Dinah asked.

"They said you make silly voices when you read to them," Evie replied, "but I have yet to hear it for myself."

"And you won't," Dinah said. "I only put on the performances for the girls."

Evie grinned as she turned her attention towards Marielle. "Dare I hope that you are here to read to the girls, as well?"

"I am," Marielle said. "I hope that it will help the girls and keep me away from the humdrum of puttering around the house."

Dinah gave her a knowing look. "What about the excitement from last night?"

Evie glanced between them. "What happened last night?"

"Someone threw a rock through a window in the drawing room," Dinah shared.

"Not someone," Marielle interjected, relieved that Dinah wasn't referring to her threatening to leave. "We know it was Mr. Emerson."

"Did he confess to throwing the rock?" Evie asked.

"No, but there was a note attached to it, and it alluded to the money he believes Hugh owes him," Marielle replied.

"Why does he believe Hugh owes him money?" Evie inquired.

"Mr. Emerson lost a great deal while gambling with Hugh, and he wants it back," Marielle said. "He even accused Hugh of cheating."

Evie's eyes grew calculating. "What did Nathaniel say about all of this?"

"He offered to speak to Mr. Emerson, but Hugh said that he would take care of it," Dinah informed her. "But he was rather incensed about the situation."

"I would say so," Evie stated. "Have you spoken to the constable?"

"For what purpose? We both know that they are useless," Dinah asserted.

Evie bobbed her head in agreement. "That is true, but it might stop Mr. Emerson from inflicting more damage on your townhouse."

"Nathaniel did tell me that Mr. Emerson threatened Marielle while they were at White's," Dinah shared.

Evie's brow shot up. "That was bold of him, to do so in front of witnesses."

Marielle shook her head. "I don't believe that Mr. Emerson will make good on his threat."

"Why, because he is handsome?" Dinah questioned.

"He is rather handsome, but I met the man, and he seemed quite pleasant," Marielle said.

Evie gave her a disapproving look. "Do not be fooled by wolves in sheep's clothing."

"Mr. Emerson is hardly a wolf," Marielle contested.

"No, but he did throw a rock through a window," Dinah said. "I'm not quite sure what he is capable of."

"Throwing a rock is hardly the same thing as hurting someone," Marielle pressed.

Dinah cocked her head. "Why are you defending Mr. Emerson?"

"I'm not," Marielle said. "I am only saying that I do not believe he is as dangerous as we have led ourselves to believe."

Evie exchanged a concerned glance with Dinah. "I would urge you to be cautious. Law abiding citizens do not go around threatening people."

"Hugh is taking precautions to ensure that I am safe," Marielle said.

"That's good." Evie glanced towards the doorway as a thin lady with brown hair walked by. "Mrs. Hughes! Will you come in here, please?"

It was hardly a moment before Mrs. Hughes stepped into the room with a smile on her face that looked more like a grimace. "Yes, Miss Ashmore?"

"I wanted to introduce you to Miss Wymond," Evie said, gesturing towards her. "She will be reading to the girls today, along with my sister."

"That is wonderful news. I have no doubt that the girls will enjoy that," Mrs. Hughes said. "Will there be anything else?"

"Not at this time," Evie replied.

Mrs. Hughes acknowledged Dinah with a tip of her head. "My lady," she said before departing from the room.

Dinah looked at Evie with a look of stunned disbelief. "Was it just me, or did it seem that Mrs. Hughes was being somewhat cordial?"

"She was," Evie replied. "Most likely due to the fact that we came to an understanding yesterday."

"Did you threaten her?" Dinah asked.

Evie gave her a wide-eyed look. "Dear heavens, I would never do such a thing."

"We both know that you would," Dinah said knowingly. "But if you didn't threaten her, how did you convince her to play nice?"

"You have your secrets, and I have mine," Evie said as she walked towards the door. "Now, let's go see the girls."

Hugh stared at the amber liquid in his glass as he sat in the parlor. He wasn't used to being up at this hour, since he usually slept his days away, but Marielle's arrival on his doorstep had altered his whole schedule.

Just as he finally took a sip, Balfour stepped into the room and announced, "Mr. Donovan has requested a moment of your time, my lord."

"Send him in," Hugh ordered, happily abandoning the glass on the table.

A moment later, Mr. Donovan stepped into the room. "Thank you for agreeing to see me, my lord."

Hugh gestured towards a chair. "Have a seat."

Mr. Donovan walked over and sat down across from him. "I thought it would be best if I came in person to tell you the news," he said. "Mr. Cadell has dropped his appeal for guardianship of Miss Wymond."

"That is good news."

"I buried him with paperwork, and the cost to fight would have certainly been beyond his means," Mr. Donovan said.

"Well played."

"Indeed," Mr. Donovan said. "But Mr. Cadell has filed a civil suit against you."

"On what grounds?"

"He is suing you for lost revenue, the cost associated with caring for Miss Wymond for the past month, and theft for stealing his ward."

"I did not steal Miss Wymond."

Mr. Donovan put his hand up. "It's a baseless lawsuit, but we can't prevent him from filing it."

"How much is he suing me for?"

"Ten thousand pounds."

Hugh's brow shot up. "That is quite a hefty sum."

"I agree, which is why I believe we should take it seriously," Mr. Donovan said. "I do fear that this case will spark Society's interest and will be played out in the morning newspapers."

"Most likely that is what he wants."

Mr. Donovan shifted in his seat. "You could always try to settle with him before it goes to trial."

"Absolutely not!" Hugh exclaimed. "I refuse to pay that scoundrel one penny, especially when I did nothing wrong."

"That is true, but if it goes to trial, it could damage Miss Wymond's reputation further."

Hugh frowned. His solicitor did have a point, and it irked him. "Will you speak to Mr. Cadell's solicitor about a possible settlement?" he asked. "I am not sure that is the best course of action, though. Paying him off implies fault on my part."

"Sometimes we must put pride aside for the sake of the ones we care for," Mr. Donovan remarked.

"You are right, of course, but I really do not like Mr. Cadell. He treated Miss Wymond terribly and shouldn't be rewarded for that."

"It is better than the alternative of dragging her name through court." Mr. Donovan rose. "I will see what I can do and will report back to you the moment I have something of note."

"Thank you," Hugh said.

Mr. Donovan tipped his head. "The most important thing is that Miss Wymond is safe from Mr. Cadell."

Safe. Was she safe? Perhaps from Mr. Cadell, but now they had Mr. Emerson to contend with. Hugh had yet to return the money that Mr. Emerson claimed that he owed, and he wouldn't do so. He had won that money fairly.

Hugh barely acknowledged Mr. Donovan as he excused himself. He had more important things to dwell on than Mr. Cadell. He was making himself a nuisance, but he wasn't truly a threat. Why wouldn't he just go away and leave Miss Wymond in peace? The only thing he seemed to care about was money.

He couldn't blame Mr. Cadell for wanting a fortune. Money was the solution to most problems. The more you had, the more freedom you had. But it did come at a cost. Hugh had acquired a fortune from the card tables, but his father still thought of him as a failure. Nothing he did would please that man.

Hugh reached over and grabbed his drink. He took a sip, listening to the sound of the crackling fire in the hearth. He should be content, but he was far from it. When had his life gone so terribly wrong? Unfortunately, he already knew the answer. It was that blasted case that caused him to question everything.

He tightened his hold around his glass. His misery was his penance for his role in those women's deaths.

He was broken out of his thoughts by Lord Simon's concerned voice. "Are you well?"

Hugh looked up and saw his friend standing over him. How had he not heard him enter the parlor?

"I am," he replied.

Simon sat on the chair across from him. "I have been trying to get your attention for a few moments now. What has you so preoccupied?"

"It's nothing," Hugh dismissed.

"It didn't appear to be nothing. You look troubled," Simon remarked.

Hugh sighed. "I was thinking about my father." At least there was some truth to his answer.

"Ah. I should have assumed."

Hugh finished off his drink, then said, "He's been rather hard on me since I took Marielle on as a ward."

"I can only imagine how my father would act if I arrived home with a ward in tow."

"Fortunately, my father seems to be taken by Marielle."

"That's good."

Rising, Hugh walked over to the drink cart. He picked up a decanter and poured two drinks. "Marielle has the fortunate, if uncanny, ability to charm everyone that she associates with."

"Has she charmed you?" Simon asked with a curious look.

"Not in the way that you are implying," Hugh replied as he picked up the two glasses, "but I do think she is pleasant enough."

After he extended a glass to his friend, Simon asked, "When do I get to meet Miss Wymond?"

"She is at the orphanage with Dinah, but she should be returning soon."

"You let Miss Wymond go to an orphanage?" Simon asked in disbelief.

"I did."

Simon gave him a disapproving look. "What if she catches something from those urchins?"

"Then we shall call for the doctor."

"An orphanage is not a place for a lady," Simon pressed. "They are terribly filthy, and the orphans will no doubt steal from her."

"Clearly, you haven't been to this orphanage. It has a butler and a cook on staff."

Simon stared at him in disbelief. "How is that possible?"

"Dinah is one of the patrons of Lord and Lady Grenton's orphanage, and she has gotten many of her friends to donate to their cause."

"Their cause being?"

"Lady Grenton is determined to educate the children so they can obtain employment as lady's maids."

"Educated orphans," Simon huffed as he brought his glass to his lips. "I have never heard of such lunacy before."

"I think it is quite brilliant."

"Why am I not surprised by that?" Simon asked.

Hugh set his drink down on the table. "If you want to enact change, you need to start with the children. They are the future."

"They are simple urchins who don't have a future."

Annoyed by his friend's pretentious attitude, Hugh asked, "Do you not have some place to be?"

Simon leaned back in his seat. "I believe I struck a nerve."

"I just think more can be done to help the people in the rookeries," Hugh said. "The moment they are born, they are given a death sentence."

"What do you intend to do about it, then?"

"I don't know."

"I prefer to ignore their plight, because it is far too great to do anything about," Simon said. "You should take my lead and just focus on yourself."

"I have been doing just that for far too long already."

Simon lowered his glass to his lap. "I did come to see if you are well, since you didn't go to the gambling hall last night."

"I was busy."

"Too busy for gambling?" Simon tsked. "You'll have to do better than that."

Hugh glanced over at the empty doorway. "A rock was thrown through our window last night with a note attached."

Simon grew serious. "What did the note say?"

Reaching into the pocket of his jacket, he removed the slip of paper and extended it towards Simon. "Read it yourself."

Simon accepted the paper and read it. "I must assume that this is from Mr. Emerson, based on what you've told me."

"That is what we believe, as well."

"What do you intend to do?" Simon asked as he returned the paper to him.

Hugh slipped the paper back into his pocket. "Nathaniel offered to speak to Mr. Emerson, but I told him that I would take care of it."

"Why not let the constable handle it?"

"Nathaniel and Dinah are of a mind that they are useless," Hugh said with a small shrug.

"But that is your only clear course of action," Simon said. "Unless you intend to confront Mr. Emerson on your own?"

"I haven't decided yet."

Simon leaned forward and put his empty glass on the table. "If you would like me to accompany you to speak to Mr. Emerson, I would be happy to do so."

"I think it would be best if I had my brother accompany me."

"Your brother does have a rather commanding presence about him," Simon said. "Truth be told, he frightens me a little."

Hugh chuckled. "I will be sure not to pass that along."

"I would appreciate that." Simon rose and tugged down on his blue waistcoat. "I assume you will be joining me at Gilded Crown this evening?"

"I haven't decided yet."

"What is there to decide?" Simon asked.

"I need to ensure that Marielle is being properly cared for before I go anywhere," Hugh replied as he rose.

"Is your mother not seeing to that?"

"She is, but Marielle is my responsibility."

"I am beginning to think it isn't much of an imposition for you," Simon smirked as he walked over to the door. "I hope to see you tonight."

Hugh picked up the empty glasses and took them over to the drink cart. He paused, undecided as to what he should do next. He was spared the need to come up with something, however, as his mother stepped into the room.

"I'm glad that I caught you," his mother said as she came to him. "We are going to the opera tonight."

Hugh let out a groan. "Please say that you are not in earnest."

"It is important that Marielle be seen in Society."

"If that is your concern, I could take her on a carriage ride through Hyde Park during the fashionable hour," Hugh said.

His mother slowly bobbed her head. "I think it would be best if we did both."

"Both? I don't think that's necessary—"

"Nonsense," his mother said, not letting him finish the thought. "We need to show Society that we have fully embraced Marielle and have thrown our support behind her."

"Isn't that why you are hosting a ball for her?"

"It is, but Marielle should be seen as many times in Society as possible before her ball."

"Are you sure that is wise after what happened last night in the drawing room?"

"That is why you will be accompanying her," his mother said simply. "I have confidence that you can keep Marielle safe."

He opened his mouth to object, but his mother spoke first. "Do not bother trying to talk me out of this," she asserted. "I have asked very little of you to this point, but it is time that you step up, for Marielle's sake."

How could he contest that? He stifled another groan and said, "For Marielle."

Chapter Ten

Marielle descended the stairs in an ivory gown with blue net overlay. At the base of the stairs, she saw Hugh pacing back and forth as he tugged on his intricately tied cravat. A smile came to her lips at the mere sight of him. She hadn't seen him since breakfast, and she found that she rather missed conversing with him.

As she stepped down from the last step, Hugh stopped and turned to face her. His eyes roamed over her, and she saw approval shining in them, making her feel even more beautiful than she had when she first donned the exquisite dress.

Hugh brought his gaze up to meet hers and his words were soft but in earnest. "You look lovely, Marielle."

"Thank you," she said, holding out the skirts of the dress. "Dinah let me borrow this dress, since none of mine would have been sufficient for the opera."

"Did you not order new gowns?"

"I did, but they haven't arrived from the dressmaker yet."

He held her gaze as he said, "I have no doubt that you will be the envy of the *ton* this evening."

Marielle tried to resist the blush that she could feel

forming on her cheeks at his kind words. "You are being rather complimentary this evening."

"I believe that is the job of a good guardian." Hugh paused. "Or at least, I think it is, as I am making it up as I go along."

"If it helps, I do believe you are doing a spectacular job as my guardian."

Hugh smiled. "I can only imagine what that admission must have cost you."

"Hardly anything," she replied as she returned his smile. "Besides, I haven't been the easiest ward."

"It has been entirely my pleasure." He took a step closer to her and tucked an errant lock of hair behind her ear, his fingers lingering. "Now you look perfect."

Marielle could feel her heart beating rapidly and wondered if Hugh could hear it pounding in her chest. She hoped not, but he was so very close.

Trying not to appear completely undone by his touch, she managed to force out a quiet, "Thank you." The words were simple enough, but she couldn't have said any more, even if she tried. Not when he was looking at her like that.

Hugh made no attempt to move, to create more distance, as he withdrew his hand. "You are most welcome," he said.

Marielle searched his eyes, finding a vulnerability in them that she hadn't seen before. His eyes dropped to her lips, and she suddenly hoped that Hugh would kiss her. It would complicate everything, but she would welcome complication if it meant that she could feel his lips on hers.

Hugh's expression was troubled as he brought his gaze back up to meet hers. "We mustn't do this."

"Why?" she whispered.

"You are good and kind, and I am not." His expression grew even more troubled, and it felt like Marielle's heart seized in her chest.

"I believe you are." Why had she said something so bold? Women weren't supposed to be so forward.

"You are not a good judge of character, then," he joked, though the words seemed to pain him.

Marielle placed a hand on his sleeve. "I wish you could see how I see you, Hugh," she responded.

He winced. "The person you believe me to be does not exist."

"He does," she said. "He is standing right in front of me."

He shook his head. "No, you are wrong. I have done things in my life that you couldn't ever understand."

"Help me understand."

Hugh reached for her gloved hand and gently held it. "I'm afraid if I tell you the truth, the light in your eyes will dim when you look upon me, and I do not believe I could endure that."

"Surely it can't be so bad."

"I hate myself for what I have done," Hugh admitted. "As much as I've tried, I can't forget my past. The events that shaped me into the man I am continue to weigh on my soul."

"Let me in, Hugh," she said, half hoping, half pleading.

Hugh tightened his hold on her hand. "You can't help me; no one can."

"No one is past saving, especially you."

"I am."

"You aren't," she asserted. "Let me prove that to you."

Hugh opened his mouth to respond, but his mother's chipper voice came from behind them, startling them both. "What fun we shall have this evening!"

They jumped apart, and Marielle smoothed down her gown as she tried to calm her flittering emotions. She had no doubt that Edith had witnessed their interaction. Would she chide them for their familiar behavior?

When no chiding came, Marielle snuck a glance at Hugh and saw that his jaw was clenched. What must he be thinking?

Edith smiled, but it appeared strained. "I'm afraid that Dinah and Nathaniel will not be joining us this evening," she revealed. "They were already committed to Lady Aston's soirée."

"That is most unfortunate," Marielle said, pleased that she'd found her voice. "Will Lord Montfort be joining us?"

"He is just finishing some work in his study," Edith responded. "He should be along shortly."

As if on cue, Lord Montfort stepped into the entry hall with his hands outstretched. "I do hope you weren't waiting too long on me."

"We all found ways to occupy ourselves. Did we not?" Edith asked as she turned to face them with a knowing look.

Marielle ducked her head in embarrassment, hoping no one could see her reddening cheeks. What must Edith think of her brazen behavior?

Lord Montfort approached his wife and offered his arm. "Shall we?" he asked as Edith accepted it.

As Lord and Lady Montfort breezed through the door, Hugh stepped closer to Marielle and held his hand out. "May I escort you to the coach?"

"That is most kind of you," Marielle said as she placed her hand into his.

Hugh arranged her hand in the crook of his arm and led her to the coach in complete silence. Marielle didn't dare speak for fear of saying something that would sound intolerably stupid. Talking about the weather seemed so insignificant to what they had been discussing before.

Marielle took her seat across from Edith and tried not to show her discomfort when Hugh claimed the open seat next to her. He smelled of sandalwood, and she resisted the urge to lean closer to him.

The coach merged into traffic and their shoulders occasionally brushed up against one another. Marielle tried to pretend that it didn't affect her, but it did. What had transpired back at the townhouse? She clasped her hands in her lap as she remembered how she'd felt when Hugh had taken her hand in his. It had seemed so natural, as if it were supposed to be natural for them.

What was happening to her? She couldn't develop feelings for her guardian!

Edith's voice broke the silence in the coach. "I understand that you accompanied Dinah to the orphanage today," she said as Marielle met her gaze.

"I did," Marielle replied.

"What was it like?" Edith asked.

A smile came to her lips. "It was wonderful, and not at all what I had expected," Marielle revealed.

"Were the girls appreciative of you reading to them?" Hugh asked.

Marielle bobbed her head. "They were," she said. "To my delight, one of the younger girls even read to me."

"I think it is a fine thing what Lord and Lady Grenton are doing for those girls," Edith said in approval.

"I agree," Marielle said. "They are giving them a chance for a real future."

"Speaking of futures..." Lord Montfort's voice trailed off as he reached for his wife's hand and turned his attention towards Hugh. "Your mother and I were discussing yours, and we have decided that you will inherit the Brookhaven estate upon my death."

Hugh didn't speak for a long moment, and judging by his clenched jaw, he wasn't pleased. "May I ask why you are being so generous?"

"We know that Brookhaven holds a special place in your heart, and it is the only one of our properties that isn't entailed," Lord Montfort replied.

"Are those the only reasons?" Hugh pressed.

"They are," Lord Montfort said. "I was thinking you

would want to retire to the estate after the Season so you could see to managing it."

"Ah," Hugh said. "You wish to get rid of the prodigal son by sending me off to Brookhaven."

"That is not our intention," Edith interjected. "We just felt that you would benefit from the responsibility of managing an estate."

"If I left Town, then I wouldn't be able to go to gambling halls," Hugh said. "But you probably already thought of that."

Lord Montfort looked displeased by his response. "It is time for you to do your duty to your family."

"I did my duty once, and look where it got me," Hugh said.

"You gave up being a barrister so you could cheat people out of their money," Lord Montfort snapped.

"I do not cheat anyone out of their money," Hugh defended, "and I am not going to quietly disappear into the countryside so you don't feel the sting of embarrassment by having me as your son!"

Edith glanced between her husband and son. "We are not embarrassed by you—" she attempted.

"I am!" Lord Montfort said, speaking over her.

Hugh sighed. "And there it is," he said. "The truth will set you free, as they say."

"Brookhaven is profitable, and even a fool could manage it," Lord Montfort declared. "I have high hopes that you won't mess it up."

Edith pressed her lips together. "William, that was uncalled for."

"Hugh wanted the truth, did he not?" Lord Montfort asked. "I am merely giving him what he asked for."

"You want the truth, then?" Hugh inquired as his hands balled up into tight fists.

Edith put her hand up. "Can we not do this now?" she

asked, her voice holding a hint of a plea. "For Marielle's sake."

Hugh's jaw was clenched so tightly that a muscle pulsated below his ear. "As you wish, Mother, but Marielle is a part of this family now, whether she wants to be or not. She is entitled to the truth."

Lord Montfort scoffed. "Your version of the truth."

Hugh puffed out his chest to reply when the coach came to a jerking stop. The silence grew uncomfortable as they waited for the footman to open the door. Once they had exited the coach, Hugh offered his arm and led Marielle into the opera house, not bothering to wait for his parents.

Hugh's gaze remained straight ahead. "I do apologize for what transpired in the coach."

"You have no reason to apologize."

"But I do," Hugh said as he politely tipped his head at a couple near a column. "I should have known better than to let my father get a rise out of me."

Marielle furrowed her brow. "Why did you react in such a fashion to receiving the Brookhaven estate?"

"It matters not." His words were dismissive. "I would prefer to discuss more pleasurable things this evening."

"But—"

"Leave it," Hugh ordered, and his tone brooked no argument.

Marielle knew it was for the best if she let the matter drop —for now. She needed to find a way to convince Hugh to trust her, to let her in, before approaching it again.

Hugh stiffly watched the stage from his family's box, but his mind was on anything but the performance. He kept chiding himself for letting his guard down around Marielle.

What had he been thinking? He had almost kissed her. If his mother hadn't interrupted them when she did, he would have succumbed to what had become a desperate desire to kiss Marielle.

Botheration! Marielle was his ward, and she was under his protection. He couldn't act on this kind of feeling under any circumstance. She was just the only person lately who didn't hold some sort of judgement over his head, and he found solace in that.

But he meant what he'd said earlier at the townhouse. She was good and kind, and he was not. She deserved someone as upright and benevolent as herself, and that was most assuredly not him. He knew that, but no matter his determination to stay away, he couldn't abide being apart from her. She was like a breath of fresh air.

He snuck a glance at the subject of his thoughts. Marielle was leaning forward slightly in her seat, enthralled as she watched the performers onstage. Her blonde hair was pulled back into an elaborate coiffure with a string of pearls interwoven in it. Why did his ward have to be so blasted beautiful? Her physical person was stunning, yes, but the very essence of Marielle was truly attractive. She was good from the tips of her fingers down to the very depths of her soul.

The sound of clapping broke him out of his musings, and he politely joined in. Once the clapping had subsided, Hugh rose and assisted Marielle out of her chair.

"Did you enjoy yourself?" he asked, although he already knew the answer.

"Oh, yes!" Marielle gushed as she removed her hand from his. "I have never been to an opera before."

"Never?"

Marielle shook her head. "My father wouldn't set foot inside. He likened attending a performance to death by boredom."

Hugh chuckled. "I find that I agree with your father's sentiments."

"That is a shame," Marielle said.

His father spoke up from behind them. "Truth be told, I would much rather be sitting in my study with a glass of port," he shared. "I attend only because it makes Edith happy."

Marielle turned around to face him. "My mother couldn't hear very well, and she couldn't make out what the singers were saying," she explained, "so she didn't mind foregoing the opera either."

"Perhaps she was just using that as an excuse to not attend," Hugh teased.

His mother slipped her arm through her husband's. "That is terrible of you to say," she reproved lightly. "Many people enjoy the opera."

"No, they like to be seen," Hugh corrected.

"There is nothing wrong with that," his mother remarked. "Being seen in Society is just as important as a polished reputation."

"If that is the case," Hugh said, gesturing grandly towards the doorway, "then your audience awaits."

Marielle gave him a puzzled look. "What audience?"

"After the performance, everyone congregates in the main hall to make polite small talk," Hugh explained. "It is the worst part of the night."

"I disagree," his mother said. "It will be a chance for our Marielle to shine amongst the other patrons."

"She is, indeed, a beacon to us all." Hugh offered his arm and was pleased when Marielle placed her hand on his sleeve. "Just be yourself, and the *ton* will adore you."

He followed the crowds towards the hall in the front of the theatre. He had the urge to not stop but continue on towards the coach. Frankly, he didn't want to share Marielle with anyone this evening. But he knew that was being selfish and it wouldn't serve her. It was important for her to be embraced by the *ton*.

His eyes roamed over the crowd in the hall, and he was rewarded with the sight of Lord and Lady Graylocke near a column along the side. "Come, I want to introduce you to someone," Hugh said, raising his voice to be heard above the crowd.

Hugh navigated through the clusters of people and came to a stop in front of Lord and Lady Graylocke.

"By gads, I never thought I would see you at the theatre," Graylocke said, his face stretching with a broad smile.

"And I doubt you will again." Hugh gestured towards Marielle. "Lord and Lady Graylocke, allow me to introduce you to my ward, Miss Wymond."

Graylocke bowed. "My condolences, Miss Wymond."

"For what?" Marielle asked.

"You are forced to contend with Hugh day in and day out now," Graylocke said with a mock shudder. "That must be truly awful for you."

Lady Graylocke swatted her husband's arm. "That is terrible of you to say, dear," she said lightly. "Lord Hugh has only ever been kind to me."

Hugh bowed. "You are an easy woman to be kind to," he stated. "Although, I do question your judgement, since you did marry Graylocke."

Lady Graylocke laughed, as he had intended. "I am happy with my decision."

Hugh shifted his gaze to Marielle and said, "Graylocke showed up drunk to his wedding, and Lady Graylocke refused to marry him."

"Which I have sufficiently apologized for," Graylocke interjected.

"That he has," Lady Graylocke agreed. "But it will still make a charming story for our children one day."

"Perhaps we should forego that part," Graylocke suggested.

"I wouldn't change anything about how we fell in love with one another," Lady Graylocke said, gazing into her husband's eyes. "Would you?"

Graylocke reached for his wife's hand and kissed it. "Not one thing, because it allowed me to win your heart."

Marielle sighed softly. "It's evident that you two love each other very much."

"We do," Lady Graylocke said, meeting her gaze. "I do hope you won't settle for anything less than a love match."

"She won't," Hugh said.

Lady Graylocke gave him an amused look. "Isn't that for Miss Wymond to decide?"

"Yes, of course." Hugh turned towards Marielle. "My apologies."

Marielle offered him a smile. "No harm done," she said before addressing Lady Graylocke. "I am not sure if I wish to marry."

"May I ask why that is?" Lady Graylocke asked.

"I will inherit my father's shipyard, and I'm not sure if I want to relinquish control of his legacy to my husband," Marielle shared.

"I understand that more than you know," Lady Graylocke said, "but I can assure you that true love is worth the risk."

Marielle didn't appear convinced, but she was polite enough not to contradict Lady Graylocke. Instead, she asked, "How long have you two been married?"

Her question had barely left her lips when Mr. Emerson broke through the crowd and approached their group.

Hugh didn't want to make a scene for Marielle's sake, as any whiff of a scandal would draw unwanted attention. Unfortunately, that meant he had to at least give the appearance of cordiality with the insufferable man.

"Good evening," Mr. Emerson greeted. "I apologize for

the intrusion, but I was hoping to take a turn around the room with Miss Wymond."

"Absolutely not," Hugh said, taking hold of Marielle's hand and moving it to the crook of his arm. "This is not a drawing room, and there are too many prying eyes."

"Isn't that the point, since we aren't alone?" Mr. Emerson said, his smile remaining intact. "Besides, shouldn't Miss Wymond have a say in the matter?"

"I am her guardian," Hugh defended.

"It would appear that she is your prisoner," Mr. Emerson pressed.

Hugh tensed. "Miss Wymond is free to do as she pleases, but she is wise enough to not consort with the likes of you."

"I believe you and I are much the same, Lord Hugh," Mr. Emerson said.

"I am nothing like you."

Mr. Emerson's eyes roamed over Marielle's face, and she looked away in discomfort. "We both appreciate beautiful women," he remarked.

"Walk away while you still can," Hugh said through gritted teeth.

Mr. Emerson tsked and gestured widely. "You aren't attempting to threaten me in front of all these people, are you?" He leaned closer. "That would not bode well for Miss Wymond."

"What do you want?" Hugh asked.

"You already know what I want," Mr. Emerson said. "Return my money, or I will destroy Miss Wymond's reputation."

Hugh narrowed his eyes. "You wouldn't dare."

"I guess you are going to have to trust me," Mr. Emerson said. "I tried to ask nicely before, but you didn't take me seriously."

"Throwing a rock through my window is asking nicely?" Hugh demanded.

Mr. Emerson put a hand to his chest. "A rock through your window? I'm afraid that wasn't me." His affected words were not convincing. "It would appear that you have made more enemies than just me."

"What gives you the audacity to believe you command the *ton*'s opinion of Miss Wymond?" Graylocke interjected.

Mr. Emerson turned his gaze towards Graylocke. "Simple," he said. "All I have to do is spread a few well-placed words about Lord Hugh having gotten rather close to his ward and let the *ton* come up with their own conclusions."

"That is a lie," Hugh growled.

"Is it?" Mr. Emerson asked. "I don't think it sounds too farfetched, considering your less-than-ideal reputation amongst the *ton*."

Marielle spoke up. "Hugh has only ever treated me honorably."

"With all due respect, Miss Wymond," Mr. Emerson started, "the *ton* doesn't give a fig about that. They are only interested in the latest scandal."

"You are an awful man," Marielle said.

Mr. Emerson grinned. "If only circumstances were different. I find you to be a delight."

"I do not feel the same."

"What a shame," Mr. Emerson said. "Be that as it may, I'm afraid that I do not want Lord Hugh's castoffs."

Marielle's eyes grew wide at his insinuation. "How dare you say something so crass to me!"

Mr. Emerson glanced over his shoulder. "You might want to keep your voice down. Someone might overhear our conversation."

"It is time for you to leave, Mr. Emerson," Graylocke commanded.

"You are right," Mr. Emerson replied with an exaggerated bow. "I wouldn't wish to overstay my welcome. I believe I have sufficiently made my point." He turned to leave but halted. "I expect to see my money in two days' time, plus interest."

"I should have challenged him to a duel," Hugh said as he watched Mr. Emerson walk off.

"That would have solved nothing," Graylocke responded.

"I could have at least wiped that smug look off his face," Hugh said before he met Marielle's worried gaze. "I am sorry that you were forced to witness that. "

"You tried to warn me about him, but I didn't want to believe he would be so..." she paused, searching for the right word, and settled on, "awful."

"I tried to protect you from the truth," Hugh said.

"I'm sorry," Marielle said. "I should never have doubted you."

Hugh placed his hand over hers. "Consider it forgotten. And I do not want you to worry unnecessarily."

"How can I not?" she asked.

"I will take care of it, but you must trust me."

Her face softened. "I do trust you," she said. "A part of me always has."

Hugh felt buoyed up by her words. "Then we shall get through this together." He turned to Graylocke. "Let's meet tomorrow at White's to discuss this."

"I will be there."

"Thank you," Hugh said. "If you will excuse us, it is time for us to depart."

As he led Marielle away, he saw Mr. Emerson watching them from where he was leaning against a column, and their eyes locked. Hugh had little doubt that Mr. Emerson would make good on his threat.

He cared little about his own reputation, as it was already in ruins, but he refused to let Marielle's be tarnished. That wasn't fair to her, especially since the only thing that she had done wrong was being associated with him, and she'd had no choice in the matter.

Chapter Eleven

Hugh sat alone in the parlor the next morning, hoping no one would interrupt his solitude so he could sort through his thoughts. He needed to find a way to stop Mr. Emerson from spreading terrible lies about Mariclle.

Perhaps he should just give him back the money he had won that night. But what if others caught wind of what Emerson had accomplished? Would they try to blackmail Hugh, too? And if they did, where would that leave him? He would end up being poor and forced to rely on his allowance to survive, something he'd vowed never to do. If he started drawing from his allowance, then he would be dependent on his father. No, it was unthinkable. He may currently live under his parent's roof, but he refused to be controlled.

His father had offered him the Brookhaven estate, but it would come with strings attached. By taking ownership of the estate, Hugh would not only be forced to leave Town and live a boring life in the countryside, but he'd be forever indebted and at his father's whim.

Balfour stepped into the parlor. "Mr. Britt has requested a moment of your time, my lord."

"Who the blazes is Mr. Britt, and why does he think he is important enough to just show up unannounced?"

Balfour stepped forward and extended him a calling card. "He claims to be the late Sir James Wymond's man of business."

Hugh read the card and dropped it on the table. "Send him in," he ordered.

As Balfour turned to do so, Hugh continued. "Will you inform Miss Wymond that I would like her to join us?"

Balfour tipped his head. "Yes, my lord."

Hugh rose from the chair he was sitting in and walked over to the window. He stared unseeingly out over the expansive gardens as he waited for this Mr. Britt.

A lanky man with a long face walked into the room and bowed. "Thank you for agreeing to see me, my lord."

"What is it that you want, Mr. Britt?" Hugh asked gruffly. He knew he was being rude, but he didn't have the energy to exchange pleasantries.

Mr. Britt removed a satchel from his shoulder. "I do apologize for coming to call unannounced, but I was just at Mr. Cadell's townhouse. He informed me that you are now Miss Wymond's guardian."

"I am."

Mr. Britt reached into the satchel and pulled out a stack of papers. "I have come with the quarterly report for Miss Wymond's shipyard," he revealed. "The company has been quite successful, and I think you will be pleased by the growth."

"That is wonderful news, but I do believe we should wait until Miss Wymond joins us before we continue."

Mr. Britt's face went slack. "Why would you wish for that?"

"Is it not her company?"

"Well, it is, but she is just a woman," Mr. Britt said. "She couldn't begin to comprehend these reports."

"I do not think you are giving her enough credit."

Mr. Britt put his satchel on the ground at his feet. "I mean no offense, but you are her guardian. You have full control over the shipyard until she comes of age. Why burden her with these trivial details?"

"Trivial?" Hugh repeated. "You believe quarterly reports are trivial?"

"Not I, but a gentlewoman such as Miss Wymond is much more interested in embroidering or shopping than trying to make sense of these reports."

"I hadn't realized that you were acquainted with Miss Wymond," Hugh said, eyeing him critically.

Mr. Britt shifted in his stance. "I'm not, but I still feel—"

"Do you take issue with working with Miss Wymond?" Hugh asked, cutting him off. "I only ask because in seven months, Miss Wymond will receive her inheritance, and she intends to run the company herself."

"Do you think that is wise?" Mr. Britt asked.

"It is not up to me, Mr. Britt," he said. "Miss Wymond is a clever woman, and I have no doubt that she will rise to the challenge."

Mr. Britt shrugged a shoulder. "I suppose I can work with her until she gets married. I can only assume her husband will take over then."

"What if she does not wed?"

Mr. Britt frowned. "That would certainly complicate the matter. I do not have time to coddle her."

Hugh was growing tired of Mr. Britt's condescending attitude. He didn't know what the future held for Marielle, but he wanted to ensure she was set up for success. From the sound of it, Mr. Britt would not be a good fit.

"Leave the report, and you are dismissed," Hugh said.

"I beg your pardon?" Mr. Britt asked.

Hugh put his hand out for the sheaf of papers. "Miss Wymond will be running her father's company soon enough, and she needs a team around her that will support her and lift her up. Not someone who will discriminate against her based on her gender."

"Lord Hugh, you misunderstood me," Mr. Britt rushed out. "I was just saying—"

"I know what you were trying to say, and I am unimpressed."

Mr. Britt handed him the quarterly report. "I have been running Sir Wymond's company for over ten years now. No one will be able to do it as well as me."

"We shall see," Hugh said as he placed the report on a writing desk. "Good day, Mr. Britt."

Mr. Britt stood there for a moment, stunned. "I beg for you to reconsider," he said. "I have a family to care for."

As Hugh was preparing to dismiss him again, Marielle's voice came from the doorway. "I do believe we should give Mr. Britt a second chance." She walked further into the room. "After all, he did work with my father for ten years."

Mr. Britt gave Hugh a hopeful look.

"I do worry that Mr. Britt is not the right fit for when you run the shipyard," Hugh said, not ready to concede yet.

Marielle offered Mr. Britt a smile. "I have great confidence that Mr. Britt will be a patient teacher."

"I will be," Mr. Britt rushed out.

Hugh suspected that Marielle had overheard the majority of their conversation, but he wanted to ensure she understood what she was agreeing to. "Mr. Britt," he started, "will you wait for us in the entry hall? I would like to speak to my ward for a moment."

Mr. Britt tipped his head before he departed from the room.

Hugh approached Marielle and kept his voice low. "By chance, did you overhear our entire conversation?"

"If you are asking if I eavesdropped, then I must admit that I did so," Marielle said.

"Could you work with Mr. Britt, knowing his thoughts on working with a woman?" Hugh asked.

Marielle nodded. "My father thought very highly of Mr. Britt, and I do believe he will come around," she said. "Besides, anyone you hire will share the same sentiment he does."

"You have a point. After all, it is unusual for a woman to run a shipyard."

"It was my father's legacy," Marielle said. "I want to ensure that it continues to thrive even after he is gone."

"That is noble of you, but it won't be easy. Running a company takes hard work and discipline," Hugh advised.

Marielle tilted her chin stubbornly. "I am not afraid of hard work."

"I know you aren't," he said, "but you will experience much opposition as a woman. I worry that you might become jaded with it all."

"I hope not." She paused. "Thank you for standing up for me."

Hugh smiled. "I am your guardian. That is my job."

"It's more than that," Marielle said. "You believe in me, even when no one else does."

The smile slipped from Hugh's lips. "I hope that doesn't include yourself. You are capable of great things, Marielle. Now you just need to believe that as well."

Marielle's eyes became downcast. "What if I fail?" she whispered.

Hugh took his finger and lifted her chin until she met his gaze. "I don't think that is possible," he said. "You are far too clever to ever fail. But if you do, you're clever enough to find a way to fix it."

"I have so much to learn, though."

"I can help you, if you would like," he said. "I don't know much about quarterly reports, but I can read ledgers."

Marielle gave him a weak smile. "I would like that very much."

"Then we will learn about how to run a shipyard together."

Hugh watched as emotions flittered across her face and wanted very much to know what she was thinking. In that moment, he wanted to know everything about her. No detail was too small.

"Why do you have so much faith in me?" she asked softly.

Hugh's lips quirked. "Because I know you, and my life is better because of it."

Her eyes searched his, and he was afraid what she might see in them. Would she see that he was completely, utterly beguiled by her? Heavens, what would happen if she told his mother?

"I am glad that you are in my life, too," Marielle said.

Hugh needed to distance himself, or else he would gather her up in his arms and kiss her senseless.

With great reluctance, Hugh dropped his hand and took a step back. "Shall we bring Mr. Britt back in to explain the quarterly report to us?"

"I think that is a splendid idea," Marielle replied, visibly summoning her courage for the encounter.

"I will also see to refreshments being served," Hugh said as he walked over to the door. He had to take a moment away from Marielle. Why did she affect him in such a fashion? He seemed to lose rational thought when he was around her.

As he stepped into the entry hall, he saw Mr. Britt staring at the flowers on the table as if they held the answers to his conundrum. Hugh approached the man of business and stopped in front of him. "You have one chance at this," he threatened in a low voice. "If you even blink wrong, I will dismiss you."

Mr. Britt swallowed slowly. "I understand, my lord."

"You will treat Miss Wymond with the respect that she deserves," Hugh said. "Do I make myself clear?"

"Yes, absolutely."

Hugh held his gaze for another moment before he stepped back. "Miss Wymond is interested in learning more about the quarterly report."

"I shall explain it to her."

"See that you do." Hugh turned his attention towards Balfour. "Will you see to refreshments being brought in for Miss Wymond?"

Balfour acknowledged him with a bob of the head. "I shall send them up at once, my lord."

Once Balfour had departed from the entry hall, Hugh gestured towards the parlor. "We'd best not keep Miss Wymond waiting a moment longer."

***

Marielle sat in the drawing room later as she embroidered a handkerchief. Dinah sat across from her, but she felt no need to converse. Her thoughts were already taking up all of her attention. They were a confused jumble as she tried to sort out all the pieces of her new life: being without a family, changes to her guardianship, threats from Mr. Emerson, and now, taking care of her father's business. Her new guardian played a key role in most of them. With every interaction, she was becoming more confident that Hugh held her in some regard. Something was stopping him from acting on it, though.

Which was good—they couldn't act on feelings of that nature. Not only was he her guardian, but she had no intention of ever marrying. She didn't want to relinquish control of her life after her experience being repressed by Mr. Cadell. It was an awful feeling to be forced to rely on another's good graces.

Once she reached her majority and received her rightful inheritance, Marielle would happily return home to her estate and run her father's company. She wouldn't have to worry about the demands of Society because she would live far away from Town. Sadly, that meant she would be distanced from Hugh, as well.

Dinah broke through her musings. "You are awfully quiet this morning," she remarked.

"I suppose I have a lot on my mind," Marielle replied.

"Anything you would like to share?"

Marielle pushed the needle through the fabric and pulled it through. "Not particularly," she said.

Undeterred by her lukewarm response, Dinah asked, "Did you enjoy yourself at the opera?"

"I did, until Mr. Emerson threatened to ruin me if Hugh didn't return the money that he lost at gambling," Marielle revealed.

Dinah blinked. "Perhaps you should start at the beginning."

Lowering the handkerchief to her lap, Marielle said, "Mr. Emerson approached us and demanded the money be returned or else he would inform the *ton* that Hugh and I had formed an intimate attachment."

"What did Hugh say?"

"He wanted to challenge Mr. Emerson to a duel, but Lord Graylocke encouraged him not to."

"That was a wise thing to do," Dinah said. "I wonder if that is why Nathaniel is meeting Hugh at White's later today."

"Hugh indicated that he wished to speak to all of his friends at White's."

"Is that what you were discussing with him this morning?" Dinah asked. "I happened by the parlor and saw you both engrossed in conversation."

"We were discussing the status of the shipyard, since we

had just gone over the quarterly report with my father's man of business," Marielle said.

"Wouldn't he be your man of business, now?"

"He is, but I am not used to all of this," Marielle admitted. "Mr. Cadell met with Mr. Britt himself and refused to discuss the shipyard with me."

"That was wrong of him, since it is your company."

"Mr. Cadell doesn't believe that women have a mind for business. He intended to sell it the moment the probate court released it to me."

"Could he do that?"

Marielle nodded. "As long as he was my guardian, he had full control over my affairs and could do as he pleased."

"I'm glad Hugh came along when he did, then."

"As am I," Marielle said. "Being around Mr. Cadell made my skin crawl."

Dinah gave her a concerned look. "Was he ever too familiar?"

"I think, given more time, he would have been," Marielle replied. "I always made sure to lock my bedchamber at night, because he became flirtatious when he'd been drinking. It made me rather uncomfortable."

"That sounds awful."

Marielle glanced over at the door before sharing, "One time he came home drunk and offered for me."

"What did you say?"

"I politely turned him down, but he grew irate," Marielle shared. "He started shouting and tossed a glass dish into the fireplace. It scared me."

"I can only imagine. You had every right to be afraid."

"Shortly after that, Mr. Cadell came home and announced that he had lost me in a card game," Marielle said. "I worried that I was going into a worse situation, but I was pleasantly surprised when I met Hugh."

"I, for one, am glad that you are here," Dinah said. "It is nice to have another lady around to converse with."

"I agree." Marielle leaned forward and abandoned the handkerchief on the table. "I enjoy being a part of this family, even if it is for a short time."

"Why do you say that?"

"Once I reach my majority, I am going to return to Brightlingsea and run the shipyard," Marielle replied.

Dinah lifted her brow. "What does Hugh say to this?"

"He is in favor of it."

"He is?" Dinah asked. "That doesn't seem like Hugh."

Marielle smiled. "He has been incredibly supportive of me. I even overheard him chastising Mr. Britt because he felt that he was disrespecting me."

"I just worry that you are giving up on the marriage mart too soon," Dinah said. "You might find a gentleman you can't live without."

"I doubt that." An image of Hugh came to mind, but she quickly banished it from her thoughts.

Dinah didn't look convinced. "Do you honestly believe Hugh will let you just live on your own?"

"I'm sure he will be happy to be free of me."

"I do not believe that to be true." Dinah reached for her cup of tea and took a sip. "It is obvious as day that you and Hugh have formed some kind of attachment."

"Nothing untoward has happened."

"Whyever not?" Dinah asked.

Marielle furrowed her brow. "Pardon?"

"I do not know how I can make it any simpler," Dinah replied with a knowing smile. "You have feelings for him, and he has feelings for you."

"I do not dare assume that Hugh has feelings for me."

Dinah returned her cup to the saucer. "Let's say for the sake of argument that he does. What would you do about it?"

"Nothing."

"Nothing?" Dinah repeated. "May I ask why?"

Marielle pressed her lips together, then said, "He is my guardian, and it is wholly inappropriate to even consider such a thing."

"It would cause a scandal, but I do believe it would be relatively short lived."

"I think you are being wildly optimistic," Marielle said. "Besides, I do not have any intention of marrying."

"Even if it was Hugh?"

"Even then."

Dinah leaned back in her seat. "Running a company is admirable, but there is so much more to life than reviewing ledgers and managing workers."

"For some, yes. But it is my duty now that my brother is gone." She choked up on the end of her sentence and looked down.

"You must miss him terribly," Dinah said compassionately.

"I do," Marielle replied as she reached up to wipe a tear that threatened to fall. "I half expect him to walk through the door at any moment, but I know that isn't likely to happen."

"I understand that your brother was a captain of a naval ship."

"Yes, he was," Marielle replied. "My father was against him returning to his ship after my mother died, but he said it was his duty to serve king and country. He lived and breathed the Royal Navy."

"It must have been hard to not hear from him for many months at a time."

"It was, and I looked forward to every letter I received from him," Marielle said. "I still have them in a keepsake box."

Dinah gave her an understanding smile. "I'd have done the same thing," she shared. "I lost my parents many years ago, and I kept every scrap of paper that had their handwriting on it."

"May I ask how they died?"

"In a carriage accident."

Marielle gasped. "How awful!"

An anguished look came to Dinah's eyes. "It was an unnecessary loss," she murmured.

"My condolences." Marielle didn't quite know what else to say.

Dinah blinked and the pain disappeared. "It is something that I have to live with every day, just as you do."

"Does it get any easier?"

"Grief never ends, but it does evolve over time. It is the price of loving someone deeply enough that their passing forever alters us."

Marielle nodded her head in agreement. "My mother always said that grief was not a sign of weakness or lack of faith, but a necessary part of this life."

"Your mother sounds like a wise woman."

"She was," Marielle agreed, "and I miss her dearly."

A silence descended over them as they both reached for their cups and sipped of their tea. They'd each endured losing their parents at a young age, and knowing she wasn't alone in her grief helped buoy Marielle up.

Balfour stepped into the room. "Miss Ashmore has arrived and has—"

"Thank you, Balfour," Evie said as she stepped into the room. "You have done your duty, and you can go about your other work now."

Balfour's lips twitched. "Yes, Miss Ashmore."

Evie sat down next to her sister. "I don't know why Balfour insists on announcing me."

"Because that is his job," Dinah pointed out.

Evie waved her hand in front of her. "Next time, I will just climb in through the window and forgo him completely."

Dinah shook her head. "I hope you don't do something so foolish, especially when you are wearing a dress."

"Perhaps I should wear trousers next time I come to call," Evie said. "They might give Balfour a fit!"

"Do you truly own a pair of trousers?" Marielle asked.

"A few, actually," Evie replied. "You never know when you are going to rip a pair and need a spare."

"How would you rip a pair of trousers?" Marielle asked.

"You could always get it stuck on a nail when you are climbing through a window."

"Do you often climb through windows?" Marielle inquired.

Evie half shrugged. "It depends on the day."

Marielle wasn't quite sure if Evie was telling the truth or not, but she suspected that she was, which made her the most extraordinary person.

Evie reached for her sister's teacup and took a sip.

Dinah arched an eyebrow. "Would you care for your own cup of tea?"

"That isn't necessary," Evie replied as she placed the cup back on the saucer. "Georgie ensured that the orphanage was well stocked with tea before she left."

"Then why are you drinking mine?" Dinah asked.

Evie smiled. "I thought it would be rude if I drank Marielle's."

Dinah gave her sister an amused look. "What brings you by today?" she asked.

"The girls were hoping you would come by the orphanage tomorrow and read to them." Evie turned towards her. "Both of you, in fact."

"I am amenable to that," Dinah responded.

"As am I," Marielle said.

Evie's smile grew. "Wonderful!" She abruptly rose. "I'm afraid I must depart now."

"So soon?" Dinah asked.

"I'm afraid I have a meeting at a tavern, and I'd best not

be late," Evie replied. "But I look forward to seeing you both at the orphanage tomorrow."

Marielle watched as Evie hurried out of the room and found she had more questions than answers. She turned back towards Dinah and asked, "Do you suppose she is truly going to a tavern?"

"Most likely, yes," Dinah replied, unconcerned.

"How fascinating," Marielle muttered.

Dinah placed her teacup on the tray and said, "Evie has always done things in her own way. That is just one of the many things I love about my sister."

"What do you think a tavern is like?" Marielle asked.

"I assume it is like a coaching inn, and those are notoriously filthy, from what I have been told," Dinah replied.

"Then why would Evie arrange a meeting there?" Marielle pressed.

Dinah rose from her seat. "I cannot speak for my sister," she said. "I think I will go rest while Nathaniel is out for the afternoon."

Left alone, Marielle reached for her embroidery and glanced at the long clock in the corner. She wasn't quite sure when she would see Hugh again, but she hoped it would be soon.

Chapter Twelve

Hugh sat in their usual corner of White's as he waited for his friends to assemble. He needed their help to stop Mr. Emerson's little game. He refused to let Marielle's reputation become tarnished because of the choices he had made. Taking Mr. Emerson's money had been easy, but now Hugh couldn't seem to get rid of him.

Hugh smiled as he thought about Marielle. She had stood her ground with Mr. Britt, being agreeable but firm with him, and had easily grasped the contents of the quarterly report. Hugh knew she was clever, but she continually managed to impress him with her wit and intellect.

Graylocke approached the table, looking bemused. "Why are you smiling like a blasted fool?"

Hugh's smile vanished. "You're late."

Graylocke's eyes took in the empty seats around the table as he sat down. "As are Haddington and your brother, I see."

"It's not surprising," Hugh said.

"How is Miss Wymond faring?" Graylocke asked, taking on a more somber tone.

"She is well," Hugh replied. "I told her that I will take care of this, and I meant it."

"It might not be easy."

"I hadn't taken you for such a naysayer," Hugh said as he brought his glass up to his lips.

Graylocke leaned back in his seat and considered him for a moment. "I couldn't help but notice that you appear rather close to Miss Wymond."

"She is my ward." Hugh didn't like where this conversation was heading.

"That she is, but you couldn't seem to stop smiling when you were conversing with her," Graylocke observed.

"I'm afraid you were mistaken."

"I was not, and my wife commented on that fact, as well."

Hugh placed his empty glass down on the table. "I do enjoy Miss Wymond's company, but that is because we are friends."

"You are friends now?"

"We have always been friends."

Graylocke gave him a knowing look. "Do you not think it is odd to be so familiar with your ward?"

"I am not overly familiar with her, and I resent your allegation," Hugh said, his tone taking on a warning.

Putting his hand up, Graylocke remarked, "There is no allegation, just concern for you."

"You do not need to be concerned about me."

"Don't I?" Graylocke asked. "You are falling for your ward, putting yourself in the most precarious situation."

Hugh pursed his lips together. "You know not what you speak of."

"I think I do," Graylocke said. "Just think of the scandal that will ensue if you marry Miss Wymond."

"I have no intention of marrying her—or anyone, for that matter."

"Then you must create distance between yourself and Miss Wymond," Graylocke advised. "If not, you are in danger of jeopardizing her reputation."

"I would never do anything to hurt her."

"I know, which is why you need to let her go," Graylocke hesitated, "for her sake."

Hugh lowered his gaze to the table as Graylocke's words echoed within him. He knew that he had formed an attachment to Marielle, and it would be in her best interest if he stayed away from her. So why did that sound like a terrible idea?

His brother's voice came from next to him. "May I ask why you look like death?" he asked. "Did something happen?"

Hugh's eyes snapped back up. "I was just thinking."

"It's always hardest the first time, is it not?" Nathaniel joked as he took the seat next to him. "Am I interrupting something?"

"No," Hugh and Graylocke responded at the same time.

Nathaniel glanced between them, not appearing convinced. "You are both terrible liars, but I am much too tired to try to root out the truth."

"I'm surprised they let you in here, wearing that worn jacket," Hugh said, looking pointedly at Nathaniel's tattered brown jacket.

Nathaniel tugged at the ends of the sleeves. "I didn't have time to go home and change."

"What were you doing that required you to wear those clothes?" Hugh pressed.

"I had an appointment in the rookeries," Nathaniel replied.

Graylocke lifted his brow. "With whom?"

"It is of little consequence," Nathaniel responded dismissively. "I am more concerned as to why I was summoned to White's by my brother."

Hugh shifted in his seat to face Nathaniel head on. "I need your help."

"Perhaps we should wait for Haddington to continue this

conversation," Nathaniel said as he gestured towards the door Haddington had just stepped through.

Haddington approached the table with a smile on his face, but it was quickly replaced with a frown. "Whatever is the matter?" he asked.

"I need your help," Hugh said.

Pulling out a chair, Haddington sat down, his expression solemn. "What do you need?"

"When we were at the opera last night, Mr. Emerson threatened to ruin Marielle's reputation if I didn't return the money he lost to me," Hugh explained.

Nathaniel leaned back. "I wouldn't give it much heed," he said. "This isn't the first time Mr. Emerson has threatened you."

"True, but I think he actually means to act on it," Hugh responded.

Graylocke spoke up. "I was there, and Mr. Emerson was rather convincing," he said. "I worried that Hugh was going to challenge him to a duel, right there and then."

"I'll be your second," Nathaniel and Haddington said in unison.

Graylocke huffed. "Need I remind you that duels are illegal?"

"Only if you get caught," Nathaniel remarked.

"Regardless, a duel will not solve Hugh's problem," Graylocke said. "We need to come up with a plan to stop Mr. Emerson."

Hugh sighed. "I could always return the money."

"Then he wins," Nathaniel pointed out.

"But Marielle's reputation will remain intact," Hugh said.

Haddington caught the eye of a passing server and indicated they needed drinks, then met Hugh's gaze. "What about next time?" Haddington asked.

"Next time?" Hugh asked.

"There will undoubtably be a next time that Mr. Emerson

will come to blackmail you," Haddington said. "Are you just going to roll over and pay the man again?"

"I am not rolling over," Hugh replied. "I just don't want to hurt Marielle."

"What is it that Mr. Emerson is threatening to do?" Haddington asked.

Hugh frowned. "He intends to start rumors that Marielle and I have developed an intimate relationship as guardian and ward."

Nathaniel gave him a pointed look. "Which isn't entirely untrue."

"Nothing untoward has happened between Marielle and myself," Hugh declared.

"Yet," Nathaniel said. "I would be a fool to not notice how you two look at one another."

"I know not what you are talking about," Hugh said gruffly.

Nathaniel shook his head. "You are walking on a fine line right now, brother, and you don't even realize it."

Graylocke gave Hugh a smug smile. "I said something similar."

Hugh shoved back his chair and rose. "I thought I could recruit your help, but I guess I was mistaken," he said, his voice rising.

"Sit down," Nathaniel ordered.

"I don't take orders from you," Hugh said.

"No, but you are making a scene," Nathaniel pointed out.

Hugh's eyes roamed the hall and he saw that people had turned their heads to watch him. He returned to his seat and muttered a curse under his breath.

"I never said that we wouldn't help you," Nathaniel said. "I just wanted to point out that Mr. Emerson isn't entirely wrong in his assumption."

"Marielle and I are just friends," Hugh grumbled.

Haddington exchanged a look with Nathaniel. "Perhaps

we should just make a visit to Mr. Emerson and ask him politely not to threaten our friends."

"Mr. Emerson wouldn't respond to politeness," Hugh said.

"No, but he might respond appropriately if I asked with a pistol in my hand," Haddington remarked.

"You mean you would threaten him?" Hugh asked.

Haddington shrugged. "A threat for a threat. I think that might just do the trick."

"What if your threat doesn't work?" Hugh asked.

"Why wouldn't it work?" Haddington questioned.

"You wouldn't actually shoot Mr. Emerson," Hugh asked hesitantly, "would you?"

"I wouldn't kill him, if that is your concern," Haddington replied.

Nathaniel interjected, "No one is going to shoot anyone."

"Pity," Haddington muttered.

"Why don't we go speak to Mr. Emerson, together, and we will resolve this matter amicably," Nathaniel suggested to Hugh.

"I like Haddington's idea better," Hugh said.

Haddington smirked. "It is a good plan."

A server approached the table and placed four drinks in the center of it. Hugh reached for a glass and asked, "What makes you think that Mr. Emerson will be reasonable?"

"I can be quite persuasive when I want to be," Nathaniel remarked.

Hugh took a sip of his drink, then said, "We will try it your way first. If that doesn't work, then Haddington can shoot him."

Nathaniel bobbed his head. "I can assure you that it won't come to that." He reached for a glass before he continued. "You do understand the scandal that would always follow you if you married Marielle."

"I have no intention of marrying Marielle," Hugh grumbled.

"A guardian marrying a ward is looked down upon," Haddington stated.

"Yet it does happen on occasion," Graylocke pointed out.

"Not without repercussions," Nathaniel said.

Hugh tightened his hold on his glass. "Why are we even discussing this?" he asked. "I know my duty as Marielle's guardian."

"Do you?" Nathaniel asked. "Because I saw you two in the parlor this morning. Marielle was giggling."

"We were discussing her father's shipyard. I had probably just said something amusing," Hugh said.

"I doubt that; you aren't terribly funny," Haddington teased.

Hugh tossed back his drink. "Why am I friends with a bunch of fools?" he asked, rising.

"Because we are the only friends you have," Graylocke said as he raised his glass.

Nathaniel looked up at him. "We will go visit Mr. Emerson tomorrow."

"I look forward to it," Hugh said. "If you will excuse me, I intend to go to the Gilded Crown tonight."

"Will you not be joining us for dinner this evening?" Nathaniel asked.

"I won't be," Hugh replied. "Will you inform Mother?"

"What about Marielle?"

Hugh shoved his hands into his pockets. "What about her?" he asked. "I have no doubt that she is capable of dining with my family without me."

Not bothering to wait for a reply, Hugh walked away, skirting the neighboring tables. He didn't want to talk about Marielle anymore. It would be for the best if he created distance between them. Well, it would be best for her. For him, it would be agony.

Marielle walked down the dark hall to return a book to the library. It was late and everyone had retired to bed long ago, but she couldn't sleep. She'd been disappointed that Hugh hadn't joined them for dinner and found that she missed his company. But she didn't dare admit that to anyone. If she did, they would know that she was already halfway in love with Hugh. So instead, she'd retreated to her room and stayed up too late finishing the book she'd been reading.

Marielle opened the door of the library and pushed it open. She walked over to the table and set the book down, then lit the candle, bringing a small amount of light into the very dark room. The maids had closed the drapes, so no moonlight came through the windows.

Candle in hand, Marielle approached the shelves of books and began to search for one that piqued her interest. There were so many to choose from, but she would prefer a light-hearted read tonight. Frankly, she wasn't in the right mindset for anything too heavy.

She had just reached for a book when Hugh's voice came from the doorway. "What are you doing up so late?"

"You are drunk," she said. Just the slurred sounds of his one sentence were enough to tell.

"Perhaps I had one too many to drink tonight," Hugh said as he walked into the library, swaying slightly.

"Just one?" she teased.

Hugh grinned as he brought his hand to his heart. "But my reward is that I was able to see you one last time before I go to bed. With any luck, you will be in my dreams."

Marielle wished his words were in earnest, but she knew that he was not in the right frame of mind at the moment.

Hugh stepped closer to her. "Do you dream about me, Marielle?"

She did, but she didn't dare admit that to him. Instead, she replied, "I'm afraid I don't remember my dreams."

"That is a shame." His eyes turned towards the shelves of books. "You should see the library at Brookhaven. It is twice this size."

"I would imagine it is lovely."

Hugh brought his gaze back to meet hers. "It is, but not as lovely as you," he said, taking another step towards her.

Marielle decided it would be best if she retired for the evening before either of them did something they would regret come morning. "If you will excuse me, it is time I go to bed."

"Don't go. Not yet," Hugh said, his voice holding a hint of a plea. "Just stay for a few moments."

"Will you behave?" she asked.

Hugh nodded. "I will. I may be drunk, but I'm still a gentleman."

Marielle walked over to the table and set the candle down. "We missed you at dinner tonight."

"I went gambling."

"That's what Nathaniel said."

Hugh slowly walked over to a chair and dropped down. "I lost tonight," he announced.

"I'm sorry to hear that."

"I never lose," Hugh said.

Marielle sat down on a chair next to him. "Did you lose a lot of money?"

Hugh shrugged. "It was a decent amount, but nothing I will lose sleep over," he replied. "Do you want to know why I lost?"

"I suppose so."

"Because I couldn't concentrate on the cards," Hugh revealed. "I kept thinking about you."

Marielle tried to keep a stunned look off her face. "Me?"

"You are forever in my thoughts, even though I tried to

banish them." Hugh stopped speaking for a long moment. "Perhaps I should move to Brookhaven and live the life of a landowner."

"Would that be so bad?" she asked. She was elated that Hugh had told her he thought of her constantly, though it would have been nicer if he didn't have to be under the influence of strong drink to do so.

Hugh blinked heavily. "Brookhaven holds so many pleasant memories for me. That was the one place my father took notice of me."

"I do believe your father has always taken notice of you."

Hugh huffed. "You don't know my father like I do," he said. "He gives the appearance all is well until he has a chance to properly destroy you."

"You are not being fair to your father."

With a frown, Hugh said, "I should have assumed you would take my father's side, especially since he likes you."

"I am not taking anyone's side. I am just trying to understand why you hold such animosity towards him."

Hugh jumped up from his seat, swaying as he made the adjustment to being upright. "I am the second son, the spare," he declared. "The only time he spent time with me was to correct my wayward behavior. He was the one that brought that horrid man into my life."

"What man?"

A shield seemed to slam into place behind Hugh's eyes, and Marielle was afraid he wouldn't respond. Finally, he spoke. "Lord Wretton."

"Who is Lord Wretton?"

Hugh winced. "He ruined my life, but I do not wish to talk about him." It seemed to have taken a great deal of effort to even say the man's name.

"What do you wish to talk about, then?"

Hugh walked over to the drink cart in the corner and

picked up the decanter. "Do you think I should take Brookhaven?"

"I think you should do whatever makes you happy."

"That doesn't answer my question," he said as he poured himself a generous helping of brandy.

Marielle eyed the drink warily. "Are you sure you should be drinking more than you already have?"

Hugh put the decanter down with a clank. "I drink to forget."

"What are you trying to forget?"

That shielded look came back to Hugh's eyes. "It doesn't matter," he said as he picked up the glass. "I will never be free of those memories."

Hugh walked back over to his chair and sat down. "You are lucky," he said.

"How so?"

"You are a woman," Hugh remarked. "You are handed everything, and all you have to do is snag a husband."

"Not all women wish to 'snag a husband'," Marielle said.

"You will, though," Hugh responded. "You are far too beautiful not to be wed. I have no doubt there will be hordes of men trying to court you after your ball."

"You flatter me." It was the correct thing to say, even if it didn't feel right at the moment.

Hugh took a sip of his drink, then said, "My father and I used to go flyfishing at Brookhaven. We would spend hours at the river, and it was the only time that I had his undivided attention." He shook his head. "I should have known that it wouldn't last."

"Why don't you try to make amends with your father?"

Hugh gave her a blank look. "Why would I do such a thing?"

"Because it obviously hurts you to be estranged from him."

"My father and I have a complicated relationship. We can hardly stand being in the same room without fighting."

"You can change that."

Hugh chuckled. "You do not know what you speak of."

Marielle leaned forward in her seat. "I do believe your father extended an olive branch when he offered you Brookhaven."

"No, he was trying to get rid of me."

"If that was the case, why doesn't he just kick you out of his townhouse and make you live on your own?" Marielle asked.

"Because my mother would never allow it." Hugh took a sip and put his glass down onto the table. "It was probably her idea to give me Brookhaven."

"You have a good mother."

"I do," Hugh agreed. "I know she tires of my disreputable behavior."

Marielle lifted her brow. "Do you ever get tired of gambling?"

"I do, but I am good at it."

"Perhaps you should find something else that you excel at," she suggested. "You might find that you enjoy being a landowner."

Hugh watched her for a moment. "Will you come with me?"

Marielle sat back. "Pardon?"

"I am your guardian until you reach your majority, and the countryside is a lovely place to retire," Hugh said.

"I don't think that is a wise idea."

Hugh looked crestfallen. "I'm going to lose you, aren't I?"

"I'm not going anywhere, Hugh."

Hugh closed his eyes tightly before he reached for his glass. "Everyone says that before they leave."

There had to be more to the story, so Marielle decided to prod a little. "Who left you?"

Hugh had been about to drink and paused. "Priscilla," he murmured into the glass. "She left me, but she promised she never would."

"Who is Priscilla?"

"She was my fiancée," Hugh spat out. "She accepted my offer of marriage, but then she changed her mind."

"Why?"

"She took issue to my gambling," Hugh replied. "She said that I wasn't respectable enough anymore."

"That isn't true."

"It is," Hugh said, his voice rising. "I am an utter failure!"

Marielle reached out and placed a hand on Hugh's sleeve to settle him. "You are being entirely too hard on yourself."

"I was a respected barrister, and I gave it all up, and for what?"

"It is not too late to make a change."

Hugh glanced down at her hand. "I have amassed a fortune from the card tables. I could always sail far away so no one else need be embarrassed by me."

"That would solve nothing. You need to stay and fight for the life you deserve."

Hugh scoffed. "I don't deserve a good life. Not after what I did."

"I don't believe that."

"Those women are dead because of me," Hugh revealed.

Marielle furrowed her brow. "What women?"

Hugh pressed his lips together, and she could tell he hadn't meant to reveal that fact. "It doesn't matter," he replied. "They died long ago, and nothing I can do will change that fact."

She opened her mouth to ask another question, but Hugh continued. "I think you should go to bed."

Marielle withdrew her hand and swallowed, her heart sinking into her stomach. "That would be for the best," she said, rising.

Hugh awkwardly rose. "Would you like me to escort you to your bedchamber?"

"No, thank you."

"When I was younger, I would get so scared at night that I used to sit outside my parents' bedchambers and cry," Hugh shared. "I always hoped they would hear me and invite me in."

"Did they?"

Hugh shook his head. "They never did," he replied. "It taught me a tough lesson from a young age: that I only have myself to rely on."

Against her better judgement, Marielle took a small step closer to Hugh and tilted her head to look up at him. "No matter what happens, you will always be my hero."

"How can you say that?" he asked in disbelief. "It's because of me that Mr. Emerson is threatening to ruin your reputation."

"Did you already forget that you saved me from Mr. Cadell?"

Hugh reached out and cupped her right cheek. "I will do everything in my power to ensure you will always be protected."

"I know you will," she said, leaning slightly into his hand.

His eyes roamed over her face. "You are so beautiful, Marielle," he murmured. His eyes dropped to her lips and lingered there. "May I kiss you?"

Marielle knew that she should refuse him, especially considering his inebriated state and what he'd inadvertently revealed, but she desperately wanted to kiss him, to feel his lips on hers. She couldn't seem to form any words, but she slowly nodded, giving him permission.

Hugh leaned forward and brushed his lips against hers, and she closed her eyes. "I love you," he breathed against her mouth.

Marielle's eyes snapped open. Had she just heard him correctly? Did he really just profess his love for her?

Hugh dropped his hand and stepped back. "Good night, Marielle."

"Good night, Hugh," Marielle said before she brushed past him. One thing was for certain—she wouldn't get very much sleep tonight, not with what Hugh had just confessed. She knew he was drunk, but did he mean what he'd said?

Chapter Thirteen

Hugh descended the stairs and tried to ignore the pounding in his head. He'd woken up with a terrible headache, no doubt from his drinking, and details of the previous night were rather hazy. But one thing was clear—he'd kissed Marielle and told her he loved her. Why in the blazes had he done such a thing?

Balfour greeted him at the bottom of the stairs with a smile. "Good mor…" He stopped and lowered his voice. "I take it you are having a rough morning."

"I am," Hugh responded as he stopped next to the butler. "Can you prepare one of your concoctions for me? Those always seem to help."

"Of course, my lord," Balfour said before he headed towards the kitchen.

Hugh's mother stepped into the entry hall and gave him a disapproving look. "You look terrible," she declared. "I hope it was worth it."

"It was… or at least, I think it was," he responded. "The events of last night aren't exactly clear at the moment."

"You missed dinner."

"I normally miss dinner."

"Not since Marielle arrived," his mother pointed out.

"She has you to care for her.

"She needs her guardian."

"No, she does not," Hugh replied. "She'll do just fine without me; even better, perhaps. I am just a hindrance to her."

His mother eyed him critically. "Has something happened between you two?"

"Nothing you need to be concerned about," he replied dismissively. "Would you mind keeping your voice down? I have a terrible headache."

"I'm not raising my voice."

"You aren't?" he asked with a wince. "It feels like you're shouting at me."

His mother looked heavenward. "You can't keep living like this," she stated. "Your late nights and drinking will catch up to you, and you will be all the worse because of it."

"I thank you for your concern, but it is unfounded," Hugh said.

"I am just worried about you."

Hugh brought a hand up to his head. "You don't need to waste your energy on worrying about me, Mother."

"I will always worry about you. That is what a good mother does."

Lowering his hand, Hugh forced a smile to his lips, despite the motion making his headache worse. "You are the best of mothers; but I am old enough to live my life how I see fit."

His mother's concerned eyes roamed over his face. "You are hurting, son, and I don't know how to help you."

Hugh didn't need his mother's help. Frankly, he didn't need anyone's help. He was doing just fine on his own; although, he couldn't seem to fathom his own lie.

"Is this lecture over?" Hugh asked, taking a step back.

"It's hardly a lecture," his mother replied. "I am only saying—"

"I know what you are saying, but my position has not changed." He glanced towards the rear of the townhouse. "Is Nathaniel in his study?"

His mother sighed. "He is."

"I need to speak to him," Hugh said.

"Will you not at least eat breakfast with us?" his mother asked.

"I'm not hungry." That was the truth. The thought of food made his stomach turn.

His mother conceded with a tip of her head. "I hope to see you for dinner this evening," she said before she walked towards the dining room.

As he headed towards the study, Hugh forgave his mother for her interference. She was only trying to help; he just didn't want it.

He entered the study and saw Nathaniel hunched over the ledgers. His brother glanced up when he entered. "Welcome home, brother."

"I've been home for hours," Hugh replied as he closed the door. He thought it would be best if this conversation remained private.

"Truly? Because you look terrible," Nathaniel remarked.

"So I've been told," Hugh muttered.

With a curious look at the closed door, Nathaniel asked, "Is there something that you wish to discuss with me?"

"Yes," Hugh said as he approached the desk. "I did something stupid last night."

Nathaniel closed the ledger. "Go on," he said, his voice taking on an edge.

Hugh hesitated before revealing, "I told Marielle that I loved her."

"I see," Nathaniel said. "And do you? Love her?"

"No," Hugh rushed to reply. "It was just a slip of the tongue when I was drunk. An honest mistake."

Nathaniel leaned back in his chair and gave him an expectant look. "Perhaps you should start from the beginning."

Hugh sat down on an upholstered armchair. "I came home late, as usual, and I noticed that there was a light in the library. I went to investigate and found Marielle there."

"Why did you go in?"

"I don't know," Hugh replied. "It would have been smart to just walk away, but I lacked the good sense to do so."

"Need I remind you that we thought it was best if you avoided Marielle for the time being?"

Hugh hung his head. "I know, and with good reason," he said. "I am not quite sure what all I told her, since my brain is a little foggy, but I believe I mentioned Priscilla."

"You haven't spoken about Priscilla since—"

"Since the day she broke off our engagement. I know, but I let it slip, and now I can't take it back."

"Do you want to take it back?"

"I do," he replied. "Why do you even need to ask that question?"

Nathaniel gave him a curious look. "You appear to have taken Marielle into your confidence."

"That doesn't mean I tell her everything," Hugh defended. "A man is entitled to his secrets, as you well know."

"They are, but there is a sense of freedom that comes with revealing them, especially to someone who will hold them just as safe as we do."

Hugh shook his head. "I don't like to even think about Priscilla, much less talk about her."

"Marielle would have eventually learned of the truth when she entered Society," Nathaniel said. "It was only a matter of time before someone let it slip."

Rising, Hugh walked over to the mantel over the fireplace. "I wish I could just forget that time in my life."

"You would want to forget both the good and the bad?"

Hugh huffed. "There wasn't much good; it was

mostly bad." He placed his hands on the mantel and leaned in. "Regardless, I made a mess of things with Marielle."

"Yes, you did," Nathaniel agreed. "What do you intend to do about it?"

Hugh lowered his hands and took a step back. "I plan to avoid her for the time being."

"That is brilliant, but did it escape your notice that you two live in the same house?" Nathaniel mocked.

"No, it did not," Hugh said with a sigh. "I am at a loss for what to do."

Nathaniel rose and came around his desk. "Maybe it is not as bad as you think," he said. "With any luck, she didn't hear you utter those words."

"I doubt it, since I told her right after I kissed her," Hugh confessed.

His brother tensed. "You do realize the implications of your actions if anyone found out that you kissed Marielle, don't you?"

"She'd be ruined. I would be forced to marry her."

"What were you thinking?" Nathaniel chided. "You should have never entered the library!"

"I agree," Hugh said, his shoulders slumping. "I was drunk, and I wasn't thinking clearly. Now I've made a muck of everything."

Nathaniel leaned back against the edge of his desk. "You need to make this right with Marielle."

"How?" Hugh asked. "How can I possibly come back from telling her that I love her?"

"You can't just ignore her. You need to consider her feelings now," Nathaniel pressed. "I'm sure she is just as confused as you are."

"Maybe I should just retire to Brookhaven for the rest of the Season."

"Mother would never let you do such a thing," Nathaniel

said. "Marielle's ball is in a few days, and you have to introduce her."

"You could do it, or better yet, Father," Hugh suggested.

"Running away from your problems isn't going to solve anything."

"But it's worked before."

"Has it?" Nathaniel challenged. "You seem to have been doing a lot of running these past couple of years."

Hugh ran a hand through his brown hair. "I have, but I'm afraid you wouldn't understand my reasonings."

"We used to tell each other everything," Nathaniel said. "When did that stop?"

"I suppose when we were at Oxford and you started disappearing at all hours of the night," Hugh said. "Or when you started dressing like you were down on your luck."

"I have my reasons."

"Just as I have my reasons to not speak about my past."

Nathaniel nodded. "You are right, of course," he said. "Sorry to pry."

A knock came at the door.

"Enter," Nathaniel ordered.

The door opened and Balfour stepped in with a tray in his hands. "I prepared one of my concoctions for you."

Nathaniel chuckled. "You must be desperate."

Hugh walked over and picked up the glass off the tray. "I am," he said as he eyed the contents. "What's in it?"

Balfour smiled. "Trust me, you don't want to know, my lord." He lowered the tray to his side. "Will there be anything else?"

"Not at this time," Hugh replied.

After the butler departed from the study and closed the door behind him, Hugh placed the glass down onto a side table. "I think I need a moment before I try to drink that."

"I don't think that will help," Nathaniel joked. "Best get it over with."

Hugh grimaced. "I was hoping you wouldn't say that."

Nathaniel straightened from the desk. "We should depart soon if we want to speak to Mr. Emerson."

Picking up the glass, Hugh shook it and saw things floating around in it. "Where do you think Balfour learned to make these drinks?"

"I don't know, but they do work."

"That they do."

Nathaniel chuckled. "Drink it, don't drink it, I don't really care, but I have a meeting later this afternoon that I can't miss."

Hugh held up the glass. "Cheers."

With a rigid back, Marielle sat in the coach as it rolled down the street, pretending to take a profound interest in the passing scenery to avoid conversing with Dinah. She was afraid of what she might reveal if Dinah started peppering her with questions, especially since she couldn't stop thinking about Hugh and his declaration of love the night before.

After she'd returned to her bedchamber, she'd lain in bed for hours as she tried to make sense of it all. Did he mean it? Or was it just a slip of the tongue because he was drunk? More importantly, did she want him to mean it?

Yes.

She hoped that his words were in earnest. But would he even remember what he had said and done that night when he woke up?

"Out with it," Dinah said.

Marielle gave her an innocent look. "Out with what?"

"What's troubling you?" Dinah asked.

"Why do you assume something is troubling me?"

Dinah gave her a knowing look. "You've barely spoken a

word all morning, and you are far too interested in those decrepit buildings we're passing."

Drat. Why could Dinah see right through her so easily? It would be best if Marielle just told her the truth and be done with it.

"What I am about to tell you must stay in the strictest confidence."

"May I tell Nathaniel?" Dinah asked. "After all, we don't keep secrets from one another."

"Will he tell anyone?"

Dinah shook her head. "He is really good at keeping secrets."

"Then you can tell your husband," Marielle responded, "but no one else."

"Not even Edith?"

"Especially not Edith."

Dinah cocked her head. "Now you have my attention," she said. "After all, I must assume this is about Hugh."

"Why would you assume that?"

"What else could it be about?" Dinah asked.

Marielle looked skyward. "You're right. It is about Hugh."

Dinah smiled smugly. "What did he do this time?"

Marielle pressed her lips together, then revealed, "Last night, I couldn't sleep, so I went to the library to pick out a book…"

"What book did you select?"

"Does it matter?"

"I suppose not," Dinah replied, "but I am looking for a new book to read and thought you might be able to recommend something."

"I can recommend a few books, but that isn't what I was trying to tell you."

"Proceed, then."

Marielle took a breath. "Hugh came in to speak to me, and it was obvious he was drunk."

"That isn't good," Dinah muttered.

"He was being very flirtatious with me."

"Did that make you uncomfortable?"

"Not at all. It was different with Hugh than how Mr. Cadell was, but I didn't give it much heed," Marielle replied. "I was able to distract him by swaying the conversation to other topics." She paused. "That is, until he kissed me."

Dinah's brows shot up. "He kissed you?"

"Yes, and it was glorious and magical and absolutely perfect," Marielle said. "It was everything I thought it would be."

"Then why don't you sound pleased?"

Marielle adjusted the sleeves of her pale pink gown. "Hugh told me that he loved me," she said in a low voice.

Dinah leaned closer. "I beg your pardon?"

Marielle tilted her chin and raised her voice. "He told me that he loved me!"

"He just... told you that he loved you?" Dinah asked, stunned.

"Yes, right after he kissed me," Marielle replied.

A bright smile broke out on Dinah's face. "This is wonderful news!"

"No, it's terrible!"

"Why do you say that?"

Marielle glanced out the window. "He was drunk, and I don't know if he meant what he said. What if he doesn't even remember saying it?"

"How could someone forget saying something like that?"

"I don't know; but if he does love me, then why has he been acting distant as of late?"

Dinah shrugged. "Because Hugh doesn't deal with emotions head on. He tends to run from them; at least, that's what Nathaniel has told me."

"Do you think he is trying to run from me?"

"I wouldn't be surprised if he was."

Marielle sighed. "What am I to do?"

"Do you return his feelings?" Dinah asked.

"I care for him."

"But do you love him?"

"I don't *not* love him."

"What does that mean?" Dinah pressed.

"I have feelings for Hugh," Marielle said, clasping her hands in her lap, "but I know nothing can come from them. He is my guardian."

"It's not against the law to marry your guardian."

"No, but Society will criticize the choice, and we could be ostracized," Marielle said. "Besides, Hugh has said nothing about marriage."

"It is only a matter of time."

Marielle didn't know what she was feeling, so how could she adequately express it to Dinah? She had deep feelings for Hugh, but she didn't even know how far they went.

Dinah gave her an encouraging smile. "Can I offer you some advice?"

"Yes, please," Marielle said a little too eagerly.

"Be patient with Hugh. He is fighting many battles within himself," Dinah said.

"Aren't we all?"

"Just because someone carries their burdens well, it doesn't mean the load isn't heavy to bear," Dinah advised.

"I would agree with that statement, but I do worry that Hugh has taken upon himself too much to carry alone."

"Then help him."

"I'm trying, but he won't let me in."

"From the sound of it, you are making more progress than you realize," Dinah remarked.

"I wish that were true," Marielle murmured.

They arrived at the orphanage, and Wilson greeted them at the door with a kind smile. "Good morning," he said. "Do come in."

They were met with complete silence as they stepped into the entry hall.

Dinah glanced up the stairs. "May I ask why it is so quiet in here?"

Wilson chuckled. "Miss Ashmore is having the girls practice climbing the brick walls in the courtyard."

"Of course, she is," Dinah responded good-naturedly. "How is Mrs. Hughes handling this particular lesson?"

"She has sequestered herself in her room until the girls are done," Wilson informed her. "She wants nothing to do with it."

"That does sound like Mrs. Hughes," Dinah said.

Wilson turned and led them down the hall. "Miss Ashmore will be pleased to see the both of you."

Marielle leaned closer to Dinah. "Why is Evie teaching them how to climb walls?" she asked in a hushed voice.

"She thinks it is a useful skill to have."

"Is it?"

Dinah shrugged. "I have never had a need for it, but I do not disparage anyone who wants to learn."

They stepped into the courtyard and saw all of the girls sitting in a large circle with Evie in the middle of it.

Evie stopped speaking when she saw the new arrivals and smiled. "Girls, will you please welcome Lady Hawthorne and Miss Wymond?"

The girls turned to face them, and all murmured their hellos.

Evie clasped her hands together. "Go to the kitchen, and Miss Peters will have some biscuits for you."

A collective cheer went up as the girls jumped up and ran towards the building. Once they had all disappeared, Evie approached her guests. "You missed the most riveting lesson."

"I heard that you had the girls climb the walls," Dinah said.

Evie nodded. "'Tis true, and some of them are naturals."

"Do you think Georgie will take issue with you teaching the girls how to climb?" Dinah asked.

Evie laughed. "She was the one who left me in charge."

"That she did," Dinah agreed. "Silly me, to think that Georgie might take issue with children learning a skill that could cause them bodily harm."

"I am sensing sarcasm, dear sister," Evie said.

It was Dinah's turn to laugh. "From me? Never."

Evie pointed at the wall. "You could always give it a go," she suggested.

"I think not," Dinah said, smoothing her ivory gown. "I will leave the climbing to you."

"My aunt received an invitation to your ball," Evie said, turning to address Marielle, "and she responded in the affirmative that we would both be attending."

"I am pleased to hear that," Marielle said. "I do hope I will receive the ballgown we commissioned before then."

"If not, you can borrow one of mine," Evie said with a wave of her hand. "I have acquired quite a few, since this is my ninth season."

Dinah gave her sister a pointed look. "I do wish you would at least consider taking a suitor."

"For what purpose?" Evie asked. "I have no wish for a man to control me."

Marielle bobbed her head. "I feel the same way."

"You two are impossible," Dinah sighed. "You speak of marriage as if it's a prison sentence."

"Isn't it?" Evie joked. "Someone tells you what to do and what to think. You don't have the freedom to do as you please."

"Nathaniel doesn't do those things, and he encourages me to pursue my passions," Dinah argued.

"You were lucky," Evie responded.

"You could be just as lucky as me," Dinah responded with

an amused look, "but that would require some effort on your part."

Evie didn't respond as she walked across the room. She opened the door and stood to the side. "It's time to read to the girls."

Dinah walked up to her sister and placed a hand on her sleeve. "You take too many risks, and I worry about you."

"I know what I'm doing," Evie asserted.

"If that is the case, then one of those risks you are taking should be with your heart," Dinah said before she dropped her hand and stepped through the door.

Marielle approached Evie, who had a look of contemplation on her face.

"I have been where you are, and I regret not speaking up," Evie said.

Marielle stopped in front of her. "Speaking up for what?"

"For love," Evie said. "Don't make my same mistake."

"You were in love once?" Marielle didn't know why she found that so astonishing. Evie was a beautiful woman with an intriguing personality. But she didn't seem like a woman who would fall in love only to have her heart broken.

Evie brought a finger to her lips. "Shh, don't let my sister hear that," she whispered, "or I will never live it down."

"What happened?"

Evie's eyes became distant. "I let him slip away," she said before she stepped inside.

Marielle could tell that admission cost Evie greatly, and her heart ached for her. But how did Evie know that she was struggling with matters of the heart?

One thing was certain—she was glad that Evie was her friend.

Chapter Fourteen

Hugh sat across from his brother in the coach and tried to control his growing irritation at Mr. Emerson. He had many words that he wanted to say to the man, and his headache wasn't helping his temper.

Nathaniel met his gaze. "Let me do all the talking with Mr. Emerson."

"Why?"

"I can be quite intimidating when the situation warrants it."

Hugh huffed. "I have yet to see that."

"That's because I haven't ever gotten angry at you," Nathaniel smirked. "At least, not lately."

"I can handle my own fight."

"This is different," Nathaniel said. "Mr. Emerson is the type of person who doesn't play fair. He'll find your weakness and exploit it. It looks like he's already doing so."

"What do you know about people who don't play fair?" Hugh asked.

"I know more than you know."

"Pardon me if I don't believe that to be true, since you live the gilded life of an earl."

Nathaniel crossed his arms over his chest. "You don't know how I spend my time or who I associate with."

"Nor do I care."

"I think you do," Nathaniel said. "I think it is eating you up inside that you know so little about me."

"You flatter yourself, but I have more important things to worry about."

"Such as?"

Hugh shook his head. "I am attempting to stop a man from starting terrible rumors about my ward."

"That's why I am here," Nathaniel said, "to stop Mr. Emerson."

"Will you not humor me and tell me how you intend to do such a thing?" Hugh asked.

"I had my contacts do a little digging into the man."

"Pray tell, who are these contacts?"

"No one you should concern yourself with."

Hugh gave him an incredulous look. "Why do you do that?" he asked. "You must think me an idiot."

"I think no such thing."

"Yet you refuse to confide in me."

"I confide in very few people."

"Can I not be one of those people?" Hugh asked.

Nathaniel frowned. "It is best that you don't know."

Hugh considered his brother for a moment. "Are you involved in something illegal?"

"No," Nathaniel replied.

"That is precisely what someone who's involved with something illegal would say," Hugh remarked.

"My loyalty is to king and country, and that is all you need to know," Nathaniel said.

"I believe you, brother," Hugh said, "but whatever you are involved in, I hope you aren't taking any unnecessary risks."

Nathaniel grinned. "I'm afraid that is all I take."

"At least try not to get yourself killed," Hugh said. "I have no desire to be Father's heir."

His brother's grin slipped. "My priorities have shifted since I married Dinah," he said. "You must promise me that you will take care of her if anything happens to me."

"Nothing will happen to you—"

"Promise me," Nathaniel demanded.

Hugh put his hand up. "I promise I will care for Dinah, and she won't want for anything."

That satisfied Nathaniel. "I never knew I could love so deeply until Dinah came into my life, and I promised her that she would never regret marrying me."

"When did you get so sappy?"

"Just wait until you get married."

"I already told you, I have no intention of ever marrying," Hugh insisted.

"So you say."

Before Hugh could respond, they came to a stop in front of a modest townhouse near the outskirts of the fashionable part of town. Nathaniel reached through the window and opened the door, not bothering to wait for the footman.

"Whatever happens in there, just know that I know what I am doing," Nathaniel said as he stepped out of the coach.

"What does that mean?"

"Just trust me."

Hugh joined his brother on the pavement and glanced at him. "Just so you know, I can be quite intimidating."

"I have no doubt," Nathaniel said.

They approached the door and Nathaniel knocked. It was a long moment before it was opened, and they were greeted by an older butler with white hair brushed to the side.

"May I help you?" the butler asked.

Nathaniel removed his calling card from his waistcoat pocket. "Will you inform Mr. Emerson that we require a moment of his time?"

The butler accepted his card and glanced at it. "I'm afraid Mr. Emerson is in a meeting with his solicitor."

"I want you to interrupt the meeting and inform Mr. Emerson that my business is of utmost importance," Nathaniel said.

"But, my lord—"

Nathaniel took a step closer to the butler. "If you do not inform your master of this, then I will," he said in a firm tone. "Do we understand each other?"

The butler slowly nodded. "Yes, my lord." He opened the door wider. "Would you care to wait in the entry hall?"

"Thank you," Nathaniel said as he stepped inside.

Hugh followed his brother inside. The only sounds came from the clipping of the butler's heel on the polished marble flooring as he walked towards the rear of the townhouse, and there was nothing to look at but gold framed portraits on the blue papered walls.

"How do you know that Mr. Emerson will see us?" Hugh asked.

"He will."

"But how can you be so sure?" Hugh pressed.

Nathaniel's eyes roamed the entry hall as he explained, "Mr. Emerson seems to be a man who is used to being in control. He will not like it when someone comes into his home and disrespects him."

"Wouldn't he just turn us away—"

The butler's voice interrupted them from the end of the hall. "Mr. Emerson will see you now," he said. "Will you follow me?"

Nathaniel gave him a smug look. "Men like him are all the same."

They walked down the hall, passing by a short, rounded man who regarded them with mild curiosity—Mr. Emerson's solicitor, it seemed. The butler stopped outside a door and indicated that they should go in.

Hugh stepped in first and Nathaniel followed him in.

Mr. Emerson rose from his desk and buttoned his jacket. "I find that I am most curious as to why you two barged into my home and threatened my butler."

Nathaniel stepped forward. "It is imperative that we speak to you."

"It is?" Mr. Emerson asked, glancing between them. "I must assume that you have the money that you owe me, then."

Hugh opened his mouth, but Nathaniel spoke first. "We've decided that we will not be paying you a pound, but you will be making a generous donation to Lord Grenton's orphanage on Tryon Street."

Mr. Emerson let out a bark of laughter. "And why would I do that?"

"Because, Mr. Emerson, I know what you are involved with," Nathaniel said.

"And what is that?"

Nathaniel reached into his jacket pocket and pulled out folded pieces of paper. "I've discovered the most fascinating things about you."

Mr. Emerson looked bored. "Which are?"

"You are embezzling from your own company. I have the proof right here," Nathaniel said, holding the papers up. "I wonder how the board of directors would feel about this."

All humor was stripped off Mr. Emerson's face. "It is my company."

"It was your company," Nathaniel said offhandedly as he thumbed through the papers. "You sold most of your shares to pay for your lavish lifestyle, which you can hardly afford."

Mr. Emerson's eyes narrowed. "You're bluffing."

Nathaniel took a step towards Mr. Emerson. "I do many things, but I do not bluff—not when someone is threatening my family."

"Miss Wymond isn't your family," Mr. Emerson said.

"I consider her family, and I protect my own," Nathaniel said. "I want you to look out your window."

Mr. Emerson turned his head towards the window and his eyes grew wide. "Who are they?"

"Those men are your worst nightmare," Nathaniel explained. "They will be following you around for the next few days. Consider them a warning."

"A warning for what?" Mr. Emerson asked, turning back to Nathaniel.

"If you ever threaten any member of my family again, I can promise that you will not live to see another day." Nathaniel's voice was calm but menacing.

"You are just trying to scare me, and it won't work," Mr. Emerson said with a stubborn tilt of his chin.

Nathaniel's lips curled into a smile that didn't reach his eyes. "You don't know me, Mr. Emerson, but I assure you that you do not want to make me upset. I have killed people for far less."

Mr. Emerson's face paled. "I understand."

"Good, because I hope never to see you again," Nathaniel said.

"What of those documents?" Mr. Emerson asked.

Nathaniel dropped the papers onto the table. "They were from your ledger, so I might as well return them."

"How did you acquire them?" Mr. Emerson inquired.

"Don't ask questions you'll never have answered," Nathaniel said. "I will inform Lady Grenton to expect a hefty donation from your company."

Mr. Emerson slowly nodded. "I shall see to it at once."

Nathaniel gave him an encouraging look. "Don't look so sad. You are still alive—for now." He turned towards Hugh. "Do you have anything you want to add?"

Hugh blinked, not knowing what he could possibly say at this moment. "Um, no, I do not."

"Then we will see ourselves out," Nathaniel said as he

headed towards the door. He spun back around and pointed at the window behind Mr. Emerson. "You might want to fix the lock on that window. It catches a little."

They didn't speak as they exited the townhouse and stepped into their coach. Once the door was closed, Hugh stared at his brother. "Who are you?"

Nathaniel chuckled. "I told you to let me do the talking, and now Mr. Emerson won't ever bother you or Marielle ever again."

"You threatened to kill him."

"I did."

"Did you mean it?"

Nathaniel bobbed his head. "As I told Mr. Emerson, I do not bluff."

Hugh furrowed his brow. "Have you killed anyone before?"

"It is best if you don't know the answer to that," Nathaniel replied, his tone not giving anything away.

"And who were those two men?"

"They were the ones who stole Mother's flowers, so they owed me a favor," Nathaniel said with the slightest shrug of his shoulders. "I think they were an effective touch for persuading Mr. Emerson that I was in earnest."

"That they were."

Hugh didn't know what to think about his brother, but he had a whole new appreciation for him. More importantly, he thought it would be for the best if he never got on Nathaniel's bad side from here on out.

Marielle sat in the drawing room as she worked on her embroidery again. After they'd returned from the orphanage, Dinah had gone to rest, but Marielle wasn't tired. Her mind refused to quiet down long enough to allow her to take a nap —which was a shame, since she loved naps.

Edith stepped into the room and greeted her with a warm smile. "I have some wonderful news!" she announced.

Marielle lowered the embroidery to her lap. "I could use some of that right now."

"Your gowns have started arriving from the dressmaker, including your new ballgown," Edith revealed.

"That is good news!" Marielle said. "I was worried that it wouldn't be completed in time."

Edith sat across from her. "It is the most exquisite gown. It has an ornate overlay with embroidered flowers." She clasped her hands together. "You shall be the envy of the *ton*."

"I'll just be pleased if I don't trip on it and fall flat on my face in front of everyone."

"I have already set aside some pieces of my jewelry for you to wear," Edith shared. "I thought a pearl necklace would go along splendidly."

"That is very generous of you. I only have this gold necklace left from my mother's jewelry," Marielle said as she reached up and fingered the simple gold strand.

Edith cocked her head. "What happened to the rest of it?"

"Mr. Cadell sold it. He said it was expensive to care for me."

"That is unfortunate."

Marielle gave her a sad smile. "It is," she agreed, not knowing what else to say. Mr. Cadell had sold the jewelry almost immediately after taking possession of it.

Hugh stepped into the room, wearing an unusually solemn expression. "I was hoping to speak to Marielle for a moment," he said curtly.

Edith rose. "Not by yourself, you aren't," she said. "Why don't you take a tour of the gardens, and I'll keep watch from the window?"

"I have no objections." Hugh turned to face her. "Do you, Marielle?"

"I do not." She put her embroidery on the table and rose. "I think it is beautiful outside, a perfect day to take a stroll in the gardens."

Rather than offer his arm, Hugh gestured towards the door, indicating she should go first. She stepped out of the drawing room and was pleased when Hugh met her stride, although he maintained more than enough distance to be considered proper.

A footman opened the rear door and followed them onto the veranda. As they started walking down a path, Hugh clasped his hands behind his back and said, "It should please you to know Nathaniel and I spoke to Mr. Emerson, and he will not be an issue any longer."

"How did you accomplish that feat?"

"Nathaniel asked nicely," Hugh replied.

"Truly?"

Hugh shook his head. "He threatened him, and he was quite convincing," he said. "A part of me was afraid of what he may be capable of."

"But Nathaniel has only ever been kind to me."

"Looks can be deceiving," Hugh muttered.

Marielle stopped alongside a stretch of empty rose bushes. "Where did all of the roses go?"

"Someone stole them."

"All of them?"

"Yes; it was a devastating blow to my mother," Hugh replied.

Marielle frowned. "Who steals roses?"

"I don't rightly know." Hugh turned to face her. "I, uh, wanted to speak to you about what I said last night."

"There is no need."

"I feel as if I should explain and apologize for my actions…"

Marielle kept walking. The last thing she wanted to hear was an apology from Hugh. That would mean he regretted his words, and she didn't think her heart could take that.

Hugh quickly caught up to her. "What I said and did last night was inexcusable, and you have every reason to be upset with me."

She stopped, and her boots ground on the loose rock as she turned to face him. "Do you regret kissing me, or telling me that you love me?"

He winced. "Both."

Marielle's heart dropped at his response. She continued down the path without saying a word.

Hugh followed her. "I know I hurt you, and that was not my intention, but you must understand that it was a mistake. There can be no future between us. You must know that."

Marielle felt tears prick in the back of her eyes and blinked them back. She couldn't cry, at least not in front of Hugh.

"I have great respect for you, and I do not want this to come between us," Hugh said. "I was drunk, and I should have never entered the library in that state."

She stopped on the path but didn't turn around this time. "What women died because of you?"

Silence.

"I don't want to talk about that," Hugh eventually said.

"I assumed as much, but you brought it up last night."

"I was drunk."

Marielle turned to face him. "Are you going to blame everything on being drunk?"

Hugh sighed. "You're angry."

"Yes, I am angry," Marielle said. "You were the one who kissed me, and I felt something between us. Am I wrong?"

Hugh opened his mouth but closed it. After a long moment, he finally replied. "You aren't wrong."

"Yet you called it a mistake."

"It was."

"I don't think it was," Marielle said.

Hugh took a step closer to her. "You are young and innocent and——"

Marielle put her hand up, stilling his words. "Do not finish that sentence. I am old enough to know that you are looking for every excuse to explain what you did, but perhaps you kissed me because you wanted to."

"Of course I wanted to!" Hugh exclaimed, his voice rising. "I've wanted to kiss you from the moment I saw you, but I am your guardian."

"Is that the only thing stopping you, Hugh?" she asked. "Because when I reach my majority, you won't have that excuse any longer."

Hugh ran a hand through his hair, growing exasperated. "I already told you, I will never be good enough for you. Never."

"Shouldn't I be the judge of that?"

"I am trying to protect you."

"From what?"

"From me!" Hugh put his hands on her shoulders. "I'm doing this for you!"

She shrugged out of his arms. "No, you're doing it for yourself," she said. "You refuse to let me in, to let anyone in. Why is that?"

"Marielle..."

"Why won't you let me in, Hugh?" she asked softly.

"You don't know what you are asking of me," Hugh said.

Marielle reached for his hand. "If you don't want me, that's fine, but at least trust that I truly want to help you."

Hugh looked down at their entwined hands. "No one can help me."

"I can."

"How?" he huffed. "You can't undo the past."

She gave him an encouraging smile. "No, but I can listen, and isn't that a good place to start?"

"You won't like what I have to tell you."

"It's a risk I am willing to take."

Hugh met her gaze. "I don't want to lose you, Marielle," he entreated in a soft voice.

"I'm not going anywhere," she responded.

He released her hand and walked a short distance away, his back towards her. Marielle didn't want to rush him, so she stayed still and remained silent, hoping he would confide in her.

"I was in love once," he said, slowly turning around.

"With Priscilla?"

He nodded forlornly. "She was like you in so many ways," he said. "She laughed freely, and her smile could light up the darkest night. I was smitten from the moment I saw her at a soirée. She was dancing, and our eyes met."

Hugh sighed before he continued. "I offered for her shortly thereafter, and she accepted. My parents were thrilled by the prospect, and my father even told me that he was proud of me for securing such an auspicious match." He hesitated. "He'd never told me he was proud of me before that. Not once."

"I'm sorry to hear that." Marielle knew her words were inadequate, but she didn't quite know what to say. Her father had always showered her with love, and she'd always known precisely where she stood with him.

Hugh gave her a sad smile. "I worked so hard to become a barrister. I wanted to prove to my father that I was worthy of his love, but it was all for naught. My father will never view me as anything but worthless."

"You are not worthless," she asserted.

Hugh shifted his gaze away from hers. "It seems that you are the only one inclined to believe that."

"It is true, though." Marielle approached, stopping in front of him. "Have you spoken to your father about this?"

"Why would I?" Hugh asked. "We can hardly be in the same room with each other without fighting."

"I just feel—"

Hugh spoke over her. "You know not what you are speaking of. Your intentions are good, but they are misplaced."

"So, you will continue to revel in your misery?"

"It is all I know."

Marielle reached out and placed her hand on his sleeve. "You can be so much more than what you are giving yourself credit for."

"And what is that?"

She held his gaze as she replied, "Happy."

"You are so naïve," Hugh scoffed.

She stepped forward until she was close enough that she had to tilt her head to look up at him. "Only you are stopping yourself from being happy."

"It's not that simple, Marielle."

"It can be."

Hugh's eyes roamed over her face, devouring her image with a sweet intensity. "The last time I was truly happy was when Priscilla accepted my offer of marriage, but when she left me, I swore that my heart would never recover. Apparently I was wrong in that assumption."

"I am glad to hear it." That was all that she could manage to say with him looking at her like that.

He leaned closer. "I know one thing that makes me happy," he said, his warm breath on her cheek. "You make me happy."

Marielle's heart skipped a beat.

As she stood on her tiptoes to press her lips against his, Edith's voice came from behind them. "It is such a beautiful day, is it not?"

They jumped apart and turned towards Edith, each trying to hide guilty expressions.

Edith's face was impassive as she said, "I think you two have toured the gardens for long enough." She turned to Marielle. "Why don't you go inside and start getting dressed for dinner?"

Marielle bobbed her head too eagerly. "I think that is a grand idea."

"I will escort you," Hugh said.

Edith put her hand up. "I think you have done far too much for Marielle today. I am confident that she can see herself to her bedchamber."

Marielle knew it was time to take her leave and took a step back. "If you will excuse me, I shall see you both at dinner." She quickly spun on her heel and hurried towards the townhouse.

Chapter Fifteen

Hugh watched Marielle hurry away as he prepared himself for his mother's ire.

"Why, son?"

Hugh met his mother's gaze. "You have to be more specific than that."

"Why do you insist on playing with fire?"

"Again, I don't know what you are talking about." He knew precisely what his mother was speaking of, but he didn't want to have this conversation.

His mother sighed. "I did not raise you to be a fool. You know I am speaking of Marielle."

"What about her?"

"You were about to kiss her when I interrupted you," his mother said.

Hugh shook his head. "We were just talking, and things got out of hand."

"Have they gotten out of hand before?"

He remained silent, having no desire to lie to the woman who'd given him life.

She tossed her hands up in the air. "Do you not think about the repercussions of your actions?"

"I do."

"If anyone even suspected that you had feelings for your ward, you could ruin this whole family's reputation."

"I don't have feelings for her."

Apparently, he could lie to his mother.

She gave him a chiding look. "You are a terrible liar."

Never mind.

"Regardless of my feelings for Marielle, I have no intention of acting upon them," Hugh said. "I know what is at stake."

Taking a step forward, his mother said, "I know you want what is best for Marielle. We all do. But you can't carry on the way that you have."

"It won't happen again."

"See that it doesn't, Hugh," his mother warned. "You are her guardian, and I do not want Marielle to be ostracized by the *ton*. The fallout would be swift and devastating for her."

"I understand, Mother."

"I am not trying to be unfeeling, but it is time you put someone else's needs above your own," his mother said.

With a tip of his head, Hugh walked past his mother and headed towards the rear of the townhouse. He was tired of being reprimanded and just needed a moment alone.

No matter how much he tried to pretend otherwise, he *had* fallen in love with Marielle, and there was nothing he could do about it. He was stuck in a vicious cycle where, time and time again, only he came out the loser. If he acted on his feelings, he would put Marielle's future in jeopardy.

Marielle tried to convince him that he could be happy, but that only seemed a possibility if she was in his life. She had breathed fresh air into him, and he didn't want to go back to the way he was. He was a better man because of her.

As he headed towards the stairs, he saw Mr. Donovan in the entry hall.

Hugh's steps faltered. What now?

"Did I miss a meeting with you?"

"You did not, but I was hoping for a moment of your time," Mr. Donovan replied as his eyes roamed the vast hall. "It would be best if we spoke in private."

Turning towards the drawing room, Hugh said, "We can speak freely in here."

After they'd both stepped into the room, Hugh closed the door and walked over to the drink cart. "May I get you a drink?" he offered.

Mr. Donovan shook his head. "No, thank you," he replied. "I have come with some distressing news."

"Which is?"

"Mr. Cadell has filed documents in court that claim he had an understanding with Miss Wymond," Mr. Donovan revealed.

"Now he is just grasping at straws," Hugh said as he poured himself a drink. "That is a blatant lie."

Mr. Donovan removed a handkerchief and wiped sweat from his brow. "I don't doubt that, but he was her guardian," he said. "They were living in the same home, which could lead to speculation that he may have compromised her."

Hugh tightened his hold on his glass. "Nothing untoward happened," he growled.

"Miss Wymond assured me of that."

"I don't doubt that, but he is asking for Miss Wymond to be returned to him or for a sum of forty thousand pounds to compensate him for his losses."

"Forty thousand pounds," Hugh repeated. "Surely he cannot be in earnest!"

"I'm afraid that Mr. Cadell refuses to go away quietly."

Hugh took a sip of his drink and walked over to a settee. "What am I to do?" he asked. "I refuse to hand over Miss Wymond to that scoundrel, and I won't pay that enormous amount."

"I do not have to tell you what would happen if this case

went to trial," Mr. Donovan said. "I have every assurance that Mr. Cadell would lose, but the court of public opinion would be much more unforgiving to Miss Wymond."

"Curse that man," Hugh grumbled.

"You could always try to negotiate with him," Mr. Donovan advised. "He was originally suing you for ten thousand pounds; perhaps he would settle for that."

Hugh lifted his brow. "Are you suggesting that I pay Mr. Cadell to go away?"

"It is merely an option."

"A terrible option," Hugh said. "I will not stoop to his level and give him that power over me."

"You must think of what a trial will do to Miss Wymond," Mr. Donovan said. "It would ruin the poor girl."

"I am well aware of that." Hugh rose from his seat. "I need to speak to my brother and see if he can help me with this delicate issue."

Mr. Donovan tipped his head. "Very good, my lord."

Hugh found Nathaniel in the study conversing with Haddington in hushed tones.

Nathaniel halted their conversation when he saw him. "What's wrong?"

"I need your help," Hugh said.

"With what in particular?"

Hugh wasn't entirely sure if Haddington knew about Nathaniel's uncanny ability to threaten people, so he decided to tread cautiously. "I, um, need you to do what you did with Mr. Emerson to Mr. Cadell."

"You need me to threaten him?" Nathaniel asked.

"I do."

Nathaniel exchanged a worried glance with Haddington. "And why am I threatening Mr. Cadell?"

"He's claiming that he had an understanding with Marielle and wants to take the case to trial."

"Which would ruin Miss Wymond's reputation if word ever got out amongst the *ton*," Haddington supplied.

"Precisely," Hugh said. "Which is why Nathaniel needs to speak to Mr. Cadell."

Nathaniel crossed his arms over his chest. "I can't go around threatening everyone who makes allegations against Miss Wymond."

"Whyever not?" Hugh demanded.

"Doing so distracts from my purpose," Nathaniel explained.

"What purpose?" Hugh asked.

Nathaniel gave him a pointed look. "Mr. Emerson was a despicable man who deserved what was coming to him," he said. "I cannot say the same of Mr. Cadell."

Hugh's mouth dropped open. "He is trying to extort forty thousand pounds out of me!"

"That is quite a sum, but——"

"You aren't going to help me?" Hugh interjected.

"I don't know yet," Nathaniel said, uncrossing his arms. "I will make some inquiries and see what type of person Mr. Cadell is."

"He is a boldfaced liar!" Hugh shouted. "He is claiming that something untoward happened between Marielle and himself."

"You are upset," Nathaniel commented.

"Of course I'm upset!" Hugh exclaimed. "The woman that I love…" He stopped speaking and closed his mouth, wondering if he should just cut his damnable tongue out and be done with it.

Nathaniel sighed deeply. "You are too close to this situation," he said. "Let me handle it."

"What will you do?" Hugh asked.

"You don't need to concern yourself with that," Nathaniel responded. "I think it would be best if you left for Brookhaven soon and put some distance between you and Marielle."

"I think it's amusing that the gambler gambled with his heart and lost," Haddington quipped as he leaned back against the windowsill.

Hugh cast him a disapproving look. "Are you quite done?"

"Not yet," Haddington replied. "The gambler got dealt a hand that his heart couldn't handle."

"That was terrible," Hugh said.

Nathaniel grinned. "You might want to work on your puns."

Haddington opened his mouth to no doubt say another terrible joke, so Hugh spoke first. "Enough of those," he commanded. "Surely you have a better use of time than to revel in my misery."

"Not at the moment," Haddington smirked.

Hugh turned his attention back towards his brother. "I am unable to depart for Brookhaven until after Marielle's ball. If I did so, Mother would be furious."

"I am sure Mother would understand," Nathaniel said. "I'm worried about you. This will not end well for you if you continue to spend time with Marielle."

"I am trying to avoid her, but it is proving to be more difficult than I anticipated," Hugh admitted.

Haddington interjected, "Even with a handful of spades, Hugh still couldn't dig himself out of a hole."

Hugh groaned. "That was the worst one yet," he said. "Are you finished yet?"

Haddington chuckled. "I am now."

"Thank heavens for that," Hugh muttered.

Nathaniel walked over to his desk and sat down. "I urge you to proceed with the utmost caution when dealing with Marielle."

"I'm trying."

"Try harder," Nathaniel asserted.

Hugh walked over to the door and stopped. "Just help Marielle. Please. She is all that matters right now."

"I will see what I can do," Nathaniel said.

The conversation flowed around Marielle in the dining room. She was too preoccupied to join the discussion, however. Thoughts of Hugh were consuming her, body and soul.

She knew he cared for her, perhaps even loved her, but he was putting his duty before his heart. It was the honorable thing to do, but she was beginning to think that she didn't care about being honorable.

As she snuck a glance at Hugh, who was sitting next to her, Dinah's voice broke through her musings. "Are you all right, Marielle?"

She bobbed her head. "I am."

Dinah didn't look convinced, but she didn't press her. "I was wondering if you wanted to accompany me to the orphanage tomorrow."

"I would like that very much," Marielle said. "I enjoy reading to the girls."

"As do I," Dinah added.

"I wonder what peculiar lessons Evie will have in store for the girls tomorrow," Marielle said as she reached for her glass.

"Maybe she'll teach them how to throw a dagger," Dinah remarked.

Marielle's eyes widened. "Evie can throw daggers?"

Dinah smiled. "She can, and she is quite good at it."

"Miss Ashmore would best remember that she needs to behave if she wants to secure a husband," Edith interjected.

"I do believe that is the least of her concerns," Marielle said.

"It should be the most important," Edith responded.

Marielle took a sip of her drink before returning it to the table. "Not every young woman wishes to be married."

"The smart ones do," Edith stated.

"My mother didn't want me to only look for security when I marry," Marielle shared. "She used to tell me that I needed to choose a husband who would love me above all else."

Lord Montfort spoke up from the head of the table. "That was some sound advice."

"I was fortunate that I was raised in a home filled with love and laughter," Marielle said. She looked downward. "I didn't realize how fortunate I was until it was gone."

"Will you tell us about your mother?" Hugh asked.

Marielle smiled. "My mother found everything amusing and taught us that laughter was the best medicine," she shared. "After our lessons were done for the day, we would go into the woods and spend hours exploring them."

"I do not see our mother traipsing through the woods," Nathaniel said with a glimmer of merriment in his eyes.

Edith shook her head. "I most assuredly would not."

"My father would join us on occasion, but he was busy managing the shipyard," Marielle said. "But we spent an enormous amount of time with Mother."

"Did you have a governess?" Edith asked.

"I did, but Mother thought it was important that we spent time outdoors each day, and we'd often do so together," Marielle said. "When my brother went to Eton, she and I were practically inseparable."

"I am glad that you were able to spend so much time with her, especially since she died so young," Edith said.

Marielle lowered her gaze to the table. "Yes, I was lucky." She blinked back tears, not wanting to cry in front of everyone.

Hugh cleared his throat. "Perhaps we should talk about something else."

A tear escaped her eye, and she reached up to wipe it

away. "I, uh, just need a moment," she said as she pushed back her chair.

She barely acknowledged the men rising from their seats as she rushed from the room. She retreated to the entry hall to gain control of her raging emotions. Would there ever come a time that she could think of her mother without growing emotional?

Hugh's voice came from behind her. "Marielle," he said in a concerned voice, "are you all right?"

She kept her back to him as she swiped at her wet cheeks. "I will be," she replied.

"I must admit that I don't like it when you cry."

Slowly, she turned around and faced him. "Oh?" she inquired.

"It means that you are hurting, and I don't know how I can help you." Hugh removed a handkerchief from his pocket and extended it towards her.

Marielle stepped forward and accepted the handkerchief. "Thank you," she murmured. "You'd best hurry back before your food grows cold."

"I care little about my food right now."

"I bet your cook would be disappointed you said that," she said, attempting humor.

Hugh watched her. "I am more concerned about what has you so upset."

"I love talking about my mother, but…" Marielle's voice trailed off as she found the courage to say her next words, "my mother died because of me."

"I can't believe that."

Marielle gripped his handkerchief tightly. "You are not the only one with a past that they regret."

"I thought your mother died from falling off her horse."

"She did, but I was the one who encouraged her to jump the hedge," Marielle said. "If I hadn't, she would still be alive."

Hugh took a step closer. "You couldn't have predicted that your mother would fall."

"True, but—"

"It was a tragic accident, and you shouldn't think otherwise."

"That's easy for you to say," Marielle said as she hugged herself. "You weren't responsible for your parents' deaths."

"Parents?" Hugh asked. "You aren't blaming yourself for your father's death too, are you?"

Marielle nodded. "After Mother died, Father was never quite the same," she replied. "It was as if he lost his will to live."

"That must have been difficult to face, considering he still had you to care for."

"He withered away right in front of me, and it was my fault." Marielle's voice broke on a sob. "I couldn't stop it."

"Oh, Marielle," Hugh sighed. "You did nothing wrong."

"I told you that I—"

"Neither one of those deaths are your fault," Hugh asserted. "Sometimes bad things happen, and you can't do anything to stop it."

"I miss them every day," Marielle admitted, "and every day I wonder what life would be like if my mother was still alive."

Hugh approached and placed his hands gently on her shoulders. "I can't answer that, but I know that your parents would be proud of the woman that you have become."

"You don't know that."

"How could they not be?" Hugh asked. "You tell me to look inward, but you don't take your own advice. If you did, you would know how truly special you are."

Marielle lowered her gaze to the lapels of his jacket. "I don't feel special."

"Then let me assure you that you are," Hugh said. "You

have a greatness inside of you. You have the ability to do more than you ever thought possible."

Tears welled up in her eyes. "I can't seem to forget the moment that I held my mother in my arms as I screamed for help."

She was suddenly wrapped up in Hugh's comforting embrace, and she leaned her head against his chest.

"I wish I could take that memory away from you," Hugh whispered next to her ear.

The rise and fall of Hugh's chest was soothing, and Marielle began to feel more at peace. She had never revealed the truth of her mother's death to anyone for fear of their reaction, but she was beginning to think she was wrong to do so.

Hugh leaned back far enough to look into her eyes. "I want you to stop blaming yourself for something that was most assuredly not your fault."

He gazed at her with an intensity she didn't understand, and she could only nod in agreement.

His lips twitched. "Good," he said. "Now, shall we go finish our meal?"

"I think that is a brilliant idea."

Hugh dropped his arms and stepped back. "Frankly, I am surprised my mother hasn't come looking for us already."

"I think she was distracted by the venison."

"Ah," Hugh said. "I, too, can be distracted by food."

Marielle held up his handkerchief. "I am afraid this is quite soiled. I'll see to it being washed and will return it to you at once."

"I want you to keep it," Hugh encouraged. "It will be a token for you to remember me by."

She cocked her head. "That sounds as if you are saying goodbye."

Hugh looked hesitant. "After your ball, I intend to retire to Brookhaven for the remainder of the Season."

"What about after the Season?"

"You will be accompanying my mother to our country estate in Sunderland," he shared. "Where you will reside until next Season."

Marielle furrowed her brows. "I'm afraid I don't understand," she said. "Why are you leaving me?"

Hugh's gaze left hers. "It is for the best."

"How can you say that?" Marielle asked.

"You must trust me."

"I do trust you, but I don't want you to leave."

"Neither do I."

"Then stay," she encouraged.

Hugh's jaw clenched. "I have already made my decision, and I must ask you to respect it."

Marielle took a step back as she attempted to school her features. "I thought you didn't even want Brookhaven."

"My situation has changed."

Marielle stared at him, dumbfounded. How could he do this to her? He was just abandoning her, and she had no say in it.

"I want you to take your mother's advice to heart," Hugh said quietly. "Find a suitor who will love you above all else. You deserve nothing less."

"You wish for me to take a suitor?" she asked in stunned disbelief. Why couldn't he see that she wanted him? It would always be him.

"I do." His words seemed forced, but he said them nevertheless.

Her breath caught in her throat. "Why are you doing this?" she breathed.

"Because it is the only way." He leaned forward and kissed her cheek, his lips lingering. "You deserve to be happy, Marielle."

She wanted to respond, but Hugh stepped back and

offered his arm. "It would be for the best if we joined everyone in the dining room."

Marielle put her hand on his arm and let him lead her. How could he treat her so tenderly, but in the next breath, encourage her to take a suitor? Her heart had already been claimed by him, and she worried that no man would ever compare to Hugh.

Chapter Sixteen

Marielle sat on her bed and leaned her back against the wall with a heavy heart as she watched her lady's maid tidy up the dressing table. She didn't want Hugh to leave her, but he had made up his mind. He would disappear after her ball, and she would be left behind to pine after him.

He wanted her to find a suitor, but she had no desire to do so. She hadn't been planning on marrying in the first place, and had only considered it because of her feelings for Hugh. He had somehow claimed her whole heart, and he would always have a special place within it.

Grace picked up a discarded gown on the settee and asked, "Will there be anything else, miss?"

"Why are men so infuriating?"

"I assume you are speaking of Lord Hugh," Grace said with a knowing smile.

"I am," Marielle said as she sat up straight. "He intends to depart for Brookhaven after my ball with no intention of returning."

"Did he explain his reasoning?"

"Vaguely," Marielle replied, "but I know he's running from me."

Grace stood by the bed next to her. "Why would he run from you?"

"He is my guardian, and a courtship between us would be frowned upon," Marielle responded. "But I care little for that."

"I think you might feel differently when the *ton* gives you the cut direct."

"Do you think they would?"

Grace shrugged her thin shoulders. "I cannot say, but it does appear that Lord Hugh is attempting to do the honorable thing."

"By letting me go?"

Grace eyed her curiously. "Did you have an understanding with him?"

"No, but I know he cares for me," Marielle said. "He even let it slip when he was drunk that he loved me."

"Do you think he meant it?"

"I hope so, because I feel the same."

Grace carefully folded the dress in her arms. "Have you considered that you are attracted to Lord Hugh because the romance is forbidden?"

"I can assure you that is not the reason why," Marielle said. "I see him for the man he truly is."

"I just think you should be cautious with your heart."

Marielle let out a puff of air. "I know what is at stake, but I believe that Hugh is worth the risk."

"What about running the shipyard?" Grace asked. "Do you truly believe Lord Hugh would allow you to sully your hands with work if you were wed?"

Marielle paused. "I would like to believe that he would allow me to run the shipyard."

"But you aren't sure?"

"Well, no," Marielle replied, "but we aren't in a position to even discuss marriage."

Grace took a step away from the bed. "I think time is a good thing. It will help you decide what you truly want in life."

Marielle leaned her head back against the wall. "When did life become so complicated?"

"I'm afraid you are asking the wrong person," Grace said lightly. "You have been given a great opportunity to reside here with Lord and Lady Montfort, and you shouldn't waste it."

"I suppose you are right," Marielle sighed.

"I am, but you don't sound very convinced."

"What if I never see Hugh again?"

"Then it wasn't meant to be."

"Surely it can't be that simple."

Grace smiled. "When two people are truly in love, they will overcome whatever obstacles are in their way to be with one another."

"I hadn't taken you for such a romantic," Marielle teased.

"True love is hard to find," Grace said, "and those who are lucky enough to find it should hold on to it."

"So, you are saying I should fight for Hugh?"

"What does your heart tell you to do?"

Marielle thought for a moment. "It tells me that I need chocolate."

"I can see to warming some up for you, if you would like," Grace laughed, "but drinking chocolate will not solve all of your problems."

"It could solve some of them."

"You are hopeless," Grace remarked with a shake of her head, "completely hopeless."

A faint knock came at the door, drawing their attention, and a slip of paper was pushed under it.

Marielle put her feet over the bed and rose. "Whatever is that?" she asked as she walked over to the door.

She picked up the note and read it.

· · ·

I will be waiting for you in the gardens. Tell no one.

Marielle held the paper to her chest as a burst of happiness came over her.

Grace approached her. "What did it say?" she asked.

"Hugh wants me to meet him in the gardens alone," Marielle replied. "Isn't that romantic?"

Her lady's maid didn't appear convinced. "Are you sure that is wise?"

Marielle walked over to the dressing table and set the note on it. "I don't see an issue with it. I'm sure Hugh just wants to talk to me without having to worry that anyone will overhear us."

"What if he kisses you again?"

Her fingers went to her lips as she remembered how it felt when Hugh had kissed her before. His kiss, accompanied by his words, had felt like a beginning of something wonderful. She just had to convince him of that. "I hope he does."

"You would be ruined if anyone found out."

Marielle waved a hand in front of her. "No one will find out," she said. "Everyone has already retired for the evening, and I can easily make my way to the gardens undetected."

"This doesn't seem like a good idea."

"You worry too much," Marielle stated. "I will be back in my bedchamber before anyone is the wiser."

Grace sighed. "I'm not going to be able to talk you out of this, am I?"

"Were you not the one who spoke earlier about true love and whatnot?"

"I was, but I never meant that you should have a clandestine meeting with Lord Hugh in the gardens."

Marielle reached for her wrapper and put it on over her nightgown. "Perhaps he is going to confess his love."

"Didn't he already do that?"

"He did," Marielle said, "but he was drunk."

Grace gave her a pointed look. "Even if he confesses his love for you, it changes nothing. He is still your guardian."

"You are being quite the naysayer."

"I just worry you are getting your hopes up for nothing," Grace remarked.

Marielle walked over to the door. "I have to go," she insisted. "I can't live my life wondering what if."

Grace nodded her understanding. "Just be careful."

"I will be." Marielle opened her door and glanced out into the hall. She stepped out, closing the door behind her, and made her way towards the stairs.

She heard a door closing somewhere else in the house, and it threatened her resolve. What if someone did catch them in the gardens? Was she prepared for the repercussions of her actions? They might be forced into a marriage. Frankly, that didn't sound so terrible.

Surely Hugh had known the risks when he wrote that note. If they were forced to wed, would he hold it against her?

Marielle glanced back the way she had come. Perhaps it would be for the best if she turned around now and didn't meet Hugh in the gardens. But could she live with herself if she did such a thing?

No. She needed to speak with him.

With squared shoulders, she hurried down the stairs with light steps and made her way towards the rear of the townhouse. Hushed speaking came from the study, and Marielle darted towards the shadows.

She recognized Nathaniel's voice. He was speaking to someone, but she couldn't quite make out what they were saying. Why was he up at this late hour? Hadn't he retired to bed with Dinah earlier in the evening?

Marielle had to pass by the partially opened door to get to the rear door of the townhouse. Would Nathaniel see her? And if he did, what excuse would she give him?

Taking a deep breath, Marielle stepped out from the shadows and tiptoed over to the edge of the door. She peeked inside and saw Nathaniel was sitting at his desk, speaking to a man who had his back towards the door. The conversation must be serious, judging by the solemn look on Nathaniel's face.

"I can do this," Marielle whispered under her breath. She calculated that it would take three small steps to reach safety on the other side of the door.

As she took her first step, Nathaniel's booming voice asked, "Who goes there?"

Drat. How had he heard her?

She hadn't even moved from her position when Nathaniel was upon her with a pistol in his hand.

"Marielle," Nathaniel said with a hard tone she was unfamiliar with. "What are you doing here?"

"I, uh, wanted to go to the gardens," she started, her eyes darting to the pistol.

He lifted his brow. "In your wrapper, and at this late hour?"

"Yes," she said.

Nathaniel tucked the pistol in the waistband of his trousers. "Were you eavesdropping, by chance?"

Marielle shook her head, vehemently. "Heavens, no!" she exclaimed. "I have been known to eavesdrop in the past, but I promise you that I was doing no such thing now."

Nathaniel studied her for a long moment before his face softened to an expression she was more accustomed to. "It isn't wise to loiter in the halls at night. I wouldn't want you to overhear a private conversation." His words held a warning.

"Of course not, my lord," Marielle said.

With a glance into the study, Nathaniel asked, "May I ask why you are going to the gardens?"

Marielle pressed her lips together as she attempted to come up with a believable lie. "I wanted to see the stars."

"Can you not do that from your bedchamber window?"

"I could, but it was so lovely this evening that I wanted to do so outside," Marielle replied.

"Come along, then," Nathaniel encouraged. "I shall escort you."

Marielle panicked. "That won't be necessary," she rushed out. "I do not mean to keep you from your guest. That would be intolerably rude of me to do so."

"It is no imposition at all," Nathaniel said with a flick of his wrist. "Unless you are not telling me the whole truth about why you wish to be in the gardens?"

She laughed nervously. "Why would you assume such a thing?" she asked. "I just really want to see the stars by myself."

Nathaniel tipped his head. "As you wish."

Marielle murmured her thanks as she walked past him and down the hall to the back door. As she stepped outside, she glanced back and saw that Nathaniel remained rooted in his spot.

Dear heavens, that man could be intimidating. Her eyes roamed over the gardens as she looked for any sign of Hugh. When she found none, she stepped down onto one of the paths and started walking. Hugh probably knew his brother was awake and was hiding behind one of the trees to prevent being noticed.

The moon was high in the sky, giving her plenty of light as she continued down the path. She heard the sound of booted footsteps coming up from behind her at a rapid pace, but before she could turn around, everything went black.

"Wake up!"

Hugh's eyes cracked open, and he saw Nathaniel standing

over him. "Why are you bothering me at this late hour?" he grumbled as he started to turn over.

"Marielle is missing."

Hugh sat up in his bed. "What do you mean, she is missing?!" he exclaimed.

"I don't think I can make it any clearer," Nathaniel said as he took a step back from the bed. "She went into the gardens, and she didn't come back inside."

"Why did she go into the gardens at night?"

Nathaniel gave him an expectant look. "I was hoping you could tell me."

"Tell you what?"

"I don't believe Marielle went into the gardens with the intention of being alone," Nathaniel said. "Which makes me wonder, who was she meeting?"

Hugh tossed his feet over the bed and rose. "If you're wondering if I arranged a meeting with her, then you would be wrong in that assumption."

"Why else would she go out there?"

"I don't rightly know," Hugh replied as he walked over to the wardrobe. He pulled clothes out and started dressing. "Did you ask her lady's maid?"

"I intend to," Nathaniel said. "I asked Balfour to bring her to my study."

"Then what are we waiting for?" Hugh asked as he pulled a white linen shirt over his head.

As they walked down the hall, Hugh made quick work of tying his cravat. "How did you know Marielle went into the gardens?"

"She was loitering in the hall outside my study, and I found her explanation as to why she was there to be inadequate."

"What reason did she give?"

"She claimed she wanted to look up at the stars."

"But it was cloudy this evening. She might glimpse a few stars here and there, but they're otherwise covered."

"I am well aware, but Marielle apparently didn't know that," Nathaniel said. "When she didn't return in a timely fashion, I went to ensure she was all right."

"Why did you even let her go outside?"

"It wasn't as if I could stop her, and I assumed she was meeting you."

Hugh frowned. "Why would you assume that?"

"It just made sense at the time."

They were about to descend the stairs when his mother's frantic voice came from the doorway of her bedchamber. "What on earth is going on?" she asked. "It would appear that the house is in a frenzy."

Hugh stopped and turned to face her. "Marielle is missing."

"Missing?" his mother repeated. "How could that be?"

"That's what we are trying to find out," Nathaniel replied.

They quickly descended the stairs and headed towards the study. They stepped inside, where Balfour was waiting with a petite, red-haired young woman.

Balfour gestured towards her. "This is Grace," he introduced. "She is Miss Wymond's lady's maid."

Nathaniel came to a stop in front of the young woman. "Do you know why Miss Wymond went into the gardens this evening?"

"I do," Grace said.

"Can you tell us?" Nathaniel asked with an impatient look.

Grace lowered her gaze to the floor. "I would rather not say, my lord."

"I know you are trying to protect your mistress, but she is missing," Nathaniel said. "The longer we waste time trying to get to the truth, the harder it will be to find her."

Bringing her gaze up, Grace offered Hugh an apologetic look before saying, "She was meeting Lord Hugh."

Hugh crossed his arms over his chest. "Why did she think I would be in the gardens?"

"Because of your note."

"What note?" Hugh asked.

Grace looked at him like he was a simpleton. "The one you wrote."

"I didn't write a note," Hugh said. "What did it say?"

Grace glanced between them. "It told her to come to the gardens and tell no one."

Hugh turned to face his brother. "I did not write that note. You must believe me," he said. "I wouldn't have done something so foolish."

"I do believe you," Nathaniel said, turning back to Grace. "How did she receive this message?"

"It was slipped under her door," Grace replied.

Nathaniel shifted his gaze towards Balfour. "I want you to wake up every servant in this household and find out who slipped that piece of paper under the door."

Balfour tipped his head. "As you wish, my lord," he said as he spun on his heel to do so.

Grace looked unsure. "Will there be anything else?" she asked.

"Not at this time," Nathaniel replied.

Hugh watched as the lady's maid walked swiftly out of the study with her head down. "Why are you letting her go?" he asked.

"She knows nothing," Nathaniel said as he came around his desk and sat down.

"What if she's lying?"

Nathaniel leaned back in his chair. "For what purpose?" he asked.

"I don't know!" Hugh exclaimed, tossing his hands up in the air. "But Marielle couldn't have disappeared into thin air."

"I agree, which leads me to believe she was abducted."

"By whom?"

228

Nathaniel shrugged. "I don't rightly know," he said. "I sent Haddington to speak to the two men who were following Mr. Emerson, but I do not believe he would be foolish enough to abduct Marielle."

"Then who else could it be?"

"You tell me," Nathaniel said with a pointed look.

"Why would I know who abducted Marielle?" Hugh asked.

"You spent time with disreputable people at gambling halls," Nathaniel pointed out. "Perhaps one of those men took issue with losing to you."

Hugh shook his head. "That's impossible. Those men are gamblers; they don't abduct women."

"Even to get to you?"

"Even then," Hugh replied as he walked over to the drink cart. He picked up the decanter and poured himself a generous helping of brandy.

Nathaniel arched an eyebrow. "Are you sure that is wise?"

"I don't see why not."

"You need a clear head."

Hugh put the decanter down and picked up his glass. "I think better with a drink inside of me."

Nathaniel didn't say anything, but the disapproval etched on his face convinced Hugh to put the glass down on the tray.

"Fine," he muttered. "I will do it your way."

Nathaniel gestured towards a chair, indicating that he should sit. "Has anyone made any threats towards you or Marielle?"

"Besides Mr. Emerson, no," Hugh replied.

"Have you gotten into any fights as of late?"

"No." Hugh sighed. "The only issue is Mr. Cadell suing me for breach of contract. He claims that he had an understanding with Marielle."

"Did he?"

"How could you even ask that?" Hugh asked. "He is lying

to try to garner money out of me. You should know this, I've told you as much. You said you'd make inquiries."

"Do you think he would abduct Marielle?"

Hugh huffed. "I do not think he is capable of such a thing. He is a coward threatening to damage a young woman's reputation to swindle a substantial sum from me. He's been relatively civil about the matter, doing everything through the courts."

"Would you have paid him off?"

"I don't know—"

Nathaniel cut him off. "Would you have paid him off?" he demanded.

"Yes!" Hugh shouted. "I would have paid him off rather than have it go to court! I couldn't—no, I wouldn't—do that to Marielle. She means everything to me."

"If that is the case, what would Mr. Cadell have gained if he abducted her?" Nathaniel mused.

"Nothing."

Nathaniel made a clucking noise with his tongue. "He wouldn't have risked abducting her for nothing."

"Why do you assume Mr. Cadell abducted her?" Hugh asked.

Before Nathaniel could speak, Balfour stepped into the room and announced, "We found the person responsible for delivering the note."

"Well, send him in, then," Hugh snapped.

Balfour put his hand out towards the hall. "Come along," he ordered.

A young boy with freckles on his face stepped into the room and stayed close to Balfour.

"Who is this?" Hugh asked.

Balfour placed a hand on the boy's shoulder. "This is Thomas," he replied. "He's the cook's son."

Nathaniel rose from his chair and walked over to Thomas.

He crouched down next to him. "Thomas, do you know who I am?"

The boy nodded slowly.

"Do you understand why we need to speak to you?" Nathaniel asked.

Thomas spoke up. "It's about the note."

"It is," Nathaniel replied. "Who asked you to deliver the note to Miss Wymond's room?"

Thomas glanced up at Balfour. "I was playing near the stables before dinner and a man approached me. He asked me to deliver the note after everyone was in bed."

"Did you get a good look at this man?" Nathaniel asked.

"Not really, no," Thomas replied.

"Can you tell me anything about him, anything at all?"

Thomas pressed his lips together. "His ears seemed really big, and he had dark hair."

Rising, Nathaniel turned his attention towards Hugh. "Does that remind you of anyone you know?"

"Mr. Cadell," Hugh growled.

Nathaniel smiled down at the boy. "That will be all, Thomas," he said. "You did well."

"Should we go speak to the constable now?" Hugh asked after Balfour and Thomas left.

"For what purpose?" Nathaniel went around his desk and opened the top drawer, removing a pistol. "I intend to speak to Mr. Cadell myself."

"You can't take the law into your own hands."

Nathaniel met his gaze. "Do you want Marielle back here alive?"

"I do."

"Then we do things my way," Nathaniel said in a firm tone. "Do we understand one another?"

Hugh would do whatever it took to get Marielle back, even if that meant he had to blindly trust his brother. "We do."

Nathaniel tucked the pistol into the waistband of his trousers and asked, "Do you have a pistol?"

"I've never had a use for one."

Reaching into the drawer, Nathaniel removed another weapon. "This is an overcoat pistol. Keep it on your person and pray you won't need to use it."

Hugh stepped forward and accepted the pistol. He attempted to tuck it into the waistband of his trousers as he'd seen his brother do, but it slipped out and fell onto the floor with a thud.

"Impressive, brother," Nathaniel mocked.

Haddington walked into the room with a purposeful stride. "I found Worsley and Talbot. They confirmed that Mr. Emerson was nowhere near your townhouse this evening."

"That's good, but we believe we know who the culprit was," Nathaniel said.

"Who?" Haddington asked.

"Mr. Cadell," Nathaniel replied as he came around his desk. "We were just about to go speak to him. Would you care to join us?"

Haddington bobbed his head. "I think that sounds like a fine idea."

Chapter Seventeen

Hugh tapped his foot against the floor of the coach. He was anxious to see Mr. Cadell and attempt to sort this all out. Although, if Mr. Cadell had harmed a hair on Marielle's body, Hugh wouldn't think twice about using the pistol Nathaniel had given him.

His brother gave him an encouraging look. "It will be all right," he assured him.

"How?" Hugh demanded. "Marielle is missing, and we don't even know for certain that Mr. Cadell abducted her."

"It is only logical to start with him," Nathaniel said. "You need to remain calm."

"Calm?" Hugh repeated. "You wish for me to remain calm? Are you mad?"

Nathaniel exchanged a worried look with Haddington. "Perhaps we should have left him at the townhouse."

"I think not," Hugh said. "If Mr. Cadell had anything to do with this, then I need to know."

"It might be best if Hawthorne and I did the talking," Haddington said.

"I can agree to that," Hugh responded.

The coach finally stopped in front of a brick townhouse with an iron railing around it in a less affluent part of Town.

Hugh stuck his hand out the window and opened the door. Without waiting for his brother or Haddington, he rushed to the door and started pounding on it.

It was eventually opened a crack, and a voice from within asked, "What business do you have here?"

Hugh didn't have time to answer bothersome questions. He shoved the door open, pushing the butler back. "I am here to see Mr. Cadell."

The dark-haired butler held a candle up. "And who is asking?"

"I'm not asking, I'm telling," Hugh replied. "Go fetch Mr. Cadell, or I will search every room in this house for him."

The butler had just turned when Mr. Cadell's voice came from the top of the stairs. "What is the meaning of this, Lord Hugh?"

"Where is she?" Hugh demanded.

Mr. Cadell gave him a blank stare. "Where is who?"

"Marielle!" he exclaimed.

"Why should I know?" Mr. Cadell asked. "I haven't seen her since I dropped her off at your townhouse."

"You're lying!" Hugh started towards Mr. Cadell but stopped when Nathaniel put a firm hand on his shoulder.

Nathaniel leaned closer and said, "You need to let us handle this."

Hugh realized how rashly he'd behaved and knew he was in no position to be rational at the moment. He reluctantly nodded his head.

Nathaniel removed his hand and turned his attention towards Mr. Cadell. "Perhaps we could speak in your drawing room."

Mr. Cadell let out a disapproving huff as he descended the stairs. "Could this not wait until morning?"

"I'm afraid not," Nathaniel said.

Mr. Cadell tramped into a room off the entry hall, and they followed closely behind him.

Once Mr. Cadell had reached the center of the room, he turned to face them. "Would you mind explaining why you are in my home and making wild accusations?"

Nathaniel gestured towards a chair. "Would you care to sit?"

"No, I would not," Mr. Cadell replied.

"I insist," Nathaniel said sternly.

Mr. Cadell eyed him for a moment before he sat down on the proffered chair. "I do not take kindly to being bullied in my own home."

Nathaniel stepped in front of the chair and pulled out a dagger from his left boot. "I am not a very patient man, and I am only going to ask each question one time. If you fail to answer the question truthfully, the retribution will be swift and very painful. Do we understand one another?"

Mr. Cadell swallowed slowly, and fear showed in his eyes. "I understand."

"Good," Nathaniel said. "When was the last time you saw Miss Wymond?"

"When I dropped her off at your townhouse," Mr. Cadell replied.

Nathaniel let out a sigh. "I thought we decided on telling the truth," he said. "Now I am going to have to do something that will no doubt inflict great pain on you."

Mr. Cadell put his hand up. "All right!" he shouted. "I saw her a few days ago when she was shopping, and I tried to approach her."

"What stopped you?" Nathaniel asked.

"Miss Ashmore stopped me," Mr. Cadell admitted.

Haddington interjected, "How do you know Miss Ashmore?"

"I don't," he replied. "I only know of her, but she met my gaze, and it just stopped me right in my tracks."

"She didn't say anything to you?" Haddington asked.

Mr. Cadell shook his head. "No, but it was as if she could read my thoughts," he said. "All I wanted to do was talk to Marielle."

"What did you want to talk about?" Hugh asked.

"I miss her," Mr. Cadell attempted.

Hugh frowned. "I think not," he said.

Mr. Cadell glanced between them. "I was going to try to convince her to return home with me, but I didn't dare with Miss Ashmore there."

Nathaniel touched the tip of the dagger with his finger. "Did you miss her enough to abduct her?"

"I did no such thing," Mr. Cadell replied, shaking his head.

"Well, we have a problem," Nathaniel said, leaning closer to Mr. Cadell. "Marielle is missing, and someone recalls seeing you outside of our townhouse."

Mr. Cadell's face grew splotchy. "That is impossible! I was nowhere near your townhouse."

"Why should I believe you?" Nathaniel asked. "And try to remember that these words could be your last."

Shrinking back in his chair, Mr. Cadell said, "I was at the Gilded Crown all evening. You can ask anyone that was there."

"I don't have the time to do that," Nathaniel replied. "What I do have time for is to gut you and leave you for dead."

Mr. Cadell dropped to his knees in front of Nathaniel. "Please don't hurt me!" he cried. "I swear I didn't touch Marielle. You have to believe me! I did throw a rock through your window, but that was only because I was angry." He motioned towards the door. "Search my townhouse. I promise that you won't find her."

Nathaniel assessed Mr. Cadell for a moment with cool

eyes. "I do believe you," he said, returning his dagger to his boot.

"*What?!*" Hugh shouted. "He is clearly lying!"

"He's not," Nathaniel said. "Mr. Cadell has nothing to do with Marielle's abduction."

"How can you be so sure?"

"I have made a great study of knowing when people are lying," Nathaniel replied. "It is a matter of life or death for me."

Hugh had heard enough and retrieved his pistol. He was not so easily fooled. As he pointed it at Mr. Cadell's forehead, he demanded, "Where is she?"

Mr. Cadell covered his head with his arms. "I don't know!" he whimpered.

"You lied about having an understanding with Marielle. How do we know you aren't lying about this?" Hugh pressed.

"I will withdraw my suit," Mr. Cadell pled. "Please, just don't kill me!"

Haddington turned to face Hugh. "You don't want to kill this man."

"Yes, I do," Hugh replied. "He knows where Marielle is."

"I don't believe he does," Haddington said.

Hugh's gaze darted to Haddington. "How can you and Nathaniel be so sure?" he asked.

"I know you want to find Marielle, but this is not going to help us do that," Haddington said. "You must trust us."

With great reluctance, Hugh lowered the pistol to his side.

Haddington nodded in approval. "We should go," he encouraged as he clapped a hand on Hugh's shoulder.

As they walked to the door, Nathaniel kept his gaze on Mr. Cadell. "If I ever hear you say one more disparaging word about Marielle, I will be back to speak to you about it, and I won't be as generous the next time."

Mr. Cadell brought his head up in a quick nod. "You have my word, my lord," he said shakily.

They didn't speak as they exited the drawing room and ignored the gaping butler as they went out the main door. Once they were situated in the coach, Hugh extended the pistol to Nathaniel. "You should have this," he said. "I can't be trusted with it. I almost shot Mr. Cadell."

Nathaniel smirked. "I think you can be trusted with it, considering it isn't even loaded."

Hugh turned the pistol to examine it. "It's not?" How had he not noticed that?

Haddington chuckled. "That's why you were so calm."

"By the way, you can't go around threatening people," Nathaniel said, the humor stripped from his face.

"Isn't that what you have done?" Hugh asked.

"I ask nicely; there is a difference," Nathaniel replied. "You can't go in weapons drawn or you could make a deadly mistake."

Hugh glanced between Haddington and Nathaniel. "What exactly are you two involved in?"

"It's best that you don't know," Haddington replied. "But we will help you find Marielle."

"But what if you can't?" he asked.

"Don't give up hope," Nathaniel encouraged.

Hugh huffed. "How can I not?" he asked. "We were wrong about Mr. Cadell, and we don't know any more now than we knew at the beginning."

"It is just the beginning of our investigation," Haddington attempted. "You need to give us time."

"What if the person who abducted Marielle has already killed her?" Hugh asked.

"You mustn't think that way," Nathaniel stated. "Whoever abducted Marielle did so for a specific reason. We just have to find out what that reason is."

Hugh's hands balled into tight fists. "When I find the person responsible for her abduction, I will kill him."

Nathaniel gave him a meaningful look. "No, you won't.

Have you ever killed a man?" he asked. "It isn't something you should do lightly. There will be consequences. It will haunt you, dwelling in the back of your mind every moment of every day."

"I know that feeling all too well," he admitted. "I may not have killed them, but I was just as responsible for their deaths as he was."

Nathaniel gave him a puzzled look. "What are you speaking of?"

Hugh didn't answer, not wanting to confess to what he had done. He turned his attention towards the window and hoped that Marielle would be home when they arrived, although he knew that was unlikely. If he could only trade places with her, he would do so in a heartbeat.

Marielle's nightgown and wrapper offered little protection against the cold and dark. The only sliver of light came from a boarded-up window along the far wall. She leaned her head against the tattered papered walls as she sat on the dusty floorboards, as there was no furniture in the room.

To make matters worse, she had a terrible headache from being hit over the head. She had woken up in this room, and it had been hours since she did so. No one had come to explain why this was happening. She was alone. And afraid.

She brought her knees up to her chest and let the tears flow down her cheeks. How was she going to get out of here? She didn't even know where 'here' was. She could be anywhere, and she couldn't do anything about it.

She cried until the tears stopped coming. As her eyes roamed what she could see of the room, they landed on the door, and she couldn't help but wonder what would happen if she banged on the door and cried for help.

Rising, she walked over to the door and tried the handle. Locked, just as it was hours ago. She started pounding on the door.

"Help!" she shouted. "I need out of here!"

She kept screaming until her throat became hoarse and her hand hurt. Turning her back to the door, she slowly lowered herself to a sitting position. What was she going to do? She had to get out of here, but she was trapped.

The door suddenly opened, and she fell back onto the floor.

A man chuckled. "I see that you tired yourself out."

Marielle quickly rose and stepped away from him, back into the room. "What do you want with me?" she demanded.

"I want nothing from you," he replied. "You are just a pawn in a game."

She studied the man for a moment. He was older than her, but not by much, and he had dark hair. His ears stood out from his head, but it didn't distract from his handsome features. He was dressed fashionably, and his hair was brushed forward. He spoke articulately and had the mannerisms of a gentleman.

"Who are you?" she asked.

The man took a step forward, and she took a few steps back. "A man you do not want to trifle with. You are nothing to me, so you'd best remember that."

"Then why haven't you killed me?"

He grinned. "You are feisty, but that doesn't surprise me. Hugh wouldn't have picked a timid young woman."

"You know Hugh?"

"I do, and, more importantly, he knows me," he said. "Well, he doesn't know the true side of me."

"Why are you doing this?"

"Revenge," the man said. "An eye for an eye. And you are the eye, my dear."

Marielle decided to switch tactics. "In a few months, I will have money. Loads of money. I will give you whatever you demand if you let me free."

"I don't care about money," the man spat. "I have been planning this for far too long to let something like money get in the way of it. Hugh took everything from me, so I am going to return the favor."

"What did he take?"

The man clenched his jaw. "You ask too many questions," he said. "Mind your tongue."

Marielle wanted to keep him talking, though. The more she learned, the more it might help in her escape. "Where am I?"

"Somewhere that no one will think to look for you," the man said with a smug smile.

"Am I in the rookeries?"

"You are," the man replied with a small shrug. "This place is lawless, and no one will care if they hear you screaming."

The man turned to speak to a burly man who had just approached him. They spoke in hushed tones, and she was unable to make out what they said.

When the first man turned back around, he had a thick piece of bread in his hand. "Are you hungry?" he asked, holding it up.

As if on cue, Marielle's stomach growled. "I am," she admitted.

The man extended her the bread. "Eat," he ordered. "I have a few questions of my own."

Marielle accepted the bread but stepped back afterward. She had no desire to be close to her captor. His eyes held a hardness to them, and it frightened her.

The man leaned his shoulder against the wall. "Do you and Hugh have an understanding?"

"No."

"Why?" he asked. "You two are clearly smitten with one another."

She shrugged. "He is my guardian."

"Why should that matter to Hugh?" he asked. "He is not one who generally plays by Society's rules."

"I suppose he is worried about my reputation."

The man looked amused. "Ah, so he is taking the noble high ground."

Marielle took a bite, taking a moment to savor the simple offering. The stale bread wasn't what she was accustomed to, but she was grateful for some nourishment.

"Do you regret meeting Hugh now?" the man asked.

"I do not."

"Even though it was his fault you were abducted?"

Marielle shook her head. "I don't blame Hugh for my abduction. I blame you."

"It doesn't matter to me who you blame, but I think your opinion will change once you realize that Hugh is not the man you thought he was."

"I don't believe that will happen."

The man scoffed. "You are blinded by love, my dear," he said. "You don't see Hugh for who he really is."

"And who is that?"

"A murderer."

Marielle's lips parted in disbelief. How could this man believe that Hugh would be capable of such a thing? "Hugh is not a murderer!"

The man's expression turned thunderous. "My betrothed is dead because of him!" he exclaimed.

"Hugh killed her?"

"He may as well have," the man said. "Hugh defended a monster, and because of it, he has blood on his hands." The man pounded his chest. "Helena's blood."

Marielle attempted to piece together what the man said with what she knew of her guardian, but she was at a loss. "Why would Hugh defend a monster?"

"Before Hugh became a gambler, he was a highly sought-after barrister," the man replied. "He won nearly every case that came across his desk."

"Are you saying that Hugh defended this monster in court?"

"I am, and he got the man acquitted of murder."

Marielle brushed the crumbs off her hands. "Wasn't he just doing his job?"

The man's eyes narrowed, and she feared that she had pushed him too far. "This monster should have had a noose around his neck, but instead he walked free, giving him the opportunity to kill more innocent people," the man shared.

"Is he in jail now?"

The man let out a dry chuckle. "He is dead."

"Did you kill him?"

"Yes," the man said. "I did what no one else was able to do."

Marielle knew it was best if she curbed her tongue, but she wanted to expose the man's hypocrisy. By killing that monster, he, himself, was a murderer. But it was apparent that he didn't see it that way.

"The monster got away with murdering innocent people," the man continued, "and was even assigned as an ambassador to Russia shortly thereafter by the king."

"That is most unfortunate."

"Unfortunate? No, it was a travesty! But I ensured that he suffered greatly before I killed him."

"You tortured him?"

The man's lips curled into a cruel smile. "I did, and I took great pleasure in it," he said. "It went on for hours, and he begged for death before the end."

Marielle shrank back. "You are mad. You didn't need to torture him."

"But I did," he said. "I wanted him to know what it felt like every morning when I wake up without Helena in my life."

Marielle could hear the grief in his voice, but she held no compassion for him. Not after what he had done. But she needed to keep her wits about her and pretend to sympathize with him in hopes that he wouldn't harm her, and may possibly release her.

"I'm sorry that you lost Helena, but that is something you and I share," she attempted. "I lost my mother in a tragic accident. Every morning I wake up and hope that I miss her less."

"But Helena's death was not an accident. She was deliberately taken from me," the man said, his voice taking on a sharp edge. "We are not the same, so do not pretend that we are."

"I am only saying—"

He cut her off. "You are just spouting nonsense in a vain attempt to defend Hugh's actions, but you can't. No one can."

"You are faulting Hugh for doing his job."

The man straightened from the wall and strode over to her. "Everyone knew this man was a murderer, but Hugh still took the case. Why?" he asked, putting his hands up. "Because Hugh doesn't care about anyone else but himself."

Marielle tried to pretend she wasn't affected by the man's nearness, but her shaky voice betrayed her. "That is not the Hugh that I know."

"Hugh is a master manipulator," the man said. "The fact that he has you wrapped around his finger proves that."

"That isn't true," Marielle defended. "I have my own mind."

"Just admit that you were deceived."

"I won't."

The man slapped her hard across the face. "I will not have you defend the man who ruined my life!"

Marielle brought her hand up to her cheek. It seemed she had gone too far in her defense of Hugh, but that didn't mean she regretted it.

As the man leaned closer to her, Marielle could feel his hot breath on her cheek and resisted the urge to shudder. "You are alive only because you *may* come in handy," he snarled. "I would not press your luck."

He spun around and left, locking the door behind him.

Marielle tried to ignore the pain in her throbbing cheek as she sat down again on the floor. One thing she did know with certainty, providing her with great comfort, was that Hugh would be searching for her.

She just had to stay alive long enough for him to find her.

Chapter Eighteen

Hugh hadn't slept, hadn't eaten, and was in a foul mood. He was sitting in front of a crackling fire with a drink in his hand. It had been almost two days since Marielle had gone missing, and he was at his wit's end. They were no closer to finding her than when she had first disappeared.

He could hear his mother and brother discussing him where they stood a short distance away. He knew they were concerned about him, but the only thing that mattered to him was finding Marielle.

His mother approached him. "Would you care for something to eat?"

"I'm not hungry," Hugh replied.

"What about putting down your glass and joining me for a cup of tea?"

"No, thank you."

She placed a loving hand on his shoulder. "You must take care of yourself, Hugh."

"I will once Marielle is found."

His mother exchanged a look with Nathanial before saying, "I will ask Mrs. Carpenter to make some of those biscuits that you love so much."

After she departed from the room, Nathaniel came to sit down next to him. "Mother wanted me to speak to you."

"I assumed as much, but I don't need a lecture from you. Not today."

"And I am not going to give you one," Nathaniel said. "I understand why you are so despondent."

"If this is a game…" he started.

Nathaniel put his hand up, stilling his words. "When Dinah was abducted, I nearly went mad trying to find her."

Hugh furrowed his brow. "When was Dinah abducted?"

"It is not something that I discuss, but it was before we had an understanding," Nathaniel revealed.

"How did you find her?"

"That story is for another day."

"You don't intend to tell me," Hugh said, "do you?"

Nathaniel gave him an apologetic smile. "I do not."

Hugh took a sip of his drink. "Perhaps it is time now that we speak to a constable about Marielle's disappearance."

"Constables are useless."

"What other choices do we have?" Hugh asked, his voice rising. "It has been two days, and Marielle is still missing!"

"We will find her."

"How?" Hugh demanded. "By asking these mysterious informants you've spoken of?"

"Someone knows something, I am sure of it," Nathaniel said. "We just haven't asked the right person."

"I wish I had your confidence." Hugh rose from his seat. "This is all my fault."

"No, it isn't."

"Yes, it is," Hugh asserted. "If I hadn't formed an attachment with Marielle, then she would have never been lured into the gardens."

"You don't know that."

"But I do," Hugh said, "and I can't lose her. I won't."

Nathaniel leaned back in his seat. "I know this process can

be tedious, but I assure you that some of the brightest minds are looking for Marielle at this moment."

"And who are these people?" Hugh demanded. "Oh, I forgot! You can't speak about them, but I am just supposed to trust you."

"You are upset."

Hugh slammed his glass down onto the table. "Of course I am upset!" he shouted. "I am doing nothing to find Marielle!"

"Pray tell, what would you do?" Nathaniel asked.

"I don't know, and that's the problem," Hugh said. "I have failed her."

Nathaniel sighed. "You have not failed her."

"It's because of me that she is missing. My past has come back to haunt me." Hugh sat down and buried his head in his hands. "What am I going to do if she is gone forever?"

"You mustn't talk that way," Nathaniel said. "You can't give up hope."

"Hope?" Hugh huffed. "In case you haven't noticed, life hasn't exactly been kind to me."

Simon's voice came from the doorway. "I apologize for calling unannounced," he said. "Is this a bad time?"

"Yes," Hugh said, bringing his head up. "Marielle is missing."

Simon's eyes grew wide. "What do you mean, missing?" he asked.

"It means that she isn't here," Hugh growled.

"Did she run away?" Simon asked as he walked further into the room.

Nathaniel shook his head. "No, she was abducted."

Simon's steps faltered. "Who would abduct Marielle?"

"That's what we're trying to find out," Nathaniel replied. "This is a delicate situation, so I do hope you keep this information to yourself."

"You have my word." Simon turned his attention toward Hugh. "How are you faring?"

"Splendidly," Hugh said dryly. "What do you think?"

Simon moved to sit on an upholstered armchair. "Do you have any leads?"

"No," Hugh replied. "Not one."

"May I ask what happened?" Simon asked.

Hugh didn't feel like rehashing Marielle's abduction, but thankfully Nathanial spoke up. "Someone lured Marielle out into the gardens by pretending to be Hugh," he explained.

"When was this?" Simon asked.

"After everyone had retired for the evening, nearly two nights ago," Nathaniel replied.

"Good heavens," Simon said. "Poor Marielle. I must imagine that she is cold in only her nightgown and wrapper."

Nathaniel bobbed his head. "I do believe you would be right."

Simon's voice held compassion as he asked, "What can I do to help?"

"Nothing at this time," Nathaniel said, rising, "but we shall send word if something changes. Until then, I think it is best to leave Hugh to it."

Simon rose awkwardly. "If that is what he wants."

"It is," Nathaniel responded.

Hugh glanced at his brother curiously but felt no need to contradict him. He did prefer to be alone at the moment.

Simon tipped his head. "Good day, then."

After Simon had left the room, Nathaniel walked over to the door and looked out. He closed the door and returned to his seat. "How well do you know Simon?"

"We've been friends for years."

"How did you meet?"

"We were at Oxford together, and we frequent the same gambling halls," Hugh said. "Why do you ask?"

"Did you notice that his shoes had mud along the sides of them?"

"I failed to notice that."

"Or that he assumed Marielle was dressed in a nightgown and wrapper?" Nathaniel added. "I just find that odd."

"I daresay you are reading too much into it. We did tell him it happened after everyone had gone to bed."

"Perhaps, but I would rather err on the side of caution." Nathaniel walked over to the window and opened it. "Talbot!"

A dark-haired man appeared at the window. "Yes, boss?"

"I want you to keep an eye on Lord Simon Thompson for now," Nathaniel said. "Be discreet. Don't let him know that you're following him."

Talbot gave him a mock salute. "It shall be done."

"Why was Talbot loitering outside of our window?" Hugh asked as Nathaniel closed it.

Nathaniel shrugged one shoulder. "I asked him to keep an eye on you."

"What? Why?"

"Until we know why Marielle was abducted, we wanted to ensure you remained safe," Nathaniel explained.

"That's wholly unnecessary," Hugh said. "I'd rather have Talbot out looking for Marielle."

"Let me worry about that."

Hugh retrieved his glass and walked over to the drink cart. "I think you're wasting your time on Simon. He is harmless."

"Sometimes the people that we least expect are the ones that betray us."

"Why would Simon abduct Marielle?" Hugh asked as he picked up the decanter. "It doesn't make any sense."

"Have you ever had a falling out?"

Hugh poured himself a drink and replied, "No. Simon is more of an 'eat, drink, and be merry' kind of gentleman. We bonded over being useless second sons."

Nathaniel considered his words for a moment. "I may be overreacting, but I feel it is best if I treat everyone like a suspect right now."

Hugh put the decanter down and picked up his glass. "I hate this feeling."

"What feeling?"

"Like something bad is about to happen."

Nathaniel gave him a weak smile. "That is a constant for me."

"You are a perplexing man, brother," Hugh said as he held his glass up, "but I am glad you are here, helping me."

"We will find Marielle. I give you my word."

"It's not that I don't trust you, but I'm afraid."

"Of what?"

"A life without Marielle."

Nathaniel eyed him curiously. "I thought you'd decided to end things with her?"

"I did, but that doesn't mean I wouldn't see her on occasion," Hugh replied. "She may be able to move on without me, but I most assuredly would not move on from her."

"You have to at least try, for her sake."

Hugh took a long drink before lowering his glass to his side. "Could you have moved on if Dinah rejected your offer?"

"That is a different scenario entirely."

"But would you have moved on?" Hugh pressed.

Nathaniel shook his head. "No, I would not have."

Hugh walked over to the door and stopped. "It might be best if I attempt to rest for a little while, but do inform me at once if something turns up."

"I will."

Hugh exited the study and started towards the stairs, ignoring the looks the servants were casting his way. He reminded himself that everything would be right in the world again when Marielle returned home. He was sure of that.

"Wake up!"

Hugh groaned as he opened his eyes and saw his brother standing over him. "You'd better have a good reason for rousing me," he growled. "It's the first time I've slept in two days."

"We have a lead on where Marielle might be," Nathaniel said.

Hugh shot up in bed. "Where is she?"

"I said 'might'." Nathaniel took a step back. "Talbot trailed Lord Simon to a tavern in the rookeries, and we are going to investigate. Care to join us?"

Placing his feet over the side of the bed, Hugh replied, "It might be a fool's errand. I still do not believe Simon has anything to do with Marielle's disappearance."

"We'll see." Nathaniel perused his brother's wrinkled clothing. "Would you care to change before we depart?"

Hugh rose. "There's no need."

"Do you often sleep in your clothing?"

"I was too exhausted to change out of them."

They didn't speak as they headed towards the entry hall, where they found Haddington waiting.

"What are you doing here?" Hugh asked.

Haddington grinned. "You didn't think you would go into the rookeries without me, did you?" he asked. "After all, who would keep Hawthorne safe?"

"I can take care of myself," Nathaniel said, shooting Haddington an amused look as he walked over to the door. "The coach is waiting out front."

They exited the townhouse and entered the coach.

"I should warn you that the rookeries are not for the faint of heart," Haddington told Hugh once they were situated.

"I have no doubt, but I would go anywhere if it meant finding Marielle," Hugh replied.

Nathaniel shifted in his seat to face him. "We were able to

determine that this tavern Lord Simon visited is owned by a Mr. Stevens."

"I am not acquainted with Mr. Stevens," Hugh said.

"That is not a surprise, considering he is the illegitimate son of Lord Haverty," Nathaniel shared.

Hugh lifted his brow. "Simon's father?" he asked. "That means Simon and Mr. Stevens are brothers."

"That's right, but why would Lord Simon sully his hands by going into the rookeries?" Nathaniel asked.

"That doesn't mean he has anything to do with Marielle's disappearance," Hugh pressed. "Perhaps he was just visiting his brother."

"Possibly, but a patron of the tavern reported hearing a woman screaming for help from one of the upstairs rooms," Nathaniel shared.

"Why didn't he assist her?" Hugh asked.

"It's different in the rookeries," Haddington interjected. "Everyone needs help, but no one is willing to lend a hand. It's usually safer to mind one's own business."

"Even when a woman is calling for help?" Hugh asked in disbelief.

"I never said it was right, but it is how things are done in the rookeries," Haddington said.

"That is a sad way to live," Hugh remarked.

"It is the only way they know how to survive," Haddington said. "We don't know for certain that Marielle is being held at the tavern, but we do not believe in coincidences."

Nathaniel nodded. "No, we don't."

"This doesn't make any sense," Hugh said, bringing his hand to his head. "Assuming Marielle is being held at the tavern, which is a big 'if', why would Simon abduct her?"

"We were hoping you could tell us," Nathaniel said.

"I haven't the faintest idea," Hugh admitted.

Nathaniel exchanged a look with Haddington. "Regardless, you will wait outside while we go into the tavern. You can look in through the windows."

"I'd like to go inside with you," Hugh said.

"You will only get in the way," Nathaniel said, shaking his head.

"If there is even a chance that Marielle is there, I want to be there when she is found," Hugh asserted.

Nathaniel considered him for a moment before he conceded. "All right, but you must promise not to get yourself killed." He reached under the bench and pulled out a metal container. He opened it and retrieved a pistol. "Be careful with this, it's loaded this time."

Hugh accepted the pistol and let his hand adjust to the weight of it. "I am not completely incompetent when it comes to shooting."

"I don't doubt that, but it is different when your shot could mean the difference between life or death," Nathaniel remarked.

Hugh tucked the pistol into the waistband of his trousers. "Do you often find yourself in those situations?"

"More than I care to admit," Nathaniel replied.

The coach stopped and Nathaniel opened the door and stepped out, followed quickly by Haddington. Hugh was the last to exit.

"Where is the tavern?" Hugh asked as his eyes roamed over the darkened buildings.

"A few blocks away," Nathaniel revealed.

"Then why did we stop here?" Hugh asked.

"We didn't want to alert them to our coming," Haddington smirked. "We prefer to surprise them."

Two men emerged from the shadows and approached them. Hugh eyed them with trepidation until he recognized Talbot.

Nathaniel put his hand up in greeting. "What did you discover?"

"There is a woman in the tavern, and no one attempted to smuggle her out," Talbot replied.

"How do you know that for certain?" Haddington asked.

The other man spoke up. "We went into the mangy hall and had ourselves a few drinks," he revealed. "I gave the serving wench a few coins for some information, and she confirmed that a young woman is being held in one of the upstairs rooms."

"You did well," Nathaniel said.

Talbot smiled broadly. "That is some high praise coming from you," he said. "Isn't it, Worsley?"

"It is," Worsley responded, matching his partner's smile. "I feel like all of my hard work has been vindicated."

Haddington shifted his gaze to Nathaniel and asked, "Do you think four of us can take on a whole tavern of men?"

"I do, but I thought it was best to call upon someone else to help us," Nathaniel said.

Haddington visibly tensed. "Do you think that's wise?"

"I do," Nathaniel replied. "I have no doubt that we will need her help."

"Her?" Hugh questioned.

"Whatever you see or hear this evening, you must never speak of it again," Nathaniel commanded. "Otherwise, there could be dire consequences."

The way his brother spoke, Hugh knew he was in earnest. "I understand."

"Good," Nathaniel said, glancing up at the full moon. "Does anyone have any questions before we proceed?"

Worsley raised his hand.

"Yes, Worsley?" Nathanial sighed.

"Do we have a plan?"

Nathaniel shook his head. "Just try not to get yourself killed."

"I have no intention of dying this evening, especially since our new business venture is starting to take off," Worsley said.

Talbot puffed out his chest proudly. "We turned a profit today."

"What are you selling now?" Haddington asked.

"You will have to come by and see," Talbot said, "but it is a steal of a deal."

Hugh shifted in his stance, growing more impatient by the moment. "Would you mind discussing this later? I would prefer to get on with saving Marielle."

"I agree," Nathaniel said, then gave Hugh a warning look. "Stay behind us, and do not do anything stupid."

They headed down the narrow pavement, and Hugh noticed that they were garnering some attention from a few men standing in the alleyways. He glanced at his brother but saw that he was giving them no heed.

After a few blocks, Nathaniel stopped in front of a tavern with a crooked sign above the door. He pointed towards the alley, and Worley and Talbot headed into it without saying a word.

Hugh and Haddington followed Nathaniel inside. About a dozen men were sitting around tables with drinks in their hands. Two serving wenches skirted the tables as they brought out new tankards. One of the women was older with red hair, and her dress did little to hide her curves. The other woman was younger, tall, thin, and had brown hair. Hugh blinked as he realized it was Miss Ashmore. Why in the blazes was Miss Ashmore a serving wench in the rookeries?

She met his gaze and put a finger to her lips.

Hugh turned his attention towards Nathaniel, wondering if he'd seen her, but his brother's alert eyes were busy roaming the room.

The men in the tavern barely spared them a glance as they continued drinking and chatting loudly.

Nathaniel pointed towards the stairs in the back. "That's where we should start," he said.

As they approached the stairs, two burly men stood from a

table nearby and stepped in front of the stairs, blocking their path.

"Are ye lost?" one of the men asked.

Nathaniel stopped in front of the men. "We need to get upstairs."

"I'm afraid it isn't allowed," the man said, crossing his strong arms over his chest.

"I don't suppose you'd let us just walk on by, would you?" Nathaniel asked.

The man leaned closer to him. "Are ye deaf, mister?" he asked.

"I can hear perfectly well," Nathaniel said. "But I am wondering how two of you will stop us from going up there."

The other man chuckled. "I could take all three of you in one breath."

"You seem pretty sure of yourself," Nathaniel said as he removed his jacket and tossed it onto one of the tables. "I would be more concerned about whether you will be able to make it out of here alive when I am done with you."

"Go away," the first man said. "I don't want to have to clean blood off the floor. It gets messy."

"I am going to count to three," Nathaniel said, rolling up the sleeves of his white shirt. "One... two..."

Instead of saying three, Nathaniel punched one of the men squarely in the jaw, causing him to stagger back.

"You will pay for that," the man growled as he massaged his jaw. He lowered his shoulder and ran into Nathaniel's stomach.

Hugh stood back as Nathaniel and Haddington fought with the two men. He had never seen his brother fight before, but he had to admit that he was impressed. Nathaniel was delivering well-timed blows and was quick on his feet. As the fight continued, Miss Ashmore slipped past them and headed up the stairs.

The men in the tavern had risen from their seats and were

all watching the fighting with great amusement. The crowd cheered when someone delivered a good blow on their opponent, regardless of which fighter it was.

Hugh wasn't entirely sure what he should be doing at this moment. He wanted to help, but he hadn't been in a fight since his days at Eton with Stephen Wymond.

Nathaniel was hit squarely on the jaw, and he fell back into his brother. Hugh caught him and asked, "Why not just shoot him?"

"Patience, brother. This is merely a distraction," Nathaniel said between heavy breaths before he jumped back into the fight.

Hugh stared at his brother in amazement. This was all a distraction? Could they not think of something other than fisticuffs for that?

Someone fired a gun, and everyone froze. A tall, portly man held a smoking pistol in the air. "Get out!" he ordered Nathaniel and Haddington.

Nathaniel inhaled deeply in an attempt to catch his breath. "I'm afraid not," he said. "You have something that I want."

The portly man took a step towards him. "And what is that?"

"There is a rumor that you have a young woman locked away upstairs, and I have come to collect her," Nathaniel replied.

"Oh, is that so?" the man sneered.

A familiar voice came from behind Hugh. "They have come to die."

Hugh turned around and saw Simon pointing a pistol at him.

"What is the meaning of this, Simon?" Hugh asked.

"Leave now or die!" Simon called over his shoulder to the tavern patrons. "It doesn't matter much to me."

In response, the majority of the men left their tankards on

the tables and hurried out the door, followed by the serving wench. The two remaining men rose from their seats and crossed their arms over their wide chests.

Simon's eyes were cold when he turned back to meet Hugh's gaze. "Now, where were we?"

Chapter Nineteen

Marielle's head dropped forward, jerking her awake. She looked around and felt a stab of disappointment. She was still trapped in the same room, and she had no way of attempting to get out of this situation.

What if Hugh never found her? Would the last faces she saw be of her captors? She hoped not.

She had to see Hugh again, even if it was just one last time. He intended to leave her to go to Brookhaven, but she had to confess how she felt about him. If she didn't, then she would regret it. She loved him, and always would.

She could hear men's voices below her, and she let out a sigh. She had tried for hours to get someone's attention by banging on the door and calling for help, but no one had come to her aid. Someone had to have heard her, since she could hear them. Why wouldn't they help her?

Marielle watched as the door handle turned slowly and the door was pushed open, revealing Evie in peasant clothing. Marielle quickly stood. "What are you doing here?" she whispered.

Evie put her finger to her lips and closed the door before approaching Marielle. "Are you hurt?" she asked.

"No, I'm not," Marielle said.

"That's good," Evie replied, her eyes turning toward the window. "Hm. We won't be able to pry those boards off in time."

"In time for what?"

Evie didn't answer her question as she met her gaze. "We are going to have to go out the back door."

"I will do whatever it takes if it means I get to leave this place."

Evie retrieved a muff pistol from the folds of her gown. "Follow me and stay close," she said as she opened the door.

Marielle followed Evie into the hall, and it was eerily quiet —the men's voices had stopped. They moved with quick steps to the stairs and Evie stopped short at the top. "Stay here," she whispered.

A single man's voice drifted up the stairs, but Marielle couldn't make out what he said. Evie remained close to the wall as she moved to peer down to the first level. She mumbled something under her breath before turning back.

"Change of plans," Evie said. "I need you to be brave and do exactly as I say."

"I can do that."

"Good, because your life depends on it," Evie responded. "We are going to find a window and climb out of it."

Marielle shook her head. "I can't climb out of a window."

"Then our only other option is going downstairs where there are men with guns," Evie said. "Which would you prefer?"

"I suppose, given those two options, I can climb out of a window."

Evie walked over to a door and carefully opened it. She disappeared into the room but returned a moment later. "This window isn't boarded shut. We can go out this way," she said before returning to the room.

Marielle followed her, but froze when she stepped on a

loose floorboard, causing a loud creak. She prayed that no one else had heard it.

"Who's there?" a voice shouted from below.

Marielle's eyes darted towards the door where Evie was, but she didn't see any sign of her. Boots pounded up the stairs; someone was coming for her.

A burly man reached the top of the stairs, and his lips curled into a cruel smile. "Hello, there," he said. "How did you get out of your room?"

As he drew closer, Marielle stepped back. She tripped on the hem of her wrapper and stumbled to the floor. The man loomed over her, and she shrank back in fear. He leaned down to grab her, but fell to the side, unconscious.

Marielle stared up at Evie, who was standing where the man had been with her fist around the barrel of her pistol.

Evie rushed towards her and crouched down. "All right, I've formulated a new plan."

"Another one?"

"Yes, but this one will actually work."

Marielle furrowed her brow. "The other one wouldn't have worked?"

"No, the window was nailed shut. Listen quickly," Evie replied. "In a few moments, someone is going to come looking for this man," she gestured to the man on the floor, "and you are going to go with him."

"You truly want me to go with him?"

"I do, but you need not fear," Evie said.

"Paul!" someone downstairs called.

Evie gave her an encouraging smile. "It will be all right, I promise. I won't let them hurt you," she said before she stepped back into the room and closed the door.

Heavy steps could be heard coming up the stairs before a man appeared. He glanced between Marielle and the unconscious Paul in confusion. "How in the blazes did you do that?"

He didn't wait for her response before approaching and

grabbing her arm. "You are coming with me," he ordered as he yanked her to a standing position.

Their view of the floor below gradually improved as they descended the stairs. She started in surprise when she saw Hugh, and quickly became concerned when she saw that her captor was pointing a pistol at him.

"Wonderful timing," her captor said. "You've come to watch Hugh die."

The man holding her arm released it when they stepped down from the last step, and Marielle ran into Hugh's arms. She clung to him for a few moments before he leaned back and searched her face.

"Are you all right?" he asked.

"I am," she assured him.

"I'm so happy we found you."

"As am I."

Hugh released her, and she glanced over his shoulder at Nathaniel and another man in a purple jacket. They both acknowledged her with a tip of their heads.

Her captor's voice drew her attention. "Which one of you should I kill first?" he asked, the pistol wavering in his hand.

Hugh moved to stand in front of her. "Marielle has done nothing wrong. You need to let her go, Simon."

Simon's eyes narrowed. "Helena was an innocent, too, but that didn't matter to you, now did it?"

"Who is Helena?" Hugh asked.

"Lady Helena Kimball!" Simon shouted, jabbing forward with the pistol. "Or do you not know the names of the people whose deaths you were responsible for?"

"I know all of their names," Hugh asserted, clenching his jaw.

"Helena was my betrothed, and it was because of you that she died," Simon said. "I have been plotting my revenge for years, just waiting for the right opportunity to make you suffer like I have suffered."

Hugh's face was crestfallen. "I had no idea you had an understanding with Lady Helena."

"We were about to post the banns when she was murdered by her father," Simon said, then shifted his gaze to Marielle. "Even though Lord Wretton had murdered his mistress in cold blood, he was still acquitted from murder by the jury of his peers. And do you know who his barrister was?"

Marielle glanced at Hugh but said nothing.

"Hugh represented a murderer and had no qualms about it," Simon growled. "What kind of man does that make him?"

"My father came to me and asked me to take the case," Hugh interjected. "It's not something I am proud of, but every man deserves a fair trial."

"And you gave it to him," Simon scoffed. "After he was acquitted, it wasn't long before he murdered his wife and daughter, taking every ounce of joy that I possessed."

"There is not a day that goes by that I don't regret taking that case," Hugh responded, "but no jury would have convicted Lord Wretton because he claimed privilege of the peerage. Since it was his first offense, they acquitted him."

"And the second time?" Simon demanded.

"I had nothing to do with him being assigned as an ambassador to Russia," Hugh said.

"That's true, but I made sure that Lord Wretton got what he deserved," Simon shared.

"What did you do?" Hugh asked.

Simon pasted on a wicked grin. "I made sure his death was as painful as possible and ensured that his body will never be found."

"I don't even know you anymore," Hugh remarked.

"You never did," Simon responded. "I bided my time, waiting for the perfect opportunity to enact revenge. I knew it had finally arrived when you first spoke of Marielle after meeting her. It was evident you were smitten."

"It doesn't have to end this way," Hugh attempted. "We can both walk out of here with our lives."

"The only way this will end is with your death, but I think I will kill Marielle first," Simon said. "Step aside."

Hugh remained rooted in place as Marielle clutched the back of his jacket, shielding her. "No."

Nathaniel cleared his throat, drawing Simon's attention. "I don't mean to bother you while you are threatening my brother—which is very convincing, by the way—but what is your plan, exactly?"

Simon looked peeved. "I plan to kill you; all of you."

"But there are only five of you," Nathaniel pointed out. "That won't be enough to kill us."

"We shall see then, won't we?" Simon asked as he tightened his hold on his pistol. "It is a shame that you will have to die alongside your brother."

Nathaniel looked amused. "I am not going to die here today, but I can't say the same about you," he said. "I can promise you that if you try to pull that trigger, you will die before you do so."

"How are you going to stop me?" Simon asked.

"I'm not going to, but they are," Nathaniel replied as he pointed towards a back room.

When no one emerged, Simon turned to Nathaniel with a smug expression. "It would appear that no one is coming to help you."

The door slammed open and a dark-haired man yelled, "Wait!" He stepped out with a pistol in his hand. "We were hoping for more of a dramatic introduction."

Another man followed him out of the room, also armed. "It's true," he said. "I felt that Hawthorne could have done much better."

"Who are you?" Simon growled.

"Friends of Hawthorne's," one of the men said. "I

wouldn't say that we were his best friends, but we could make a case for that."

Nathanial put his hands up to stop their prattle. "It would appear that you are now outnumbered and outgunned, Simon," he said. "I would put the pistol down while you still can."

Simon's face hardened as he shifted his gaze towards Hugh. "You always have been lucky, but your luck has run out," he growled as he pointed the pistol at Hugh's chest. "You will not win; not this time."

Hugh reached behind him and grabbed Marielle's hand.

Multiple gunshots echoed throughout the hall, and Simon immediately collapsed to the floor. One of the men behind him clasped his arm, and another two clutched at their legs. The final man had dropped his weapon and was now cowering behind a table.

Hugh dropped Marielle's hand and ran the short distance to Simon, dropping down next to him as Nathaniel kicked the pistol away.

"Simon?"

When Simon didn't respond, Hugh hung his head and sighed. "It's my fault that he is dead."

Marielle walked over and crouched down next to him, keeping her eyes on Hugh rather than the body on the floor.

"No, Hugh, this was not your fault," she said. "Simon was mad."

"But I drove him to it," Hugh responded.

"There will be time to grieve later," Nathaniel said, "but it would be best if you escorted Marielle home while we sort out this mess."

Hugh rose slowly, unable to tear his gaze away from Simon's body.

"Why didn't I see this coming?"

"No one could have seen this coming," Nathaniel replied

as he placed a hand on his shoulder. "Simon let his demons get the best of him, and it cost him his life."

Hugh held his hand out to Marielle and assisted her in rising. He didn't release her hand, instead tucking it into the crook of his arm.

"Let's get you home."

Hugh sat in the darkened coach as his eyes roamed over Marielle. Her hair was loose and looked terribly disheveled, her wrapper was filthy, and she was coated in layers of dirt and grime. But to him, she had never looked more beautiful.

Marielle met his gaze. "Why are you smiling?"

"Because you are here with me."

She returned his smile. "Thank you for rescuing me."

"I can't take all the credit for that," he said. "I did have some help."

"Thank heavens for that."

Hugh leaned forward in his seat and reached for her hand. "Did Simon hurt you?"

"Not really," she said. "He mostly left me alone in that room."

"I'm sorry that it took so long to find you."

"I'm just glad that you did."

Hugh's eyes dropped to their intertwined hands. "I would imagine that you think less of me now that you know the role that I played in the death of Lord Wretton's wife and daughter."

"My opinion of you has not changed, Hugh."

His eyes shot up to meet hers. "How can you say that?" he asked. "I defended a murderer, and because of me, he was able to kill again."

"You did your job and nothing more. You couldn't have known that Lord Wretton would kill again."

His jaw tightened. "I should have."

"No one can see the future," Marielle said. "You can only do your best with the information in front of you."

"After Lord Wretton killed his wife and daughter, I spiraled out of control," Hugh shared. "That's why I stopped working as a barrister. I lost faith in laws and justice, and I lost faith in myself."

"You have punished yourself long enough for something that you had no control over," Marielle said, her eyes brimming with compassion. "It is time to forgive yourself."

"I don't think I can."

"It won't be easy, but it will be worth it," Marielle replied. "Just living isn't enough, though. One must have a true purpose in their life."

Hugh allowed himself to relax, feeling lighter than he had in a long time. "When have you gotten so wise?"

"I have always been wise, but you have only just noticed it," she joked.

"I suppose so," Hugh said.

Marielle offered him a weak smile, but it quickly turned downward. "I'm sorry about Simon."

"He did some terrible things, but I didn't want him dead," he said.

"I know that."

"I just can't believe I never saw the hatred that he had for me," Hugh remarked. "We saw each other so often. How did I miss that?"

"You mustn't be so hard on yourself. You were fighting your own battles."

"But how could I have been so blind?"

Marielle tightened her hold on their hands. "Sometimes things are not so obvious," she said. "Simon hid a part of himself from you."

"A big part of himself," Hugh sighed. "But I understand why he did what he did."

"You do?"

Hugh held her gaze for a moment before saying, "If I lost you, I don't think I could go on with my life."

"Perhaps, but I do not see you turning into a murderous lunatic."

He chuckled. "That's true."

They arrived at the townhouse and went inside. Once Balfour had shut the door, he leaned close to Hugh and whispered, "A Mr. Stephen Wymond is in your study."

Hugh reared back. "Are you sure?"

Balfour nodded solemnly.

Hugh had just turned back to Marielle when a man's voice came from down the hall. "Marielle!"

Hugh watched as shock, then joyful surprise, registered on her face. "Stephen!" she shouted as she ran into his awaiting arms.

After a long embrace, Marielle leaned back. "How are you here?"

"I'm sorry it took me so long to get back to you," Stephen replied.

"It doesn't matter, because you are here now," she said with a bright smile.

Stephen perused her clothing with disapproval. "Why does it appear as though you have been to hell and back?"

"I was abducted, and Hugh rescued me," Marielle shared.

Stephen's eyes snapped towards Hugh, and he did not look pleased to see him. "It would appear that Lord Hugh has some explaining to do."

Hugh gestured towards the drawing room. "It might be best if we discuss this in private," he said.

Stephen's eyes softened when they landed back on his sister. "I concur," he stated as he escorted Marielle into the drawing room.

Before he followed them inside, Hugh turned to Balfour. "Miss Wymond requires some refreshment."

"Right away, my lord," the butler responded.

Hugh stepped into the drawing room, anxious about the forthcoming conversation. It was remarkable that Stephen was here—alive—but it was evident that the animosity they had for one another in their youth was still there.

Marielle was sitting next to Stephen on the settee, and her smile had not dimmed at all. Hugh knew precisely how she felt about having her brother back from the dead. It didn't surprise him; she'd made it clear that she had always adored him.

Hugh sat across from them and held his hands out wide. "Where to begin?"

In a voice that could only be described as a growl, Stephen said, "You can start with how in the blazes you became Marielle's guardian."

"That is easy to explain," Hugh said. "I won her in a card game."

Stephen's eyes narrowed. "A card game?"

"Yes, and she has been here ever since," Hugh replied.

"It has been wonderful living here," Marielle interjected. "Everyone has been so kind to me, and they are even throwing me a ball tomorrow."

"Are you sure you are up for that?" Hugh asked.

"I wouldn't dare disappoint your mother. She put a lot of effort into preparations," Marielle said.

Stephen's eyes darted towards Hugh. "How kind have they been to you?" he asked in a critical tone.

Marielle patted her brother's arm. "Hugh has only ever been a perfect gentleman."

With a huff, Stephen said, "I somehow do not believe that to be true, considering you two rode in a coach—alone. Or am I incorrect in that assumption?"

"Well, we did ride in the coach alone, but that was only

because Hugh wanted to return me home at once," Marielle replied.

Stephen gave him a disapproving look. "Pray tell, how did you allow Marielle to be abducted from right under your nose?"

Marielle shifted in her seat to face her brother.

"It was entirely my fault," she said. "I thought Hugh had written me a note to meet him in the gardens, but it turns out that it was a ruse to get me outside."

"Why would you meet Hugh in the gardens, especially in your wrapper?" Stephen demanded. "Do you not understand the repercussions if you had been caught?"

"I did, but, uh…" she hesitated, "I wanted to say goodbye."

"Where is he going?" Stephen's eyes narrowed. "Or were you going somewhere?"

Marielle's eyes shot towards Hugh. "He is retiring to his Brookhaven estate after my ball."

"But he is your guardian."

"I was going to leave her in my mother's care for the rest of the Season," Hugh interjected.

"That's the first sensible thing I've heard out of your mouth," Stephen grumbled, "although my sister should never have been your ward in the first place."

"Hugh saved me from Mr. Cadell," Marielle asserted. "He was terrible to me, and I suspected he intended to marry me once I received my inheritance."

"Was Mr. Cadell the one that abducted you?" Stephen asked.

Marielle shook her head. "No, it was Simon."

"Who is Simon?"

"Lord Simon Thompson," Hugh clarified.

Stephen's brow shot up. "Why would Lord Simon abduct my sister?"

"Because he was seeking revenge for the death of his betrothed, Lady Helena, and her mother," Marielle explained.

"What did Hugh have to do with their deaths?" Stephen asked.

Hugh met Stephen's gaze. "I represented Lord Wretton in court, where he was acquitted from the murder of his mistress," he said. "Unfortunately, Lord Wretton then killed his wife and daughter, who was Lord Simon's betrothed."

Stephen cast him a furious look. "So, it was entirely your fault that my sister was abducted by a madman."

"It was," Hugh said, seeing no reason to deny it. It was the truth.

Marielle spoke up. "But he saved me, Stephen," she stated. "He risked his life for me."

"That is no less than I would expect of any man, but it's still his fault that you were in danger," Stephen responded.

A maid stepped into the room with a tray and placed it on the table in front of Marielle. They all soon had steaming cups of tea in their hands.

Stephen glanced down at his tea before he placed it aside. "We should go," he said, rising.

"Go? Where?" Marielle asked, a line between her brow appearing.

"I have arranged for lodging until we can depart for Brightlingsea," Stephen informed her.

Panic swelled in Hugh's chest. He didn't want Marielle to leave, but it wasn't his place to say so, not anymore. Still, he couldn't just sit back and let her walk out of his life without doing anything.

"What about the ball?" Hugh asked.

Marielle turned her attention towards her brother. "Hugh is right. We can't leave before my ball."

"There will be other balls," Stephen replied, unconcerned. "It is more important to get you home, where I can keep you safe."

Hugh knew that comment was a jab at him, but he felt no need to argue with Stephen. After all, the man wasn't wrong. He had done a poor job of keeping Marielle safe.

Marielle didn't move to stand. "I am going to my ball, Stephen." Her voice was firm, unyielding.

Stephen visibly tensed. "You will do what I say, Marielle."

"I am not some sailor on your ship," Marielle said. "I will do what you say, but only if I think you aren't being a stubborn jackanapes."

Hugh hid his smile behind his teacup. It certainly appeared that Marielle could hold her own against her brother, and he found it rather amusing.

Stephen looked heavenward. "Fine," he conceded. "You can go to the ball, but we will depart the following morning."

Marielle's eyes drooped. "Do we have to leave Town so soon?"

"I'm afraid so," Stephen replied. "I have a shipyard that I need to oversee."

Marielle snuck a glance at Hugh, and he could see questions in her eyes. "I understand," she murmured before she leaned forward and set her teacup down.

Stephen held his hand out to assist her in rising. "It will do you some good to be back in the countryside, with fresh air. London is terribly filthy."

Hugh rose as he tried to think of some reason to delay Marielle's departure. He wasn't quite ready to say goodbye yet. "You will need to see to having your trunks packed," he attempted. It was his experience with his mother that packing women's trunks took an exorbitant amount of time.

"There is no need," Stephen replied. "I already saw to that while I was waiting for hours for you to return."

"Oh, that was thoughtful of you," Marielle muttered.

Hugh put his teacup onto the table and attempted to buy more time with Marielle. "It is very late. You are welcome to reside here for the evening," he offered.

Stephen scoffed. "I think not." He gestured towards the door. "Shall we, Marielle?"

Marielle turned towards Hugh, blinking back tears. She was trying to be brave, for him. "Thank you, Hugh. For everything."

Hugh's heart cracked, and he reached for her hand and brought it up to his lips. "This is not goodbye. I shall see you tomorrow."

Marielle didn't attempt to move, so he continued to hold her hand. He knew it wasn't proper, but nothing about the last few days had been proper.

Stephen cleared his throat, and his sister withdrew her hand.

Hugh watched as Stephen led Marielle out the door, and he knew that she had taken his heart with her.

Chapter Twenty

As the coach jerked forward, Marielle stared at her brother in amazement. His face was thinner than she would like, but she marveled at how much he resembled their father at this age. "I still can't believe you are here!" she gushed. "How is this even possible? You were supposed to be dead."

Stephen smiled. "It turns out that I am rather hard to kill."

"That isn't funny, brother," Marielle said. "Where have you been all this time?"

All the humor disappeared from Stephen's face. "I assure you that it was no small feat to return home to you, but failure was not an option for me," he said.

"Did you know that Father died?"

He nodded. "I received word right before my ship was attacked," he said. "It sustained heavy damage from a French frigate and went down."

"How did you survive?"

"My crew fought valiantly when we were boarded, but very few of us survived the onslaught. The ones that did were taken by the French as prisoners of war," Stephen shared.

"The conditions were horrid, the food was sparse, and we were beaten every day."

"How awful!" Marielle gasped.

"Knowing you were alone and unprotected was the only thing that kept me going," Stephen said. "What scared me the most was that I had no idea what had become of you."

"You should have been more worried about yourself. You look so thin," she said.

"I assure you that I won't have an issue gaining the weight back once I've had a few good meals."

"How did you become free of the French?"

"Eventually, the few of us that were still alive were traded in a prisoner exchange, and we boarded a ship home. The moment we arrived on English soil, I traveled home to find you, but you weren't there."

"How did you discover where I had gone?"

"From Mr. Britt," Stephen replied. "He informed me that our distant cousin, Mr. Cadell, had been your guardian until Lord Hugh took you in. I was distraught and came straight-away to retrieve you."

"Mr. Cadell was awful to me. I was profoundly grateful that Hugh won me in that card game," Marielle said. "His family has been very kind to me."

Stephen's jaw tightened. "You appeared rather close to Hugh."

"I am. He is my friend." She tripped over that last word. Hugh meant so much more to her than just a friend.

"Hugh can't be trusted."

"I disagree. He has proven himself to be extremely trustworthy."

Stephen looked displeased. "You do not know him as well as I do. He was a terrible bully at Eton and has always been very pompous."

"People can change, brother."

"Not that much," Stephen said. "He made my life unbearable when I was away. We could hardly be in the same room without fighting."

"Why did you not get along?"

"I don't rightly know, but we took an immediate dislike to one another," Stephen shared. "At one point, the headmaster made us share a room to force us to resolve our differences."

"Did it work?"

Stephen shook his head. "Heavens, no," he said. "Hugh threw all of my personal belongings out the window, and they were soaked from the heavy rain."

"That is terrible of Hugh, but I know you," Marielle said. "How did you retaliate?

"I set his clothes on fire."

Marielle's eyes grew wide. "How could you do such a thing?"

"I didn't start the fight, but I was going to end it."

"And did it work?"

"Sadly, our feud continued until I left for the Royal Naval Academy," Stephen replied.

"It sounds as if you were both culpable in your actions."

"It matters not," Stephen said as he shifted in his seat. "It would be in your best interest to avoid Hugh from here on out."

"Why do you say that?"

"Hugh is a gambler and doesn't have a pristine reputation amongst the *ton*."

Marielle lifted her brow. "When did you ascertain this information?"

"Mr. Britt informed me of it," he said. "He also informed me that Hugh insisted that you be able to run the shipyard in my absence."

"That's true," she responded. "Do you not approve?"

"I never said that, but I will admit that my respect for Hugh has gone up slightly. I am pleased that you had an advocate in him."

"Hugh and I didn't always see eye to eye, but I like to believe that we grew to respect one another."

Stephen huffed. "It appears as if you grew to more than just respect one another."

"That may be true, but nothing untoward happened," she lied as the memory of Hugh kissing her in the library came to her mind.

"I should say not, since he was your guardian."

Marielle pressed her lips together, then said, "I know you have a poor opinion of Hugh, but he saved me, on more than one occasion."

"I will be eternally grateful for that, but Hugh is your past. He is not your future."

"Hugh has become such an important part of my life," she remarked as she glanced at the opened window. "I don't think I am ready to say goodbye."

"It is for the best."

"For whom?"

Stephen gave her a knowing look. "You don't want to get the gossips' tongues wagging any more than you already have."

"I can't live my life around what the gossipmongers might whisper about."

"Our parents would have wanted you to marry an honorable man and live a respectable life away from the hustle and bustle of London," Stephen said. "They would have wanted you to remain in Brightlingsea. That is where you belong."

"I don't know where I belong anymore," she murmured.

"Yes, you do. You have just forgotten from whence you came," Stephen said. "Mr. Britt told me that you had some promising ideas for the shipyard. Perhaps we could run it together?"

Marielle perked up. "Do you truly mean that?"

Stephen bobbed his head. "I do," he replied. "I would be

a fool not to accept your help, assuming that it is what you would like to do."

"When I was told you were dead, I thought it would be best if I focused on running the shipyard rather than finding a suitor."

"Now you don't have to worry about that," Stephen said. "I have no doubt that you will charm every gentleman that you cross, and hopefully one of them will interest you enough to become your suitor."

Marielle frowned. "It almost sounds as if you are pressuring me to wed."

"That was not my intention, but I do think you should keep your options open," Stephen remarked. "I do not want you to focus solely on the shipyard. I want you to be happy."

"I am happy, now that you are home," Marielle said.

Stephen leaned forward and tucked her hair behind her ears. "You look terrible, dear sister."

"You would, too, if you were abducted by a madman who was intent on seeing you dead," she said with a smile.

"How did you manage to escape?"

Marielle opened her mouth, but then closed it. She wasn't quite sure how much she should tell him. Stephen had always been overprotective of her, and she feared that he would resent Hugh even more if he ever learned the full truth of the matter. Furthermore, she thought it was important that she left out others' involvement, specifically Evie's.

"Marielle?" Stephen asked as she was still deciding what to say. "Is everything all right?"

"It is," she replied. "I just don't feel like reliving it at the moment."

"That's understandable." Stephen's eyes grew guarded. "I try every day to block out the memories of the French prison."

"I am sorry that you were forced to endure that."

"It's better than the alternative." His words were soft, but the pain was there, nonetheless. "I lost a lot of good men, and I still need to speak to their families."

"Would you care for me to go with you?"

Stephen shook his head. "There are some things that I have to do alone."

The coach hit a rut in the road and dipped to the side. Marielle put her hand on the side of the coach to steady herself.

"I should warn you that our country house is not in the best condition," Stephen said. "Mr. Cadell dismissed all of the household staff, but Mr. Britt is trying to round them up again. Unfortunately, many of them have sought other employment."

"I do not fault them for that."

"Neither do I," Stephen said. "With any luck, we will have a functioning staff soon enough. It might be rough for the first little while, though."

"I can manage."

Stephen looked amused. "This is coming from the girl who insisted that she had to take a warm bath every morning."

"I was forced to grow up some and do without after Father died," she revealed. "And when I received word that you had died, as well, I…" her voice cracked, "I thought my life was over."

Stephen moved to sit next to her on the bench and wrapped his arms around her. "I am here, and I promise that I will never leave you again."

Tears came to Marielle's eyes. "I miss Father and Mother every day."

"That is to be expected. I miss them, too," Stephen said. "But you must remember that grieving someone is proof that that love is still there. You will always grieve for them, in your own way, because you will always love them."

Marielle bit her lower lip before she admitted, "Until

recently, I blamed myself for Mother's death because I encouraged her to jump the hedge."

"That was not your fault," Stephen asserted as he leaned back far enough to meet her gaze. "Mother jumped that hedge all the time. It was just an accident. A terrible accident."

"That's what Hugh told me."

"And you believed him?"

She nodded. "I did," she replied. "I trust him, and he took the time to listen. That made all the difference."

Stephen pulled her in close. "Hugh and I may have had our differences, but I am pleased that he did right by you."

The coach rolled to a stop and Marielle glanced out the window. "Where are we?"

"A boarding house," Stephen replied as he opened the door. "It was the only lodging I could find on such short notice."

"We could have stayed at Hugh's townhouse."

"I think not," Stephen said, stepping onto the pavement. "I do believe you and Hugh have spent entirely too much time together."

Marielle accepted Stephen's hand as he assisted her out of the coach. A wooden sign above the boarding house designated it as "The Bradford".

Stephen offered his arm. "Let's get off the street and get you cleaned up."

Hugh sat in the study with a drink in his hand. Marielle was gone. He had lost her. She would return to her home in Brightlingsea with her brother, and he would be left alone, never knowing true happiness again. He took a sip of his drink and sighed. This was not how he expected the evening to turn out. He was happy for Marielle and the family she'd reclaimed. Stephen had miraculously returned from the dead, but then he had taken everything from Hugh. Without Marielle, who was he?

Nathaniel walked into the study with a purposeful stride. "You are still awake, I see."

"She is gone."

"Who?"

"Marielle."

Nathaniel gave him a baffled look. "Where did she go?"

"Her brother, Stephen, came to retrieve her," Hugh replied as he stood. He walked over to the drink cart and picked up the decanter.

"Stephen is alive?"

"It came as a shock to me, as well," Hugh said as he poured himself a generous helping of brandy. "And I have no doubt that he will turn Marielle against me."

"How do you know that?"

Hugh gave his brother a knowing look. "We weren't exactly civil to one another when we were at Eton."

"No, but you are both adults now."

"I don't think that matters to Stephen. I could see that he still held animosity for me."

Nathaniel walked over and took the decanter from his brother. "Are you just going to let Marielle walk out of your life?"

"What can I do?"

"You can fight for her," Nathaniel said as he put the decanter down and stopped it.

"It's too late," Hugh replied.

"You're wrong."

Hugh tightened his hold on the glass. "Stephen will never give me permission to court Marielle. It is futile to even try." He went and sat down. "She is lost to me."

Nathaniel frowned. "How much have you had to drink?"

"Too much, but drinking helps me see things clearly."

"I contend that is not true." Nathaniel took a seat across from him. "I do believe you are still reeling from tonight's events."

"You mean because one of my good friends tried to kill me."

Nathaniel nodded.

"I wish he had killed me," Hugh said. "It was no less than I deserve."

"You did nothing wrong."

Hugh looked down at the amber liquid in his glass. "Simon certainly blamed me for their deaths."

"Simon was mad, and he was trying to kill you and Marielle."

"That doesn't mean I won't mourn his death."

"I wouldn't expect any less from you," Nathaniel said. "You should know that we contacted the constable, and he will inform Lord Haverty of Simon's death."

"I thought constables were useless."

"They generally are, but at times they do come in handy," Nathaniel shared. "To ease the sting of Simon's passing, we paid the constable to tell Lord Haverty that his son died an honorable death when he tried to save a woman from a robbery gone awry."

"That was most kind of you."

"We thought you would have wanted that, for Simon's sake."

Hugh gave him a grateful look. "Thank you."

Nathaniel tipped his head as he shared, "The other men are in Newgate, where they are waiting to be transported."

"I would be remiss if I did not thank you for helping me rescue Marielle and saving my life."

Nathaniel smiled. "That's what brothers are for."

"Did I truly see Miss Ashmore dressed as a serving wench?" Hugh asked.

"You did," Nathaniel replied. "Truth be told, she was the one that ultimately shot Simon."

"From the second level?"

Nathaniel bobbed his head. "She is an excellent shot."

"It would appear that Miss Ashmore is a remarkable woman."

"I am not going to disagree with you there," Nathaniel said, "but it would be appreciated if you never acknowledged Miss Ashmore's hand in all of this."

"Consider it done."

Their father stepped into the room and sighed in relief when he saw them. "You are both here," he said. "What were you thinking, going to search for Marielle yourselves? Do you not know how dangerous it is for you to be in the rookeries?"

Hugh took a sip of his drink. "Do not fear," he said dryly. "Your heir is safe."

Their father sat down next to Nathaniel. "I worried about you, too, son."

"There is no need to pretend," Hugh said.

Rather than engage him, their father shifted in his seat to face Nathaniel. "Your mother informed me that you found Marielle, but that her brother arrived to retrieve her."

"That is true," Nathaniel said.

Their father shifted his concerned gaze to Hugh. "How are you handling Marielle's leaving?"

"Superbly," Hugh muttered, then took another sip of his drink.

"How did you find her?" their father asked.

Hugh gestured grandly to Nathaniel and said, "The golden child shall reveal all, especially since he was the one who saved the day."

Nathaniel leaned forward and took the glass out of his hand. "I think you have had enough for today."

Hugh shook his head. "It doesn't matter. No matter how drunk I get, I won't be able to forget her."

"Why do you wish to forget her?" their father asked.

"Because she is gone," Hugh replied.

"Aren't you going to fight for her?" their father pressed. "After all, you're no longer her guardian."

"I know she cares for me, but in time, she will grow to despise me. I am sure of it, considering it was my fault that she was abducted."

"In what way?" their father asked.

"Lord Simon abducted Marielle because he blamed me for the death of Lady Wretton and her daughter, Lady Helena," Hugh revealed.

"But it was Lord Wretton that killed them," their father pointed out.

"True, but I was the barrister who got him off for the murder of his mistress," Hugh said. "Lord Simon was determined to kill Marielle in front of me so I could feel some of the pain that he felt from losing his betrothed."

"That was misguided thinking," their father remarked. "I am confident that Lord Simon was not in his right mind."

"No, he wasn't, but he did have a point," Hugh said. "I should have never taken that case, but I only agreed because you asked me to do so."

"I'm sorry, son," their father said. "I didn't realize what a monster Lord Wretton truly was, or else I would have never asked you to take the case."

"After Lord Wretton killed his family, I couldn't be a barrister anymore," Hugh admitted as he looked up at the ceiling. "I lost faith in the courts, and I loathed myself for the part I played in it."

"Why didn't you say anything?" Nathaniel asked.

"For what purpose? I wouldn't have believed anything that you said," Hugh said. "I turned to the only thing that made sense—gambling. And I found that I was really good at it."

"That is not something to be proud of," their father said.

Hugh shook his head. "Does it matter?" he asked.

"Nothing I ever did made you proud. I only took that case so I could win your approval, and I failed."

Their father was silent for a long moment. "I admit that I have been disappointed that you chose a life of gambling, but that doesn't mean I love you any less."

"Please," Hugh said, rising, "I do not need your pity. I have always known where I stood in the hierarchy of this family."

As Hugh walked towards the door, his father spoke. "I remember the day you were born like it was yesterday. You had brown tufts of hair on the top of your head, and you didn't cry right away," his father said, turning to face him. "I was so worried that something was wrong, but you just opened your eyes and... and looked at me."

His father's eyes moistened. "And I knew that my life was never going to be the same now that you were in it."

Hugh started clapping slowly. "What a wonderful story, but that doesn't change how you've treated me my whole life. You have always treated me as if I was second best."

"I know I have expected a lot from you—"

Speaking over him, Hugh said, "That is an understatement."

"But I knew you were capable of great things," his father continued, "and I was right. You became a well-respected barrister at a young age."

"Yes, and for a short time, I brought honor to this family," Hugh remarked.

His father stood and walked over to him. "You have so much potential, but you've always doubted yourself. I thought if I was hard on you, you would rise up and be the man I knew you could be."

"You were wrong, Father. I am not that man."

"I am not wrong," his father said, placing a hand on his shoulder. "I saw that man when you were working as a barrister, and more recently, when you were with Marielle."

Hugh glanced down at his father's hand but didn't say anything. Frankly, he wasn't sure what to say. He had never known his father to be emotional, and it caught him off-guard.

"I am sorry that I made you feel as if I have loved you any less than your brother," his father said. "That was never my intention. You are my son, and I love you."

Hugh could hear the sincerity in his father's words, and it threatened his resolve to be angry at him. "Am I supposed to just forgive you now?" he asked.

"I know that I haven't been the best father, but I have always had your best interest in mind," his father said. "I do hope that with my apology we can start healing—together."

As Hugh stared at his father in silence, he heard crying from the hall.

"Mother," he said, "you may as well come in now."

His mother stepped into the room, clutching the collar of her wrapper. "That was lovely, William," she murmured. "Just lovely."

His father removed his hand from Hugh's shoulder and walked over to his wife. "We may be an imperfect family," he said as he slipped his arm around her waist, "but we love each other."

"That we do," his mother said.

"What say you, Hugh?" his father asked with a questioning look. "Should we begin anew?"

Hugh had waited for so long to hear these words from his father, but could he let go of the bitterness that he had held on to for years? He'd blamed his father for everything that had gone wrong in his life, but he was beginning to see that wasn't fair of him. Perhaps it was him that needed to see things in a different perspective.

His father loved him and was proud of him, even after what he had done. Tears came to his eyes as he thought of all the time that he had wasted with his father. Instead of tearing each other down, they could have been trying to build each other up.

"I am willing to try," Hugh said as he blinked back tears.

His mother rushed over and embraced him. "I love you, Hugh," she murmured against his ear. "Don't tell Nathaniel, but you are my favorite."

"I can hear you, Mother," Nathaniel said good-naturedly.

"You are my favorite, too," she said, turning to him, "but only because you married Dinah."

"You can't have two favorites," Nathaniel teased.

She waved her hand dismissively. "Of course I can. That is my right as a mother," she replied. "Now, on to a more important discussion. How is Hugh going to get Marielle back?"

"I think it might be a lost cause," Hugh said.

"You are spouting nonsense," their mother asserted. "I have seen the way she looks at you."

"I love her," Hugh said. He didn't feel like hiding the truth anymore.

His mother patted his hand. "I know, dear. You did not do a good enough job of disguising that fact, but now you are in a position to do something about it."

"I suspected when Marielle defended you from me and called you a hero that it was only a matter of time before you fell in love with her," his father said. "There is a feistiness to her that I find admirable, and you would be a fool to let her go."

Hugh walked over to the mantel of the fireplace and leaned into it. "What am I to do, then?"

"You need to confess your love and convince her to marry you," his mother replied.

"What if she turns me down?" Hugh asked.

"Then at least you tried," his mother said. "You don't want to live your life not knowing if Marielle feels the same as you."

"I am sure that she cares for me, but her brother hates me," Hugh revealed.

"That doesn't surprise me, considering how often I received letters from the headmaster about your antics," his mother stated. "I could never understand why there was such animosity between you two."

"He was cocky and entirely too stubborn for his own good," Hugh shared.

Nathaniel chuckled. "That sounds like someone else I know."

"Regardless, I need to get Marielle away from Stephen long enough to declare my love and hope that she accepts my offer of marriage," Hugh said.

"I have a few ideas on how to accomplish that feat," his mother said, amusement twinkling in her eyes.

Chapter Twenty-One

Marielle stared out the window of the coach as it traveled down the road the next evening and fully realized that her heart was profoundly heavy. She had every reason to be happy now that her brother had returned to her, but she missed Hugh desperately.

How could she leave Town, knowing that she would be leaving him behind? Would he miss her? She hoped so, because she would miss him every moment of every day. But they didn't have an understanding between them. Perhaps they were just star-crossed lovers, destined to be apart from one another.

Her brother's voice broke through the silence. "You look lovely."

Marielle smoothed down her ivory ballgown. "Thank you," she said. "It was considerate of Lady Montfort to send the gown to the Bradford."

"It was, but I don't know how they knew we were staying there, considering I failed to mention it to anyone."

Marielle brought her gloved hand up to her lips to hide her smile. She knew precisely how Lady Montfort knew where she was, because Evie had been with the maid who delivered the gown. Her friend was a woman of many talents, and she couldn't wait for an opportunity to speak freely with her. She still had a lot of questions about the night that she was rescued.

Stephen looked at her curiously. "What is troubling you?"

"Why do you suppose something is troubling me?"

"You are never this quiet," he teased. "You are always rambling on about something, and I do mean that in the nicest way possible."

Marielle knew it would be best if she was just honest with her brother, even though it might upset him. "I don't want to leave for Brightlingsea tomorrow," she said. "I would like to stay in Town for the Season."

"Is there a particular reason why?"

Marielle clasped her hands in her lap as she boldly admitted, "I am not ready to say goodbye to Hugh."

Stephen frowned. "I do not understand your fascination with him, and I am beginning to wonder what truly transpired between you two."

"Hugh always behaved as an honorable gentleman."

"I doubt that," Stephen said. "You seem to forget that I knew him for many years, and he is a rogue."

"People change. You've changed," Marielle asserted.

Stephen sighed. "I fear that recent events may have befuddled your mind, and you need to take a step back and decide what you truly want out of life."

An image of Hugh came to her mind, and she smiled. "I know what I want."

"No, you don't," Stephen said, looking at her smile in apparent horror. "You just think you know what you want, but what happens when you wake up in a few years and regret your choice?"

"That won't happen."

"How can you be so sure?" Stephen asked. "I am responsible for you, and I can't watch you make a terrible mistake. Once this is done, it can't be undone."

"I daresay that you are being unfair to Hugh."

Stephen huffed. "I am being unfair to Hugh?" he repeated. "That man was a thorn in my side while I was at Eton. I have no doubt that he woke up every morning with designs on how to make my life miserable."

"You can't tell me you didn't do the same. Besides, you were just children when that happened."

"What has Hugh done with his life since?" Stephen asked. "He is a gambler and an utter drain on Society."

"You know why he turned to gambling."

"I do, but that doesn't mean he will ever stop."

"I believe he will."

"You have entirely too much faith in him," Stephen said. "I fear you are seeing something that isn't there. Sometimes a man is irredeemable."

"No one is past hope."

A pained look came to Stephen's eyes. "I do not believe that to be true. Sometimes one must do unspeakable acts, and those acts cannot be forgotten or forgiven."

Marielle cocked her head. "Are you speaking of Hugh or yourself?"

Stephen didn't respond but instead shifted his gaze towards the window. His whole body grew tense, and his eyes took on a hardness Marielle had never seen before.

"Stephen?" she asked. "Are you all right?"

"No, but I will be."

The coach arrived at Hugh's townhouse and a liveried servant opened the door. After she stepped out of the coach, she stood on the pavement and admired how nice the townhouse was when it was lit up. A small crowd of people had exited their coaches and were slowly making their way towards the entrance.

Stephen offered his arm and led her inside. They followed

the other patrons into the ballroom and her eyes roamed the crowded place. It looked different with so many people inside. The gold-papered walls seemed to glow with all of the lighted sconces. A full orchestra was warming up in the corner, and the center of the room had been chalked with illustrations of flowers.

"Marielle!" Edith greeted from where she stood in a receiving line. "You have finally arrived!"

"I do apologize for our delay, my lady," Stephen interjected. "We did not anticipate the traffic on the streets."

Edith waved her hand in front of her. "We are just glad that our guest of honor has arrived." She offered him a kind smile. "It is a true pleasure to meet you, Captain Wymond."

"The pleasure is all mine," Stephen replied graciously.

Edith beamed as she turned toward Dinah. "Allow me to introduce you to my daughter-in-law, Dinah, the Countess of Hawthorne."

Stephen bowed. "My lady."

Dinah smiled. "I have heard so much about you that I feel as if I already know you." She gestured towards Evie, who was standing next to her. "Captain Wymond, I would like you to meet my sister, Miss Ashmore."

To Marielle's surprise, Stephen's eyes sparked with interest. "Enchanted, Miss Ashmore," he murmured as he performed a bow.

Evie dropped into a curtsy.

Stephen stood there watching Evie for a moment. "Would you do me the honor of saving me the first dance, Miss Ashmore?"

"I would be delighted," Evie said.

Dinah stepped forward and looped arms with Marielle. "Would you mind terribly if I borrowed your sister for a moment?"

Stephen looked hesitant but politely tipped his head. "Not at all, Lady Hawthorne."

As Dinah began to lead her away, she leaned closer and whispered, "I daresay that I thought your brother would refuse my request."

"He is rather protective of me," Marielle said.

"Clearly," Dinah remarked. "Hugh has requested a moment of your time in the gardens. Edith has instructed me to escort you to him and remain close to chaperone."

Marielle's heart fluttered, and she felt elated at the prospect of being alone with Hugh, even if it was for just a moment.

They stepped out onto the veranda and Dinah led her down a path to where Hugh was standing. He was dapperly dressed in a black jacket, black trousers, and a white cravat. His brown hair was brushed forward, and his eyes were firmly fixed on Marielle. Would there ever come a time when her breath wouldn't hitch at the mere sight of him?

Dinah dropped her hand and stepped back. "I do encourage you to both speak freely and not waste this time." She glanced back at the townhouse. "I am not sure how long it will be before Stephen comes looking for us."

They both watched as Dinah walked a short distance away before Hugh cleared his throat. "You look beautiful," he said as he admired her in her finery.

"Thank you," she said, "as do you."

Hugh took a step closer to her, but still maintained proper distance. "I am so happy for you that Stephen has returned home."

"I must admit that it has been a bit surreal having him back from the dead."

"I can imagine," he said. "May I ask what you intend to do now that he is home?"

Marielle bit her lower lip as she delayed her response. "He wants to return to Brightlingsea tomorrow, and has even asked me to help him manage the shipyard."

Hugh smiled, but it appeared forced. "That is wonderful."

"Is it?"

Hugh gave her a baffled look. "Isn't that what you wanted?" he asked. "To continue your father's legacy?"

"It is; or at least, it was."

"What changed?" Hugh asked.

You.

Marielle knew what she needed to say, but she was scared. What if he didn't feel as deeply as she did? What if she confessed her love, only to have Hugh refuse her? Could her heart handle that rejection?

Hugh had practiced a thousand times, knowing this was, without a doubt, the most important speech he would ever give. But now that he was here with Marielle, he couldn't seem to recall one word of it.

How was he going to convince Marielle that he was worth taking a risk for when he couldn't even find the right words to say? This was not boding well for him.

Hugh took a deep breath and hoped that he wouldn't sound like a blabbering idiot. "Marielle," he began, "as you know, I am no longer your guardian, and I do believe that is for the best."

"You do?"

He nodded. "Now that I am no longer responsible for you, there is nothing stopping us from being together."

A line between her brow appeared. "I see."

"I know you care for me; I can see it in your eyes," Hugh rushed out. "I never thought I wanted to fall prey to the parson's mousetrap, but you changed my mind. I do believe us getting married is a brilliant idea." He paused. "What do you say?"

Hugh knew it was a far cry from what he had intended to

say, but he had never expected to see the hurt visible on Marielle's features, pain that he had undoubtedly caused.

"I think I should go back inside," Marielle said, her voice soft.

As she turned to leave, Hugh reached for her arm and gently turned her to face him. "What did I say wrong?" he asked.

Marielle looked up at him with tears in her eyes. "From the moment I met you, I started to fall in love with you," she said. "You have been able to speak to my soul in a way that no one ever has before."

"I don't understand. What's the problem, then?"

"I would like nothing more than to marry you," she said, tilting her head stubbornly, "but I deserve more than a marriage of convenience."

He furrowed his brow. "That isn't what I was offering you."

"It wasn't?" she asked. "Because you made no declarations of love, and you referred to marriage as 'the parson's mousetrap'."

Hugh dropped his hand from her arm. "You must forgive me, because I am not good at giving speeches, and I knew I was going to botch this up," he rambled. "I love you, Marielle, and that is why I want to marry you."

Marielle pressed her lips together before saying, "If that is the case, I want a real proposal, Hugh. Not a rushed one."

Hugh reached for her hand and dropped down to one knee. "Miss Marielle Wymond," he started, "the truth of the matter is that I am wholly, completely, unequivocally in love with you. I have never loved another as much as I have loved you."

"Why do you love me?"

His face softened as he smiled. "You have taken a broken man and made me whole again."

"You were never broken."

"But I was, even though you never looked at me that way," Hugh said. "You believed I had a good heart when no one else did, including myself." Tears filled his eyes. "You have saved me from a lifetime of misery."

Marielle gave him a playful smile. "What else do you love about me?"

He chuckled. "I love how feisty you are, and how you stood up to my father without any sign of hesitation."

"Your father isn't so scary when you get to know him," Marielle said.

Hugh tightened his hold on her hand. "I have fallen so deeply in love with you that I cannot climb out of such depths, nor can I imagine a life without you. And I can't lose you."

A tear escaped her eye, and she reached up to swipe it away. "That was much better than your first attempt."

"Is that a yes, then?" Hugh asked. "Because it is deucedly uncomfortable down here."

Her eyes twinkled with merriment. "I never thought I would see you down there."

Hugh's lips twitched. "Men will do just about anything when they are in love."

"Yes, Hugh," she responded warmly, "I will marry you."

Hugh jumped up and brushed his lips against hers. "You have made me the happiest of men by agreeing to become my wife."

Marielle's lips turned into a pout. "I believe I deserve a real kiss, then, don't you?"

"I have no objections," he replied, and pressed his lips against hers. Slowly, tenderly, Hugh deepened the kiss until he was so lost in the moment that he almost didn't hear Dinah warn them that Stephen was approaching. *Almost.*

Hugh broke the kiss and turned to see Stephen stomping towards them with a thunderous expression.

"Marielle Elizabeth Wymond!" Stephen shouted. "What in the blazes do you think you are doing?"

Marielle turned to face her brother. "I believe it is rather obvious that I was kissing Hugh."

As soon as Stephen reached them, he pulled his fist back and punched Hugh in the jaw, knocking him onto the ground. "I challenge you to a duel for dishonoring my sister!" he declared.

"Don't be ridiculous, Stephen," Marielle challenged as she went to assist Hugh in rising. "You would kill him."

Hugh coughed but bit his tongue.

"That is the point of a duel, sister," Stephen mocked.

Remaining close to Hugh, Marielle placed a hand on her hip. "Aren't you being a bit dramatic?"

"We are leaving!" Stephen exclaimed. "Now!"

"No," Marielle said with a shake of her head. "I am not going anywhere without my fiancé."

Stephen's face went slack. "Your fiancé?" he repeated. "You don't honestly want to marry this blackguard, do you?"

"I do."

"But he isn't worthy of you," Stephen said. "You must know that."

Hugh rubbed his sore jaw. "For once, I find myself in agreement with Stephen," he said. "I am not worthy of you, and I never will be. But I will try to be better, for your sake."

Marielle placed her hand on Hugh's sleeve. "You are perfectly imperfect just the way you are, and I would never ask you to change."

"He is a gambler," Stephen pressed. "You are always going to be left wondering where he is and who he is with."

Hugh shook his head. "My gambling days are over," he said. "I have amassed a large enough fortune that I can give Marielle the life that she deserves. If she has no objections, we can retire to our estate after we are wed."

Stephen scoffed before he turned back to Marielle. "I thought we were going to run Father's shipyard together."

"As much as I appreciate that offer, I have decided to marry Hugh instead," Marielle said.

"You would give up everything for him?" Stephen asked.

Marielle offered Hugh a private smile. "He already has my heart. What else matters?"

Stephen opened his mouth to no doubt object, so Hugh spoke first. "I was terrible to you when we were at Eton, and I am sorry."

"Is that supposed to make it right between us?" Stephen asked through gritted teeth.

"No, but I hope it is a start," Hugh replied. "I was young and foolish. I didn't think through the repercussions of my actions."

Stephen frowned as he thought for a moment. "Marielle hasn't reached her majority yet, so you need my permission to marry."

"I would wait for Marielle. As long as it took, I would wait," Hugh said. "My love will only increase for her."

Stephen shifted his irate gaze to his sister. "I could lock you in your bedchamber."

"I would find a way to escape," Marielle said.

"I could take away your inheritance and you would be left with nothing," Stephen pressed.

Marielle gave her brother a knowing look. "We both know that you would never do that."

Stephen's jaw clenched, but there was a sudden tremor in his lips. "I can't lose you, Marielle. You are the only family that I have left."

Marielle stepped forward and embraced her brother. "You will never lose me, Stephen. I love you, and that will never change."

"Why did you have to pick him?" Stephen groaned as he leaned back.

"Because he is the one man that I can't live without," Marielle replied.

Stephen remained close to his sister as he turned to face Hugh. "I do not like you, Hugh. You have only ever been a nuisance to me. But my sister chose you, and I must respect her decision."

"Thank you, Stephen," Hugh said, offering his hand. "I promise that I will do right by your sister."

Stephen hesitated before he finally relented and shook Hugh's. "You'd better, or I will kill you."

"I would expect no less of you." Hugh dropped his hand, and he heard a collective cheer. He turned and saw that a group of people had assembled on the verandah, including his mother, who was standing in the front. How had he not noticed that they were being watched?

"I suppose an announcement is in order," Marielle said, following his gaze.

Hugh offered his arm. "Shall we do it together?"

"Together," Marielle murmured as she accepted it. "I like the sound of that."

Epilogue

Hugh adjusted his top hat as he sat next to Marielle in the carriage. The sun was shining brightly, the birds were chirping merrily in the trees, and he was content as he listened to Marielle go on and on about how lovely Rotten Row was. Nothing could sully his mood, not even Stephen, who was sitting across from them, scowling.

Marielle offered him a rueful smile. "I do apologize for my ramblings."

"You have nothing to apologize for," Hugh said. "I do not think I could ever tire of you speaking your mind."

Stephen huffed.

Marielle turned her amused gaze towards him. "Do you wish to say something, brother?"

"No," Stephen replied, crossing his arms over his chest.

Hugh smiled. "How fortunate we are that your brother agreed to chaperone us on our ride through Hyde Park," he joked.

Stephen narrowed his eyes. "You could always end this farce of an engagement with my sister and be rid of me."

"It is not a farce," Marielle interjected. "Hugh and I are

going to marry tomorrow, and then we are leaving on our wedding tour."

"Do not remind me," Stephen muttered.

Hugh tipped his head at a rider passing by before asking, "When do you return to Brightlingsea?"

"I have decided that I will remain in Town until the end of the Season," Stephen replied.

"You will?" Marielle asked. "When did you decide this?"

Stephen shrugged. "I thought it would be best if I stuck around to keep an eye on you. Is that an issue?"

Marielle shook her head. "Not at all. I look forward to it," she said. "But may I ask what changed your mind?"

"I just thought I would enjoy all the festivities that London has to offer," Stephen replied.

"But you hate social events," Marielle remarked.

"Not all of them."

Marielle eyed him curiously. "What are you about, brother?"

Stephen uncrossed his arms. "You do not need to concern yourself with me. I am the one who should be worried about you, since you are insistent on marrying a blackguard."

"Hugh is not a blackguard," Marielle defended, "and I will not have you making disparaging comments about him."

"Do you wish for me to praise him?" Stephen asked. "Because I doubt that would ever happen in this lifetime."

Hugh spoke up. "I do not need your praise, nor do I expect it." He reached for Marielle's hand. "I am just grateful that you gave your permission for us to be wed."

Stephen's eyes landed on their intertwined hands and a growl came from the back of his throat. "You are being too familiar with my sister."

Marielle laughed. "Stop being such a prude."

Hugh withdrew his hand and reached into his jacket pocket. "I do have something for you—for both of you."

"You don't need to give me anything else," Marielle

rushed out. "You have already spoiled me with too many gifts."

"Just one more," Hugh said as he removed a diamond encrusted necklace from his pocket.

Marielle gasped. "That's my mother's necklace!"

"It is," Hugh said as he handed it to her. "My mother told me that Mr. Cadell had sold off your mother's jewelry, and I paid him a visit. He graciously told me where I could find the pieces."

"Pieces?" Marielle asked.

Hugh nodded. "I wasn't able to acquire all of the items he sold, but I did purchase everything the jewelry shop still had."

Marielle fingered her mother's necklace as her eyes filled with tears. "I can't believe you did this for me."

"I would do anything for you; you must know that," Hugh said.

After he placed the necklace around Marielle's neck, Hugh reached back into his pocket and pulled out a gold band. "I believe this was your father's." He extended it towards Stephen. "I thought you would want it."

Stephen accepted it and read the inscription on the inside. "*You are my heart, my soul.*" His voice choked with emotion. "My mother commissioned this ring for their wedding day, and I never saw my father without it on."

Stephen met his gaze and continued. "Thank you, Hugh. This means more than you will ever know."

Hugh tipped his head in acknowledgement. "You are welcome."

"This still doesn't change the fact that I am unhappy about you marrying my sister," Stephen said, his voice returning to his usual gruff tone.

"I assumed as much," Hugh responded.

"But," Stephen hesitated, "I find you to be much more tolerable than you once were."

Marielle beamed at her brother. "Was that so hard to admit?"

"It was, actually," Stephen replied.

Hugh was about to respond when he saw Nathaniel and Haddington approaching on their steeds.

Haddington put his hand up in greeting. "Good afternoon," he said. "It is a beautiful day for a ride, is it not?"

Marielle's eyes went wide with recognition as she stared at Haddington, but she didn't say anything. Hugh decided it would be best if he provided the introductions. "Lord Haddington, allow me the privilege of introducing you to my betrothed, Miss Wymond, and her brother, Mr. Wymond."

Haddington tipped his hat. "It is a pleasure to meet both of you."

"Likewise, my lord," Marielle said.

Nathaniel spoke up. "Mother wanted me to remind you that dinner is not optional this evening, for any of us."

"I know," Hugh muttered. "She has reminded me of that fact relentlessly."

"It will be your last meal as a free man," Haddington joked.

"Which I have no qualms about," Hugh said. "I would have married Marielle yesterday if I was able to."

Nathaniel gave him a knowing look. "Mother would have never allowed it."

"Neither would I," Stephen said. "Posting the banns is the respectable thing to do."

"I just received word that Grenton and his wife will be joining us this evening," Nathaniel shared. "They have returned home from their Scotland cottage."

Haddington chuckled. "Grenton was rather surprised to learn that Hugh had gotten engaged while he was gone."

"It won't be a surprise to him when he meets Marielle," Hugh said. "She has the ability to charm everyone she associates with."

"That was sweet of you," Marielle acknowledged.

Haddington turned his attention towards Stephen. "Is Hugh normally this sappy around your sister?"

"I'm afraid so," Stephen remarked with a hint of a smile on his lips.

"Then you have my apologies," Haddington jested.

"If you will excuse us," Nathaniel interrupted, "we are late for a meeting."

As they rode off, Stephen looked curiously at his sister. "May I ask why you were staring so intently at Haddington?"

Marielle waved her hand dismissively in front of her. "He reminded me of someone that I know; someone I was very grateful to for their assistance."

Stephen didn't seem appeased, but he didn't press her. "Why are we moving so slowly?" he asked, turning to look at the long line of carriages on the road.

Hugh turned to Marielle and admired her beautiful face. He could hardly wait until tomorrow to wed her. Marielle was everything that he never knew he needed until she walked into his life. She had changed his life for the better.

He would safeguard their love and never take it for granted. Only a fool would gamble with something so precious and rare.

The End

Spies were never meant to fall in love...

Reginald, Marquess of Haddington, has been assigned to determine
if a dangerous weapons dealer operating in the rookeries poses a
threat to the Crown. It appears to be a straightforward case until he
is also assigned to partner with Miss Ashmore, a beautiful but
stubborn woman he has always loved.

Miss Evie Ashmore doesn't want a partner but is forced to accept
Reginald's help. She is convinced that harm has befallen her mentor
and is bound and determined not to rest until she ensures that he is
safe, which forces her to visit the most unsavory parts of London.

As Evie and Reginald learn to work together, a greater danger looms and they quickly realize that everything is not what it seems. Can love truly conquer all, or was this doomed from the start?

Also by Laura Beers

Proper Regency Matchmakers
Saving Lord Berkshire
Reforming the Duke
Loving Lord Egleton
Redeeming the Marquess
Engaging Lord Charles
Refining Lord Preston

Regency Spies & Secrets
A Dangerous Pursuit
A Dangerous Game
A Dangerous Lord
A Dangerous Scheme

Regency Brides: A Promise of Love
A Clever Alliance
The Reluctant Guardian
A Noble Pursuit
The Earl's Daughter
A Foolish Game

Also by Laura Beers

The Beckett Files
Saving Shadow
A Peculiar Courtship
To Love a Spy
A Tangled Ruse
A Deceptive Bargain
The Baron's Daughter
The Unfortunate Debutante

About the Author

Laura Beers is an award-winning author. She attended Brigham Young University, earning a Bachelor of Science degree in Construction Management. She can't sing, doesn't dance and loves naps.

Besides being a full-time homemaker to her three kids, she loves waterskiing, hiking, and drinking Dr. Pepper. She was born and raised in Southern California, but she now resides in Utah.

Made in United States
North Haven, CT
21 December 2022

29945354R00176